3/13

TIGRIS

EUPHRATES

THE · HANGING · GARDENS
OF · BABYLON

ERUSALEM

PERSIAN · GULF

ED · SEA

M I L E S

0   100   200   300   400   500

THE
COLOSSUS RISES

The Monastery

THE
COLOSSUS RISES

PETER LERANGIS

HARPER
An Imprint of HarperCollinsPublishers

Seven Wonders Book 1: The Colossus Rises
Copyright © 2013 by HarperCollins Publishers
All rights reserved. Printed in the United States of America.

For information address HarperCollins Children's Books, a division of HarperCollins Publishers, 10 East 53rd Street, New York, NY 10022.
www.harpercollinschildrens.com

Library of Congress Cataloging-in-Publication Data
Lerangis, Peter.
The colossus rises / Peter Lerangis. — 1st ed.
  p. cm.— (Seven wonders ; bk. 1)
  Summary: Teens Jack, Marco, Aly, and Cass begin a quest to find seven pieces of Atlantis's power that were hidden long ago and that will, if returned to Atlantis, save them from certain death due to the genetic abnormality that also gives them superior abilities.
  ISBN 978-0-06-207040-1 (hardback)—ISBN 978-0-06-224939-5 (international edition)
  [1. Adventure and adventurers—Fiction. 2. Ability—Fiction. 3. Friendship—Fiction. 4. Atlantis (Legendary place)—Fiction. 5. Science fiction.] I. Title.
PZ7.L558Col 2013   2012025334
[Fic]—dc23   CIP
                                                                                                      AC

Typography by Joe Merkel

12 13 14 15 16 LP/RRDH 10 9 8 7 6 5 4 3 2 1
❖
First Edition

FOR MY FELLOW VOYAGERS.
ALL OF YOU.

THE
COLOSSUS RISES

CHAPTER ONE

RED BEARD

ON THE MORNING I was scheduled to die, a large barefoot man with a bushy red beard waddled past my house. The thirty-degree temperature didn't seem to bother him, but he must have had a lousy breakfast, because he let out a burp as loud as a tuba.

Belching barefoot giants who look like Vikings are not normal in Belleville, Indiana. But I didn't really get a chance to see the guy closely.

At that moment, I, Jack McKinley, was under attack in my own bedroom. By a flying reptile.

I could have used an alarm clock. But I'd been up late studying for my first-period math test and I'm a deep sleeper. Dad couldn't wake me because he was in Singapore

1

on business. And Vanessa, the au pair I call my don't-care-giver, always slept till noon.

I needed a big sound. Something I couldn't possibly sleep through. That's when I saw my papier-mâché volcano from last month's science fair, still on my desk. It was full of baking soda. So I got my dad's coffeemaker, filled it with vinegar, and rigged it to the volcano with a plastic tube. I set the timer for 6:30 A.M., when the coffeemaker would release the vinegar into the volcano, causing a goop explosion. I put a chute at the base of the volcano to capture that goop. In the chute was a billiard ball, which would roll down toward a spring-loaded catapult on my chair. The catapult would release a big old plastic Ugliosaurus™—a fanged eagle crossed with a lion, bright-red.

Bang—when that baby hit the wall I'd have to be dead not to wake up. Foolproof, right?

Not quite. Around 6:28, I was in the middle of a nightmare. I'd had this dream way too many times: me, running through the jungle in a toga, chased by snarling, drooling, piglike beasts, whose screeches fill the smoky sky. Nice, huh? Usually I awake from this dream when a gap in the earth opens beneath my feet.

But this time, I fell in. Down into the darkness. To my death.

At the moment of contact, the Gaseous Giant burped in real life. The sound woke me up.

The coffeemaker-volcano alarm went off. And the Ugliosaurus whacked me between the eyes.

Which, in a nutshell, is how the worst morning of my life began. The last morning I would awaken in my own bed.

"@$%^&!" I screamed, which means I can't tell you the actual words.

I sprang off my bed in agony. That was when I caught a glimpse of Red Beard on the sidewalk. Which caused me to drop to the floor, embarrassed to be seen, even by a wacked-out barefoot stranger. Unfortunately my butt landed squarely on a sharp Ugliosaurus wing, which made me scream again. That was way too much screaming for someone who just turned thirteen.

I lay there with gritted teeth, wishing I'd used the alarm clock. In my mind I saw Vanessa goading me: *You think too much, Jack.* Which she used to say about a hundred times a day. Maybe because I think too much. Always have.

I got off the floor, clutching my head. Red Beard was padding down the street, his feet slapping the pavement. "Next time, close your mouth," I grumbled under my breath as I staggered to the bathroom.

I should have wondered who he was and why he was here. But I couldn't stop thinking of my nightmare, which still lingered like the taste of moldy cheese. I tried to replace it with thoughts of math. Unfortunately, it felt about the same.

Looking in the mirror, I saw that the Ugliosaurus had made a gash on my forehead. Not too deep, but it looked pretty bad, and it stung.

I turned on the tap, dampened a washcloth, and pushed aside a mass of rat-brown hair to uncover my wound. As I dabbed it, I noticed a little tuft of blond hairs sticking out from the back of my head.

Weird. I'd never seen them before. Without Dad around to bug me, I hadn't had a haircut in a while, so those blond hairs looked like loose wires. As I leaned closer to look, a sharp creak made me spin around.

"Vanessa?" I called out.

Aha. She'd heard my scream. I imagined her cowering behind the door, planning how not to be blamed for whatever happened. But she wasn't there.

I glanced at the bathroom clock: 6:39. I had to leave the house by 6:45. But I wanted to see that little blond patch. I had enough time.

I pulled open the bathroom cabinet and reached for a hand mirror I hadn't touched in years. Dad and I had bought it at CVS when I was in second grade, for an art project. Picking it up, I looked at the message I'd carved into the plastic frame.

I turned the mirror around. On the back I'd laminated a photo to the surface. In it, I was four years old and dressed in a puffy winter coat, sliding down a gentle

hill on a sled. The white snow was tinged yellow-green with age. Mom was on the hilltop, laughing, wearing her favorite Smith College wool jacket. Dad was at the bottom, turned away. It was our game: Boom to Daddy. I'd slide into his legs and he would keel over, howling in pretend pain. Then he'd carry me back to the top and we'd do it all over again.

I smiled. Back then, I thought this game was hilarious. Every little thing we did was fun. Life was pretty perfect before Mom died. Before I started having those nightmares. Before Dad had decided home was a place to avoid.

Turning my back to the big bathroom mirror, I used the hand mirror to see behind my head. That was when I realized the blond hair wasn't blond—it was white. And it wasn't just a couple of hairs. I patted them down and noticed a pattern, an upside-down V. I tried to scrape it off with my fingernails, hoping it was some kind of weird stain. But nothing happened. My hair had just changed color—like in those cartoons where someone's hair goes white with shock. Was that what the Ugliosaurus did to me? No way were the kids at school going to ignore this.

I thought about what Mom would say: *Wear a hat.*

Quickly I brushed my teeth. I dropped the mirror into my pack, in case I wanted to investigate further at school. Then I ran into my room and grabbed my peacoat off the floor. Peeking out from under a Wendy's bag was my wool knit cap. I wiped off a crust of congealed ketchup and Chocolate Frosty from one side. It didn't smell too bad, so I jammed it on my head, shoved my math notebook into my backpack, and bolted.

It was 6:43.

As I reached the top of the stairs, my cell phone beeped. *Dad!*

Ugh. Our 6:30 Wednesday morning Skype session. I'd totally forgotten—and he was late! How could he do this on a test day?

I raced downstairs. Dad always insisted I take the call in the living room on the sofa—with the camera on, so he could make sure I hadn't trashed anything.

He's a neat freak. I'm a mess freak. And I had only five rings till the call went to voice mail. In the living room I shoved a pile of cables and joysticks to the center of the Turkish rug, along with two guitars, some comic books, three sweatshirts, a few pairs of socks, take-out containers from Wu Kitchen, a pizza box I was afraid to look into, and a half-eaten Kit Kat.

Beep . . .

From the middle of the pile I lifted a hook attached to four cables, which were linked to the corners of the carpet. I slipped the hook into a pulley I'd rigged to the ceiling chandelier support. A couple of strong tugs, and the rug rose like Santa's toy sack, leaving a pristine wood floor below.

Beep . . .

6:44.

Plopping myself on the sofa, I accepted the call.

"Hey, Dad! Um, I don't have much time to—"

"Five and a quarter! Tell them to sell at five and a half!" Dad was shouting to someone in his office. All I saw was his arm. "And close the door. I'm on a conference call!"

Then he was grinning happily at me. Which made me grin, too. It was the end of his day in Singapore. He looked really tired, like he'd just run a marathon with a dead gorilla strapped to his back. I really missed him. I wished his job could keep him closer to home.

7

But why did he have to call now?

"Heyyyy, Jackie, so sorry I'm late!" Dad said with a tight grin. "Living room looks great! But . . . uh, where's the rug?"

Oops. I tilted the phone so only the wall would show in the background. "I guess Vanessa took it to be cleaned. But, Dad, look, I have to go—"

"Did she spill something?" he asked.

"I have this math test today . . ."

"You'll do great!" Dad replied. "Hey, what's the McKinley family motto?"

"A problem is an answer waiting to be opened," I recited.

"Bravo! Hey, did you see the article I sent you about that poor kid, Cromarty? Died in the bowling alley near Chicago?"

Ugh. Current events. This always involved sad stories about kids and tragedies. Followed by a lecture. Dad's way of scaring me into being extra-careful.

I glanced at my watch. 6:46.

"I think I skimmed it. Send me the link again. So. Wish me luck!" As I stood, my leg buckled beneath me and I almost dropped the phone. I had to clutch the sofa arm to keep from falling.

"Jackie, are you okay?" Dad's brow was all scrunched now. "What's that mark on your forehead? Is that a cut? Did you fall?"

"No!" I said. "I just used a flying toy instead of an alarm."

That sounded a lot crazier coming out of my mouth than I expected. "You used a *what?*" Dad said.

I was feeling weak and light-headed. I took about three deep breaths and tried to stand tall, but I stumbled against the tied-up pulley rope.

Bad move. The rug hurtled downward. It sent up a cloud of dust as everything clanked to the floor. I swiveled away so Dad wouldn't see it.

"What was that?" Dad asked.

6:47. *How much worse could this possibly get?*

"Nothing!" I snapped.

Dad's eyes were wide. "Okay, that's it. Something's not right. I'm booking the next flight home."

"*What?*" This wasn't like him. Usually he's explaining left and right how important his job is. Usually he's the one to cut the conversation short. "Really?"

Dad was looking at me funny. "Stay safe until I get there. Do not let yourself out of Lorissa's sight. Make her take you to school."

"Vanessa," I said. "Lorissa quit. And so did Randi."

"Okay, stay close to her, Jack," Dad said. "Be safe. And good luck on that math test."

"Thanks!" I said. "Bye, Dad! Love"—the image flickered off—"you."

The screen was blank.

6:48. I had to book.

"Vanessa!" I yelled, running into the kitchen. As I snatched two bags of fruit-flavored Skittles from the counter, I saw a note taped to the fridge.

Tell yr dad I quit—b

Vanessa

I darted back to Vanessa's bedroom door and pushed it open. The little room was tidy and neat. And totally empty.

One more catastrophe to explain when Dad got home.

Shutting it out of my mind, I bolted out the back door and got my bike from the garage. The air was cold and bracing, and I quickly buttoned my peacoat.

As I sped onto the sidewalk, I leaned right and headed toward school.

If Red Beard was there, I didn't see him.

CHAPTER TWO

THE ACCIDENT

"YO, SPACE MAN, watch out!"

I didn't hear the warning. I was at the end of my bike ride to school, which involves a sharp turn around the corner of the building. You're supposed to walk your bike by that point, but I was in too much of a hurry. Not that it matters, because most people are too smart to stand close to that corner anyway.

But most people doesn't include Barry Reese, the Blowhard of Mortimer P. Reese Middle School.

There was Barry's hammy face, inches away, his eyes as big as softballs. As always, he was involved in his favorite hobby, making life miserable for littler kids. He was hunched menacingly over this tiny sixth-grader named Josh or George.

I slammed on the brakes. My front wheel jammed. The rear wheel bucked upward, flinging me over the handlebars. The bike slid out from under me. As I flew forward, Barry's face loomed toward me at a zillion miles an hour. I could see three hairs sticking out of a mole on his cheek.

Then the worst conceivable thing happened.

He caught me.

When we stopped spinning around, I was hanging from him like a rag doll. "Shall we dance?" he said.

All I could hear was cackling laughter. Kids were convulsing. Barry grinned proudly, but I pushed him away. His breath smelled like bananas and moldy feet.

Josh or George scrambled up off the ground. No one offered to help pick up his books, which had been scattered all over the playground.

I don't know why Barry was a bully. He was rich. Our school was named after his great-great-grandfather, who'd made his fortune creating those little plastic thingies that protect the toilet lid from hitting the seat. Personally, if I were rich and the heir to a toilet-thingy fortune, I'd be pretty happy. I wouldn't pick on smaller kids.

"I don't dance with apes," I said, quickly stooping to pick up my bike to lock it to the rack.

I stole a look at my watch. The bell was going to ring in one minute.

"My apologies." Barry elbowed me aside and scooped up my bike with exaggerated politeness. "Let me help you recover from your ride, Mario. From the cut on your head, I guess you had a few crashes already."

I tried to take back the handlebars, but he was too fast for me. He yanked the bike away and began walking fast toward the rack. "Hey, by the way, did you finish the bio homework?" he said over his shoulder. "'Cause I was helping my dad with his business last night, and it got late. And, well, you can't think about homework before profits. Not that I wouldn't get all the answers perfect anyway—"

I pushed him aside and grabbed the bike. "No, Barry, you can't copy my homework."

"I just did save your life."

As I locked the bike to the rack, Barry leaned closer with a twisted, smilelike expression. "Don't think there won't be some financial reward . . ."

Before I could answer, he took two quick steps to the side. Josh or George was making a break for the safety of the school yard, clutching an unruly mass of papers and notebooks. Barry thrust his arm out as if yawning. He clipped the kid squarely in the chest and sent him flying, the papers scattering again.

The blood rushed to my head. I wasn't sure if it was from

the Ugliosaurus hit, the crazy bike ride, the near crash, or Barry's extreme obnoxiousness. Math test or not, he couldn't get away with this.

"Here's my homework!" I blurted, yanking a grocery list from my pocket. "You get it if you pick up Josh's stuff and say you're sorry."

"It's George," the kid said.

Barry looked at me as if I were speaking Mongolian. "What did you say, McKinley?"

I was shaking. Dizzy. Maybe this was fear. How could I be so afraid of this doofus?

Focus.

Barry reached toward my sheet, but I pulled it away, backing toward the street. "Tell him you'll never do it again," I insisted. "And don't even think of saying no."

Balling and unballing his fists, Barry stepped closer. His white, fleshy face was taking on the color of rare roast beef. The bell rang. Or maybe it didn't. I was having trouble hearing. What was happening to me?

"How'd you get that little cut on your head, McKinley?" Barry's voice was muffled, like he was speaking inside a long tunnel. "Because I think you need a bigger one."

I barely heard him. I felt as if something had crawled into my head and was kickboxing with my brain.

I struggled to stay upright. I couldn't even see Barry

15

now. The back of my leg smacked against a parked car. I spun into the street, trying to keep my balance. The blacktop rushed toward me and I put out my hands to stop the fall.

The last thing I saw was the grille of a late-model Toyota speeding toward my face.

CHAPTER THREE

FLATLINING

BEEP...

Beep...

Harp strings? What was that noise?

The street was gone, and I could see nothing. I felt as if I were floating in a tunnel of cold air. I had dreamed my own death, and then it had really happened. I pried my eyes open briefly. It hurt to do it, but in that moment I had a horrifying realization.

The afterlife was beige.

I tried to cry out, but my body was frozen. Odd whistling sounds drifted around me like prairie winds.

Slowly I began making out voices, words.

Peering out again, I hoped to see cherubim and seraphim,

or at least a few clouds. Instead I saw nostril hairs. Also, really dark eyebrows and blue eyes, attached to a man's face that loomed closer.

I felt a hand push my head to the side. I tried to speak, to resist, but I couldn't. It was as someone had turned the off switch on all my body functions. "Extremely odd case," the man said in a deep voice. "No diabetes, you say? He had all inoculations? No history of concussion?"

"Correct, Dr. Saark," came an answer. "There's nothing that would indicate these erratic vital signs. He's a healthy boy. We haven't a clue what's wrong."

I knew the second voice. It was my family doctor, Dr. Flood. She'd been taking care of me since I was a baby.

So I was not dead, which was a big relief. But hearing your doctor's voice is never a cheery thing. I was tilted away from the voices, and all I could see were an IV stand, electrical wires, and a metal wastebasket.

It had to be Belleville Hospital, where I hadn't been since I was born. I must have been hit by a car.

The math test! I had visions of a blank sheet of paper with a big, fat zero. I willed myself to open my mouth. To tell them I was all right and had to get to school. But nothing moved.

"A highly rare set of symptoms," Dr. Saark said, "but it fits exactly into the recent research I've been doing . . ."

Dr. Flood exhaled loudly. "We're so lucky you were in town and could rush here at such short notice."

I felt fingers at the back of my head, poking around where the upside-down V was. I felt a rush of panic. I figured I was about to become the first kid in the world with a prescription for Grecian Formula.

Heavy footsteps plodded into the room. "Excuse me?" Dr. Flood said. She sounded confused, maybe annoyed. "What are you doing here?"

"Chaplain," a gruff voice answered. "New on job."

While Dr. Flood dealt with the chaplain, Dr. Saark pushed my head back and slipped something in my mouth. He held my mouth shut, forcing me to swallow. From under his sleeve, I could see a tattoo that looked like two winding snakes.

What did he just give me? Could he see my eyes were open? What kind of doctor had a tat like that?

What was a chaplain doing here?

"But . . . I never sent a request for a chaplain," Dr. Flood said, sounding completely confused. "Are you sure you're in the right room?"

"Yes, correct," the man replied. "For last rites. Hospital rules. These situations . . . you know."

Last rites? As in, the prayers spoken over people about to die—*those* last rites?

I panicked. I was obviously in worse shape than I thought. Then my body lurched violently, and everything turned white.

"He's flatlining!" Dr. Saark shouted. "Dr. Flood, notify the OR. I need a gurney, stat!"

My body convulsed. I heard choking noises—my own. And hurried footsteps as Dr. Flood left the room.

The room was a blur of colors. The two men—Saark and the chaplain—were on either side, strapping my arms and legs down. My head jerked backward, and I thought it would crack open like an egg.

Hold on. Don't die.

Dr. Saark stood over me, his face red and beaded with sweat. *"Now!"* he said.

The chaplain was nearly a foot taller than Dr. Saark and at least fifty pounds heavier, but he snapped to, fumbling for something in his inner pocket. I could see his face for the first time—green eyes, ruddy skin, curly red hair, and a deep jagged scar that ran down the left side of his cheek and disappeared into a bushy beard. He pulled out a long syringe with one hand, and with the other wiped my arm with an alcohol pad. As he leaned down, I realized I'd seen him before.

I tried to call out. I opened my eyes as wide as they could go. I stared at the man's face, willing myself to stay awake.

A word escaped my mouth on a raspy breath: "Red . . ."

I felt a sharp pain in my left arm. As the room went black, one last word dribbled out.

". . . Beard."

CHAPTER FOUR
THE DREAM

A ring of fire, screaming animals, the end of the world. I am being attacked by a hose-beaked vromaski, whose breath is like a roomful of rotting corpses. Its head is long and thin, with a snout like a sawed-off elephant's trunk. It has the sinewed body of a striped, shrunken cheetah, with long saberlike fangs and scales in place of fur.

As it thunders toward me through the burning jungle, its stocky legs trample everything in its path. In the distance a fireball belches from the top of a volcano, causing the ground to jolt.

The beast bares its teeth. Its crazed red eyes bore into me, desperate and murderous. But rather than running away, I face it head-on.

Mostly, I think, I'm an idiot.

I have a weapon in my right hand, a gleaming saber with a pearl-inlaid handle. It must weigh a hundred pounds, but it's so well-balanced I barely feel it.

I rear back. The polished blade of the saber reflects in the vromaski's red eyes. The creature roars, hurtling itself into the air, its teeth bared and aimed at my throat.

I swing with two arms. The saber shhhhinks *through the fetid air, slicing off the beast's head. Blood spatters onto my face and uniform, a brocaded tunic with a helmet and bronze chest plate, now washed in crimson.*

Before the slavering monster's head hits the ground, a creature swoops down from above, its gargantuan wings sending a blast of hot air into my face. With a screech, it grabs the bloody head in its talons and rises. I stumble back. Its wingspan alone is three times my height. I watch in fright and awe, recognizing the great beast somehow. It has the head and wings of an eagle and the body of a lion.

NO.

The dream is not supposed to be like this. Before it was more of a game, the most awesome and scary 3-D video game ever. But now it feels different. The heat sears my flesh. The weight strains my muscles and the smells sicken me.

I turn to run, and I spot . . . her. The queen. But she's not the same either. She's got darker skin than before and a long face lined with worry. Behind her, the land falls off steeply, and I see a vast plain stretching to the horizon. But I follow her glance, which is looking toward a deep valley near us, a depression in the middle of the jungle. She points to a cave opening and looks at me pleadingly. Something has pained her deeply, but I don't know what—has someone attacked her? Stolen something?

"What do you want me to do?" I shout. But she looks blankly back.

The sky suddenly darkens. In the distance, behind the queen and far below us, I see something growing. A dark blue watery mass at the edges of the vast plain. It is moving toward us, changing shape, roiling and spitting. It seems to be swallowing the earth as it charges, crashes downward, and shakes the earth.

In the valley, the cave is beginning to collapse.

The queen's mouth drops open. I see a crack growing in the earth. Trees, bushes, still aflame, drop inside the gaping maw. I must leave. I can prevent the destruction. But for the life of me, I don't know how. All I know is that I must leave. I must race downward to the ocean. I must find someone—someone who looks a great deal like . . . me.

I run. But the crack is now opening in my path. My brain is telling me I've been here before. This is where I die. I am heading for the hole.

I can't dream my own death again. Can't.

Somehow I know my brain can't take this one more time. If I follow through, if I fall into the hole and die, this time it will be for real.

The flying creature swoops down. I feel its talons burn their way into the back of my head. In the shape of an upside-down V.

CHAPTER FIVE

ARRIVAL

"GEEEAHHH!" I BOLTED upward and immediately regretted it. The back of my head felt as if it had been blasted open, and I was afraid my brains would fall out.

I had been facedown. I'd lifted myself to a push-up position, on a bed with sheets soaked in sweat. I dropped back to the mattress instantly, letting out a moan.

What had they done to me?

Partied on the back of my head, that was obvious. I was afraid to move, even to think. I lay still, face buried in the damp pillow, catching my breath. Slowly, the pain began to subside. The stillness helped.

You're okay. You lifted yourself too fast. Breathe in . . . breathe out . . .

I tried to think positively. The last thing I remembered, Dr. Flood was rushing off to notify the OR. That meant I'd had an operation. Okay. This made sense. I wasn't convulsing or dizzy or hallucinating anymore. No more wooziness. I had a voice. I could move and see. So the operation must have worked, and I was hurting because of the surgery. That had to be it. When Dad had had surgery on his back a year ago, he'd been in bed for two days. I would need to recover, that's all. I had to look on the bright side.

Surgery, I realized, was a good excuse for missing a math test.

I took a deep breath. Had they cured whatever had happened to me?

In a few moments, I cautiously turned my head. I could see that they'd moved me to another part of the hospital. Dressed me in a set of pajama pants and a neat white polo shirt. It was quiet here, not like the first room. No beeps or voices or traffic noise. The room was dimly lit by a pre-morning glow. The walls seemed to be a peaceful bluish shade, maybe turquoise. The floor was polished wood.

"Hello?" My voice was hoarse and barely audible. I wondered where I was. How long I'd been out.

A breeze wafted over me, pungent and salty.

Salty?

I moved a little more until I could see the windows. They were open. A nearly full moon was fading overhead into a shimmering, silvery sky. I'd seen that color only once before, on the day after Mom had died. Dad and I had stayed up all night and seen the sun rise.

It was warm out, but I'd been wearing a coat when I had my accident.

I thought back to what the doctor had said. *A highly rare set of symptoms.* Patients with rare conditions sometimes had to go to special hospitals with the right doctors and equipment. This seemed like California or Hawaii.

A closed door stood about ten feet away. Carefully I rolled over and sat up. The back of my head felt like an epic smackdown between John Henry and Thor. I sat for a long moment, took some deep breaths, and stood.

With tiny steps, I shuffled toward the door. I was fine as long as I didn't move my head too much. Propping myself up on the doorjamb, I pushed the door open onto a long hallway.

It had a new-building smell, like sawdust and plastic. A carpet stretched down the corridor, past a few closed doors. At the end of it, a hospital orderly sat on a stool, snoring. His back was against the wall, his face drooped down into his chest. He had broad shoulders and sharp cheekbones. A flat cap was pulled down across his eyes, and he wore fatigues and thick boots. On his belt was a holstered pistol.

What kind of hospital *armed* its orderlies?

Waking him up seemed risky. I backed into the room.

I needed to call Dad. I wondered if he'd landed yet, and if he knew where I was. How long had I been unconscious? How much time had passed since I was in Indiana?

Slowly I worked my way over to the foot of the bed. There, on top of a steamer chest, someone had placed my backpack and my clothes, neatly folded. I reached around in the pockets of the folded jeans for my phone, but it was gone. It wasn't in my backpack, either.

But Mom's birthday mirror was.

I pulled it out. Her smile seemed to blast out of the photo, cutting through the darkness. Across the room, the bathroom door was open, and I could see my reflection in shades of gray. I wondered what exactly they'd done to the back of my head.

Taking the mirror into the bathroom, I turned on the light.

I barely recognized the kid in the big mirror over the sink. My face was ghostly pale, my head completely shaved. I noticed for the first time a monogram on the polo shirt—KI.

I turned and held the small mirror so I could see the back of my head in the larger one. The white hair had been shaved off with the rest. But someone had drawn a shape in black marker, from the top to the bottom of my head, outlining exactly where the upside-down V had been. Bandages had been placed at the bottom of each line, just above the neck.

I touched one and began to pull, but the pain was too sharp. There must have been stitches underneath. Incisions.

"What the—?" The mirror slipped from my hand and crashed to the counter. The mirror cracked instantly, as did the frame, one horizontal line down the center, separating the image of four-year-old me from still-alive Mom.

As I reached to pick it up, I heard a click behind me. I spun around to see a figure standing in the door. It was a guy about six feet tall. He slipped inside and shut the door behind him. "Hey," he said. "You okay?"

I stepped toward the bed, barely feeling the pain now. "Fine, I guess," I rasped. "Who are you?"

"Marco Ramsay." He was wearing the same clothes as I was, but three or four sizes larger. His shoulders were wide, his feet enormous. He had high, chiseled cheekbones dotted with small patches of acne. Dark brown hair hung down to his brow, making his eyes seem to peer out of a cave. They darted toward the door as if he'd done something wrong. "Because I heard a noise from in here . . ." he said.

"I dropped a mirror, that's all," I said. "Um, I'm Jack."

He nodded. "Yeah, I know. Anyway, that dude outside—you know, Conan? Special Ops, Sleep Division? He should have been in here to check on you, but it's hard to wake him up. And if you do, he gets nasty. So I figured I'd check in myself. But it looks like you're okay, so I guess

I'll go . . ." He began to turn back to the door.

"Wait!" I said. "This guy, Conan? Since when do they allow guns in a hospital?"

Marco gave an uncomfortable shrug. "Maybe one of the patients is a terrorist?"

The door swung open again and two others scurried in, a skinny guy and a girl with dyed-pink hair and a mole on her left cheek. She was about my age and looked like someone you didn't cross. The guy seemed maybe a little younger and was a curly-haired version of George, the little guy from my school who'd been bullied by Barry Reese. "This is what we're doing? We're going to be in deep doo-doo, Marco," the little guy said.

"Fun's over," the girl added, her voice a tense whisper. "C'mon, back to the kennel, Big Foot."

Marco laughed. "Oh, look who's Little Miss Obedient!" he said, also in a strange, whispery voice.

"Why are you guys whispering?" I said. "And what are you talking about? *Kennel?*"

"That's supposed to be a joke," Marco said. "Aly is a one-person Comedy Central."

"Time to go!" said the shorter guy, his voice about three times as loud as the others. As he pulled the door wide open, he gave a dramatic wave. "See you at breakfast!"

"Dude, you'll wake Conan!" Marco snapped. "Last time we did that, he punctured my basketball."

"Will you guys at least tell me who you are and what we're all doing here?" I shouted.

From out in the hallway, Conan let out a snort and a mumble. Marco froze.

The little guy was halfway out the door. "I'm Cass Williams, and this is Aly Black. Look, don't get the wrong impression. We love this place, really. You will, too. It's awesome. They'll tell you everything soon. But we're not supposed to be here right now. That's all."

Aly nodded and scurried out the door. Marco backed out, too, shooting me a thumbs-up. "Seriously, dude. Best place in the world. Great breakfasts. All you can eat. We're all happy here. Later."

Before I could say another thing, they were gone.

For a moment I wanted to race after them, but I knew my head would explode with the effort. And I didn't want to risk waking the guy with the gun.

Plus, that was about the creepiest conversation I'd had in my life. Who were these losers? This felt like one big prank. Some crazy reality TV show. *Postsurgical Punk'd.*

I sank onto the bed and pinched my right arm, just to be sure I wasn't dreaming. No chance of falling back to sleep now. Morning light was beginning to filter in through the windows, and I could see the room more clearly. I noticed a flag on the wall to my right, with a symbol that matched the one on my shirt:

The initials weren't familiar. I searched for a call button, some kind of signal for a nurse. Nothing. No button, no medicine cabinet, no rolling tables or IV drips or hanging televisions. There was nothing hospital-like about this place at all.

I tried to think back to what had happened at Belleville. Had anyone said anything about moving me?

I'd had dizziness. I'd fallen into the street. In the hospital, there was this expert and Dr. Flood. She was worried. Some chaplain was there to perform last rites and

31

that confused her . . .

But I never sent a request for a chaplain . . .

The chaplain had grabbed my arm. I remembered him now. Huge face, bulbous nose. *Red Beard.* The same guy who'd passed my house only an hour earlier, barefooted and without a clerical collar. He had tied me to a table and injected me with something. He wasn't a chaplain. He was helping Dr. Saark. But helping him do what?

I wanted desperately to contact Dad. Just one phone call. I turned toward the window. The sky was brightening in the rising sun. Carefully I stood up. The pain wasn't quite as intense as it had been. I guessed it was the sudden movement that had really torpedoed me. I'd be fine if I slowed down.

I stepped toward the window and gazed out. Before me stretched a long, grassy lawn nearly the length of a football field, crisscrossed with paths. Surrounding the lawn were old-fashioned red brick buildings, most with tidy, white-shuttered windows. They seemed old, but some of them had sections with glass ceilings. If the lawn were a clock I'd be at the bottom, or six o'clock. To the left, about nine, was a grand, museum-like structure with pillars and wide stairs, kind of the centerpiece. At around two, tucked between the red brick buildings, was a sleek glass-and-steel structure that seemed out of place. The whole thing was peaceful looking, like a college campus plopped into the middle of a jungle. Trees surrounded the compound like a thick green collar stretching in all directions as far as the eye could see. Except for the left side—west.

Way beyond the big museum building, a massive black rock mountain loomed darkly over everything. It thrust upward through the greenery like a clenched fist into the softening sky. It seemed almost fluid, changing its shape with the movement of the morning mists.

A murmur of distant voices made me look across the compound. A pair of men dressed in khaki uniforms emerged from the side of a distant building. "Hello?" I called out, but my voice was too weak to carry.

As they stepped into the dim light, I saw that both of them were carrying rifles. Big ones, with ammo.

I ducked away from the window. This was no hospital. I was in lockdown. Were these people coming for me? Already they'd kidnapped me, drilled holes in the back of my head, and stuck me in some sort of bizarre prep school with a bunch of brainwashed zombies. Why? And what were they going to do for an encore?

I made my way silently back across the room. The window on the other side had a much different view. It looked away from the campus. The only thing separating the building from the surrounding jungle was a scraggly clearing, about twenty yards of rocky soil. Beyond it was a thicket of trees. In the dawn light, the jungle looked dense and almost black. But I could see a path leading into it, and that made my blood pump a little faster. Every path had a destination. Wherever this was—Hawaii, California, Mexico, South America—there had to be a road somewhere to a town or city. Stuff had been built here, which meant bricks and materials had been trucked in. If I could find a road and hitch a ride, I'd be able to locate a pay phone or use somebody's cell. Call Dad. Contact the news media. Report this place.

I sat on the bed and carefully put on my jeans and shoes. Then I went to the window and perched on the sill. Swiveling my legs around, I jumped out.

CHAPTER SIX

INTO THE JUNGLE

IT WAS ONLY a short drop to the ground, but in my condition, I felt like I'd landed on iron spikes.

Sucking in air, I held back the urge to scream. I pressed my hands to my head to keep my brain from bursting. I had to be careful. I'd just had surgery and was a long way from recovery. Even just looking left and right hurt.

There wasn't much back here: a scraggly yard of trampled soil and grass, some truck tire marks, a Dumpster. I was alone, and no one was coming after me.

Go. Now.

Each step felt like a blow. My ears rang. The distance from the window to the jungle felt like a mile. I was in full view of the windows on this side of the building. If anyone saw me and told Conan, I would be toast. Try as I might, I just couldn't go very fast.

But as I stepped into the narrow path, I heard no alarm, no voices. Only the cawing of birds, the rustling of branches and leaves. An animal skittered through the grass, inches beyond my toes, barely making a sound.

Focus.

I hobbled as fast as I could. The adrenaline was pumping now, making me less aware of the pain in my head. The path wound around narrow gnarled trees. Thorns pricked my clothing and vines whipped against my face. The air was tinted orange in the rising sun, and droplets of dew sat like glistening insects on the leaves.

I don't know how long I trudged like that—a half hour? an hour?—before all traces of coolness had burned off. My clothes were soaking wet with sweat and dew. Flies swarmed around my neck and ankles. I was slowing.

When my foot clipped something hard and sharp, I went down.

I let out a wail. Couldn't help it. I took a deep breath to avoid blacking out. I had to will my clenched jaw open, to keep from shattering my own teeth. My eyes were seeing double, so I forced them to focus on where I'd tripped. It was a flat, disk-shaped rock, hidden by vines until my foot had torn away the greenery. A snaky line had been carved into the top.

I pulled away more vines. The rock was about the size of a manhole cover, covered with a blackish-green mold. But the carving was clear—a crude rendition of a slavering beast, a frightening eaglelike head with fangs.

It looked a lot like my Ugliosaurus.

This was freaking me out. I felt like someone was taunting me. I had to keep it together. There were carvings of mythical beasts all over the world—dragons and such. The kind of stuff that ends up in the museums of natural history. I didn't care about that.

Look forward. Eyes on the prize.

The path was becoming narrow and choked. To my right, the black-topped mountain loomed over the trees. It seemed to be staying exactly the same size, which probably meant it was farther away than I thought. How far—maybe a mile, two? I felt like I was going nowhere.

I vowed to keep the mountain in sight, always to my right. That way my path would be straight. But straight to *what*? What if the next village was a half continent away? I had no idea how to survive in the wilderness—except from reading *Hatchet* and *My Side of the Mountain*, and I barely remembered those.

As I plodded on, the day grew darker. The thickening canopy blotted out sunlight like a vast ceiling. My ankle ached from the fall and my hands were bloodied by thorns. Overhead, caws and screeches rang out like playground taunts: *Check it out! New prey! It can barely walk!* The woods seemed to be closing in, dense and alive, rustling with the wind. Or maybe not the wind. Maybe hawks or a nearby pack of pumas or an angry cannibalistic tribe—or all, jockeying for position. First come, first served. A shadow passed and a buzzard landed on a branch above me, cocking its head expectantly.

"Not dead!" I called up. "See the moving mouth? Not! Dead!"

It didn't budge a millimeter. It was waiting. Birds were smart. They knew where to find dinner. They could tell when someone was about to be killed.

My resolve was crumbling. I'd gone from get-me-out-of-here to what-was-I-thinking. Suddenly the idea of a zombie prep school didn't seem so bad.

Time to bail.

But as I turned, I felt my heart drop like a coconut. I saw no trace of a path. The compound had long been swallowed up by the trees. The mountain was invisible behind the greenery.

The sun and the mountain. Those were the things that gave me direction. But I couldn't see either one now.

"Help!"

My cry sounded puny in the wild-animal chorus. I stood, hoping that would help me get some more volume. *"Help me!"*

The buzzard fluffed out its feathers.

38

That was when I caught the hint of a breeze. It tickled across my nose and pricked me with a summer memory— the deck of a ferry, a Nantucket shack with Mom and Dad, air so damp it glued envelopes closed.

I may have been from Indiana, but I knew the smell of the sea. Sea meant shore. A shore was a path along water. I could follow it to a port. Swim if I had to. Signal to a passing ship.

As I moved in the breeze's direction, I came across a pile of charred branches and vines. Excellent. With dry tinder, bright sun, and a piece of flint, I could start a fire and send up smoke signals. I gathered some of it, used my shirt as a sack, and slung it over my shoulders.

I forged on, feeling stronger. I was going to make it! I thought about returning home. Dad would be so freaked. He'd get a job in town and never leave home again. We'd work together to expose this place. My brain would recover from whatever these people had done to it.

My head had stopped pounding. The ringing in my ears was totally gone.

Unfortunately, so was the sea smell.

I stopped. I hadn't been paying attention. I sniffed left and right. I sniffed until I had to sneeze. But I had lost the scent. Completely.

I thought of retracing my steps, but they'd vanished in the underbrush. Looking desperately around, I saw a gap between trees. Animal droppings. The possibility of a path. In the distance I thought I could see a tiny, bright glint. The reflection of the sun against water?

My heart raced. I hurried toward it, thrashing through the thick brush.

And then something fell from the sky.

"EEEEEEEEEEE!" With a piercing scream, it hurtled into my path. I sprang backward. As it leaped toward me, I could see a set of knifelike teeth and bright red gums.

A monkey landed on all fours and stood chattering angrily. In one hand it held some half-eaten fruit. In the other it was jangling something metallic.

A set of keys.

I rubbed my eyes. I was seeing things.

The monkey didn't seem to want to attack. Instead it turned its back and walked into the woods. I watched it go, feeling as if my beating heart would burst out of my chest. Just as I'd gathered myself, the monkey popped out again, scolding me. Waving into the jungle.

"You . . . you want me to follow you?" I said.

"EEEEEEEEE!"

I took that for a yes.

I tried to obey, but the thing was much slipperier than I was. It would disappear into the brush and then emerge exasperatedly with its hands on its little hips. Ahead, I saw the bright glow of a clearing—and the glint again. We were approaching it from a different angle. It wasn't water. It was something in the middle of a jungle clearing, something metallic or glass.

I picked up the pace, sweeping away thatches of thorny vines. And then I saw it.

A helicopter.

I figured it had crashed long ago, a relic from some war. But as I neared, I saw it looked new and was standing intact. The words KARAI INSTITUTE were emblazoned on the side in purple letters.

KI—the same initials that were stamped on my shirt and the banner in my room. I had no idea what Karai meant. But "institute"? You didn't call a hospital an institute. Some kind of laboratory, maybe. A place where smart people got together to have smart ideas. What was I doing there? Was I some kind of specimen?

I approached warily. The monkey had dropped the keys on the ground by the helicopter's door and was jumping around, hysterically excited.

"What do you want me to do?" I asked. "Fly it?"

The monkey clapped its hands and danced.

The only chopper I'd flown was in a video game. I escaped in order to get help, not get myself killed. Maybe there'd be something inside that could help—a map, a radio, a GPS device. Limping forward, I picked up the keys. "Thanks, bud. If I get out alive, I'm sending you bananas."

I grabbed the handle by the helicopter door and pulled myself up. Standing on the platform, I carefully pulled the door open.

And I nearly fell back onto the ground.

In the driver's seat was an enormous man in a short-sleeved shirt. His legs were crossed, revealing the thick, blackened sole of a bare foot. His arm showed a tattoo of the letters KI, made of intertwined snakes. As he turned with a sigh, a pair of steely green eyes peered out from a familiar, scarred face.

I said the only words my brain would allow. "I know you."

Red Beard grabbed me by the arm and pulled me upward. With his other hand, he swiped the keys from my grip.

"Next time," he said, "I shoot that chimp."

CHAPTER SEVEN

YODA IN TWEEDS

I DIDN'T STAND a chance. Red Beard's hands were like steel bands. He hefted me up into the chopper in one effortless swoop. The movement was so jarring and such a shock to my fragile system that I blacked out.

When I came to, we were rising high above the jungle to a chorus of simian screeches. I tried opening my eyes but even the light hurt. My brain felt as if someone had pumped it full of air.

"Seat belt," the man grunted.

The chopper's blades were deafening. I was going back. Back to the institute. Taken by the same man who had injected me with who knows what while he posed as a priest. He had walked past my house on bare feet. Now he was wearing earphones, moving the controls and humming tunelessly to himself. His eyes were bloodshot, his face haggard.

I tugged on his shirt to get his attention. "Take me home!"

"Hunh?" He turned, a little startled, as if he'd already forgotten I was there. Pulling off the left side of his earphones, he said, "Can't. Got to go back. Seat belt!"

My sight was slowly clearing, the pain in my head subsiding. What was he doing here—in the middle of a jungle? What had he been doing in front of my house . . . at the hospital?

What was going on?

"You . . . you injected me . . ." I said.

He shrugged. "Job."

"Why?" I said. "Why do you want me?"

"Do what I'm told," he replied.

"What's the Karai Institute?" I pressed.

"Bosses," he said, as if it were the most obvious answer in the world.

I gazed out the window. Off to one side, the mountain was like a black wound. In the distance, the sea stretched out in a silvery sheet. I could see where the helicopter had been waiting. The spot was surrounded by acres and acres of jungle. What were the chances I'd walk right to it?

"So . . . you were just waiting at some random place in the middle of the jungle?" I asked. "What if I didn't show up?"

44

The man's face darkened. "Blasted monkey thief!" He pulled down his arm angrily and the chopper swooped. "Stole keys!"

My eyes slammed shut and my stomach jumped. *Do not get him angry. And do not hurl.*

In a moment we were descending. I peered downward to see a round helipad hidden behind the largest building on the Karai Institute compound.

"Torquin," the guy said.

I figured he had lapsed into Swedish. "I'm sorry?"

"My name. Torquin."

"Oh!" I replied. "My name. Jack."

He cocked his head curiously. "You talk funny."

The chopper landed and I reached for the door handle. But Torquin let out a grunt and held me back.

Five uniformed workers, three men and two women who looked like the Olympic weight-lifting team, had rushed out of the building. The helicopter door opened and a gloved hand reached in. I tried to pull away, but it grabbed me tight. I heard a sharp, metallic click.

Handcuffs.

* * *

"Wait here." In the basement of a KI building, Torquin pulled open a conference room door. Unhooking the cuffs, the guards shoved me in. The place smelled of fresh cement.

"Go," Torquin barked. For a moment I thought he was

45

talking to me. But the guards instantly began to grumble and leave the room. I watched them disappear into a long hallway until Torquin slammed the door shut.

He pushed me around a long, polished-wood table to the other side of the room. The place was windowless with pristine white walls, swiveling leather seats, a coffee machine, and a pile of food on the table. With his Visigoth beard, bare feet, and camo clothes, Torquin looked way out of place. "Too many people. Don't like crowds," he said.

"Me neither," I agreed. "Handcuffs, too. Can you take them off?"

"Sit." He pulled out the leather chair at the very head of the table. My eyes shot directly toward the food spread: fresh and dried fruits, doughnuts, and pastries. On top of it all was a huge, gleaming, chocolate chocolate-chip muffin. It looked awesome, and I was starving.

As he undid my cuffs, Torquin pricked up his ears. "What's that noise?"

"My stomach," I said.

"Stay here," he replied. "Eat. Professor will come."

As he left, he grabbed the muffin off the top and inserted the entire thing into his mouth.

I hated him.

At the click of the shutting door, I began cramming doughnuts into my mouth. I chased them down with enough fresh pineapple and sliced mango to feed a small Caribbean nation.

When I couldn't fit another crumb, I slid back into a comfy leather chair and closed my eyes. I would have fallen asleep, I think, and slept for a week straight if five seconds later, the door hadn't flown open. This time, it wasn't Torquin.

It looked more like Yoda in a tweed jacket.

"Well, that must have been an ordeal," the man said in a flat, high-pitched voice. "Greetings and a cordial welcome, Jack."

He was an older guy, short and lumpy looking with dark, wrinkled skin and a broad nose crossed with veins. His eyes were droopy and sad, and his salt-and-pepper hair seemed to have slid off the top of his head and skidded to a stop just above his ears, forming two messy thatches on either side.

He walked around behind me, leaned in too close, and peered at my head as if I were a lab specimen. Pushing a pair of thick glasses up his nose, he said, "Are we feeling all right?"

"I'm trapped in this room with you," I said. "I was kidnapped and handcuffed. Nobody will tell me where I am or why I'm here. They took away my phone—"

"Yes, yes, that is a lot to unpack, isn't it?" the man said, still peering at my head. "But you were hardly kidnapped. You were found wandering off into the jungle. Dear Torquin saved your life. Now please turn and let me properly see the stitches. I promise not to hurt you."

He reached toward me. I flinched, but he took my chin in his hand and pushed it gently to one side. With his other hand, he lifted one of the bandages on the back of my head. "Splendid! The surgeons did a clean job back there. Are you still in much pain?"

My patience was gone. I was always taught to be nice to grown-ups, but that had expired. "They knocked me out and dug into my brain—*yes, I'm in pain!* I want to call my dad! Why am I here? And who the heck are you?"

The man pulled up a seat. As he extended his hand, his Coke-bottle glasses slid back down his nose. "Forgive my poor manners. As I used to say to my students at Yale, 'I have three names—Professor Radamanthus Bhegad— but unlike most academics, I let you use my first name. So you can call me . . . *Professor Bhegad*!'"

He sniffed with a very satisfied expression.

"Is that supposed to be funny?" I growled.

"It slew them at Yale," he said with a sigh. "I apologize for all the secrecy here. You see, Jack, it's very simple. You need us. You have a rare genetic condition that is about to kill you, and we at the Karai Institute are the only ones who know how to treat it."

I looked at him warily. "I thought you already treated it."

"We're not done yet. This condition is complex. It has

48

lain dormant in you until now. Untreated, it will overload your circuits, so to speak, and cause death." He sighed and wiped his glasses. "The good news is that when we are finished, you will attain superpowers beyond your wildest dreams."

"Is this a joke?" I asked.

"Pardon?" he said.

"You mean, *superpower* superpowers?" I asked. "Like flying, stopping bullets, becoming invisible, having X-ray vision?"

"Dear, dear boy," Professor Bhegad said, shaking his head with a barely tolerant smile, "the radioactivity in X-ray vision would wreak havoc, wouldn't it? It is a silly comic-book myth."

"And there are some superpowers that aren't?" I asked.

Bhegad nodded. He began to get this odd, faraway look in his eye. "The brain is an amazing thing, Jack. Quite exciting for a boy, no? Whoosh . . . whoosh . . . Geronimo!" He seemed to be igniting from the inside. Beads of perspiration lined his forehead. "Of course, this goes two ways. You see, we need *you*, too. Which is the main reason I am here. To explain your connection to a lost ancient civilization."

"Wait. Lost civilization?" I said. "I'm still at superpowers."

49

Without explaining, he began lifting doughnuts and fruit and glancing underneath. I noticed his fingernails were yellow, practically bitten to the nub.

That's when it finally hit me. This guy was a nutcase. And I was alone with him. This place wasn't a lab or a hospital. The "Karai Institute" was an *institution!*

"Excuse me, Professor . . . sir . . ." I said slowly, trying to keep my temper from rising, "I need to see your bosses. Please. Tell them where I am. Tell them there's been some mistake. Tell them I don't have my phone, and I need to contact my dad now. Because if they don't, *he will sue their pants off!*"

Bhegad looked up from the plate of food. His fingers were smeared with chocolate icing. "You sound frustrated. But you needn't worry. We have taken care of all details."

"What does that mean?" I shot back.

"For reasons that will become clear, secrecy is necessary. You will understand when I show you this informational slide show, if I can find that blasted remote. . . ." Leaving the pile of food, he flicked a switch on the wall, and a screen began to lower from the other end of the room. He knelt to peer under the table. "Honestly, no one puts things back where they belong. . . ."

I had to get out of here. Slowly I stood up. The exit was just beyond him. I was sitting at the other end of the table, on the right side. On the floor behind me to the left was a pile of papers. "Oh! Is it that little black thing?" I said, pointing to the corner. "Behind that stack of folders?"

"Ah, thanks . . . let me see . . ." he said, waddling around the table.

I waited until he was leaning over, looking away.

And I bolted.

CHAPTER EIGHT

G7W

I RAN DOWN an empty, carpeted hallway. At the end
was an exit sign pointing left, with a little graphic that indi-
cated stairs. I took the corner at top speed.

I didn't expect the stairs to be so close. Or to run into a
card game in progress on them.

"Whoa, where are you going?" Aly cried out. She, Marco,
and Cass jerked backward as I tripped over the steps.

Marco caught me midfall, but didn't let go. "'Sup, Jack?
Didn't Bhegad explain everything?"

"You mean the part about him saving my life?" I said,
struggling to pry myself loose. "Or turning me into a DC
Comics hero?"

"Are you a DC guy?" Cass asked. "Emosewa!"

52

"Meaning *awesome*—Cass likes to talk backward," Aly explained. "I'm a fan of the old-school *Superman* TV series . . . with George Reeves?"

They were all crazy. "Get me out of here! I want to see the head of this place!"

"You just did," Cass said. "Well, he's not the head of the whole thing . . ."

But Marco was already dragging me back toward the room. "Just do this, okay?" he said through clenched teeth. "Don't be a pain in the butt."

"By the Great Qalani, what are you doing to him?" Bhegad's voice thundered as he came around the corner. "If he pops those stitches, we lose him!"

Marco loosened his grip. I shot upstairs and pulled open the door, to the sound of a piercing alarm.

Three guards pivoted on their heels and faced me, hands on their weapons.

I stopped in my tracks. I was trapped.

"Jack," Bhegad said softly from the bottom of the steps, "I have PhDs from Yale and Cambridge. If you think I'm crazy, then you must think your three friends are, too. And Torquin and the guards. And seventy-nine world-class experts in genetics, biophysics, classical archaeology, geography, computer science, mythology, medicine, and biochemistry. Not to mention a support staff of two hundred and twenty-eight. The Karai Institute is the finest think tank in the world. And we are patient. We can wait until you're ready to listen. But you will not escape. So it's either now or later. Your choice."

"I don't believe a word of it," I said.

Bhegad beckoned me to come down the stairs. "Marco, Cass, Aly—would you kindly turn your backs?"

Marco spun around first—and my jaw nearly dropped. Buried in his dark mop of hair was a white Λ.

Cass's, too.

"Mine is under the dye," Aly explained.

I swallowed hard. I took a couple of steps downward. The guards slammed the door shut. "So . . . you're all . . . ?"

"The lambda is a unique physical sign," Bhegad explained. "We don't understand the mechanics of it. The hair changes rather quickly, and at virtually the same age among all who have the condition. But we do know its significance. It is common to one group of people, whom we call the Select."

"Select? What are we selected for, something good?" I asked.

"Yes and no," the professor replied. "Each of you has a rare genetic marker. It is an extraordinary gift, but it also happens to be a ticking bomb. Jack, we were hoping to have five of you here—including a young man called Randall Cromarty. You know the name?"

I was about to say no. But the name did ring a bell. A

news item. A grainy video that had been circulating for the last week or so. Some kid rolling a gutter ball, throwing up his hands, dropping to the floor. The story Dad had sent me. "The kid who died in the bowling alley?"

Bhegad nodded. "At the age of thirteen, in Illinois. Cause unknown. Before him, a girl named Sue Gudmundsen fell into a fatal coma while in a San Diego mall—also thirteen. And Mo Roberts, playing catch with his little sister. In all cases, our medical team was too late. But we found you in time."

"Torquin . . ." I said. "Dr. Saark . . . But how did they know?"

"For that, you can thank our IT staff," Bhegad said. "After your last checkup, Dr. Flood made a note on your computerized medical records about the very beginnings of the lambda. Our tracking software picked it up."

"You hacked my medical records." My checkup had been about a week before the math test—a day before Dad left for Singapore. Had Dr. Flood mentioned anything about a mark on the back of my head? I couldn't remember.

"*Hacking* is such an ugly word," Bhegad replied wearily.

"So . . . what does the lambda mean?" I asked.

"Think of those nightly news headlines, the stories that float around social media like crazy." Bhegad smiled. "An ordinary person lifts an entire car to free a trapped loved one! A kid considered mentally defective draws ornate cathedrals from memory, to the tiniest detail! As humans, we access only part of our brain's capacity. But these people have tapped into a vast unused area of the brain that we call the ceresacrum."

"What does that have to do with us?" I asked.

"Some people breach the ceresacrum temporarily, in response to crisis," Bhegad replied. "Some are born with a bit of access, not much. But what if the ceresacrum's gate could be lifted? Not just the rare flash of genius or the momentary feat of strength, but total access? Imagine! In each of us lies the potential to do superhuman things. Feats of great physical daring, art, science. The ability to defy laws of nature. Am I clear, Jack?"

Aly, Cass, and Marco were grinning at me now. My mind was a big fog of duh. "No."

"Some genes are buried deeply in our DNA," Bhegad continued. "For example, we all possess the code for a tail . . . for gills! But these are not *expressed*, as we say. Nature has shut the mechanism, except in extremely rare cases. Being able to open the ceresacrum gate is like having a tail. The genetic ability is there, but ninety-nine point nine nine nine nine percent of the world's people do not express it. You four"—he glanced slowly at each of us— "are the point zero zero zero one."

Now it was becoming clear. And the clarity hurt. "You mean . . . we're all genetic mutants?"

"Yes, in a good way," Bhegad said. "You four possess what we call G7W. It's a marker. A piece of genetic code. We do not understand how it works, but we know what it indicates. You are the elite. The top of the top. The ones whose ceresacrum can be cracked wide open. Millennia ago, this ability may have existed in many, if not all, humans."

"Wait," I said. "Evolution is survival of the fittest. So if you had dudes who were superhumans way back then, why wouldn't they have survived to now?"

"Because those who die early are, by definition, not the fittest." Bhegad leaned forward. "Jack, we ran a genetic map of Randall Cromarty's DNA after he died. And Sue Gudmundsen's and Mo Roberts's. They all had G7W."

I looked from Aly to Marco to Cass. Their faces were drawn. "So I'm—all of us—we're going to die?" I asked.

"No one who has had this marker has lived past the age of fourteen," Bhegad said. "For whatever reason, the gene kicks into action around your age—and its actions are too powerful to be withstood by the body. Which is why we brought you here. We have developed a treatment. The operation on your head was the first step. You will be required to undergo regular procedures every ten days or so. Your first will be in about seventy-two hours. But we cannot keep you alive forever. There is a point after which nothing can be done—a sort of expiration date we can read in your genome. And that is what scares me. The fact that all our science is still not enough to keep you alive."

I sank to the stairs. The carpet felt clammy. The walls felt cold. It was as if the stairwell itself were my coffin. I wouldn't leave here without dying. I wouldn't see my dad ever again. I might develop a power or two in the meantime. Maybe paint a cathedral or twirl a helicopter in my bare hands. And then . . . ?

"So your job is to study us," I said. "We're your superhero guinea pigs. So what happens when we're dead? Will you call our families and friends—or just have Torquin dump our bodies in the sea?"

"Yo, hear him out, brother," Marco said.

"I'm not your brother!" I snapped. "Here's a deal, Professor Bhegad. Call my dad. Give him your location. Let him come here so I can see him—"

"Jack, please," Bhegad said. "Your father would snatch you back in an instant—the worst thing that could happen to you. Besides, it would be impossible to give him these coordinates. This place is not visible by ordinary means. Radar, sonar, GPS—none of them register here. There are forces on this island even we do not understand—"

"Then go get him and bring him here," I said. "If he knows I need the treatments, he'll stay. He'll help!"

"We can't risk that!" Bhegad shouted. "Your lungs

need air, your eyes need light—but your ceresacrum needs something here, in the earth itself. Eons ago, this island was a continent. Its people created grand architecture, made extraordinary music, governed with fairness and sophistication. It was protected by a curious flux point of natural forces within the earth—electromagnetic, gravitational, perhaps extraterrestrial. When the place was destroyed, the forces were, too." Bhegad's phone beeped. He snatched it angrily from his pocket and looked at the screen.

"Dude, man up to this," Marco said to me. "We're on what's left of Atlantis. And we're, like, great-great-great-to-a-zillionth descendants."

"Atlantis? Very funny," I said, attempting a laugh.

No one else laughed with me. I looked toward Professor Bhegad, but he was texting, his face lined with concern. As he snapped it shut, he said, "I must go. But, yes, Marco is correct. You are connected to Atlantis by blood. Your ceresacrum must feed off the ancient power in order to survive. But that power must be found."

I swallowed hard. Aly and Cass were looking pale and frightened. "How?" I asked.

Bhegad stood. He pocketed his phone and began edging up the stairs toward the building's exit. "We don't know where it is now. The power of Atlantis was stolen. Broken up and hidden all over the world. You must find what was taken. Your lives will be saved, Jack, if you locate all the elements of that power. You must bring them together and return it to Atlantis."

Bhegad's phone beeped again, and before I could say a word, he was up the stairs and gone.

CHAPTER NINE

THE SELECT

I FELT LIKE I'd been run over by a three-ton tank. Or squashed by Torquin's feet.

Aly, Cass, and Marco were all talking at once. Really loudly. We were walking out of the building and onto the path that ringed around the quad. They were telling me what a smart guy Bhegad was and how he was our only hope and how famous we would become.

Half of me felt like a caged orangutan in the zoo. The other half wanted to burst out laughing. Either Bhegad was going to save my life or I had been pranked by some island Yoda who was two sandwiches short of a picnic.

"Atlantis . . ." I muttered. "Superpowers . . . I'm supposed to believe this?"

Aly put her arm around me. "Hey, we all doubted it, too!" she said in a loud, affirming voice, like she was talking to someone at the other end of a room. "It's a tough transition!"

I looked at Cass. "I think Bhegad is nuts. No offense, but I'm not sure about you guys either. You all don't mind not seeing your parents?"

"Um, no." Cass's face clouded over. "Not really. Well, I do, I guess. I mean, I *did*."

My heart dropped. I felt like an idiot for asking the question. "Oh, I'm sorry. Are they . . . ?"

"No!" Cass shot back. "They're not dead. But we . . . my family isn't close."

Marco ran ahead of us on the path. He grabbed a basketball that was lying against the side of a building and began dribbling.

"Trust us," Aly said. "This is no *Truman Show*."

"She likes old movies." Cass stepped up onto the path's narrow stone border, and began flapping his arms rhythmically. "Be grateful, Jack. Just think what would have happened if they didn't find you."

I had to admit that one. "Okay, I might have died. But I feel totally cured now. Do you really believe this skeezy story—they're keeping us alive so we can find our inner superpowers, but only if we find the lost power of Atlantis?"

"I believe him!" Aly exclaimed.

"Brother Jack, we are surrounded by world experts," Marco said, spinning the basketball on one finger. "Wicked smart people. If they just wanted goons to travel and find the Atlantean powers, they could get them. They got Torquin, didn't they?"

I looked around. Teams were working hard, mowing lawns, repairing roofs, paving walkways. A group was wiring a small maroon half globe to the side of a building. It looked to me like the surveillance cameras in Dad's old office building. They waved to us as we passed.

"I used to feel the same way you do, Jack," Aly said, toning her voice down. "I was on a plane flight home from Washington, DC, watching *Citizen Kane* for like the thirtieth time, and just when I got to the election scene, I had a seizure—and then I was here. The only other person was Marco. *That* was depressing."

"Thanks a lot." Marco threw the basketball at her head, but she caught it. "One minute I'm about to break the scoring record in a middle school basketball game, the next minute I collapse on the court—and I wake up here. I was the first one."

"You're in middle school?" I asked. I'd been assuming Marco was at least fifteen.

"I'm thirteen. Big for my age. I think they almost flew me back home, just to get rid of me. But then I started getting the treatments." Marco faked left, stepped across my path, and quickly snatched his ball back from Aly. "I can't wait to become invincible."

Cass had veered off the path and was moving diagonally to the right.

"Where are you going, brother Cass?" Marco asked.

"Nowhere. Just trying to retrace the exact path I took at three o'clock or so." Cass shrugged. "I committed my foot placements to memory. The patterns of the little pebbles in the blacktop. And the ssarg."

"Ssarg?" I said, and immediately got it. "Oh. Grass."

"Humor him," Aly murmured. "He's just that way with directions, trivia, you name it. World-class memory."

"Just about the only thing I don't remember is how I ended up here," Cass said. "I was in a parking lot, and then I was here. Hey, tell me the name of the town where you live, Jack. And then name any other place in the United States."

"Belleville, Indiana," I offered. "And . . . um, Nantucket, Massachusetts."

Cass stood stock-still for about thirty seconds. "Belleville. Take Route Thirty east to Fort Wayne; Route Sixty-nine north to Route Eighty all the way across Ohio, Pennsylvania, and New Jersey to the George Washington Bridge to the Cross Bronx; the Hutch to the Merritt, swinging down to Ninety-five via Route One at Milford; One Ninety-five in Rhode Island, Four Ninety-five to the

Cape, and Six to One-thirty-two to the ferry in Hyannis."

"Which shipping channel does the ferry take?" Marco asked.

"Ynnuf ton," Cass drawled.

I couldn't believe what I'd just heard. "He's right. I used to follow the route on a map on our vacations. That's freaky."

"The ceresacrum takes your biggest talent and makes it awesome," Aly said. "The treatments allow G7W to do its thing."

"What's your big talent?" I asked. "Something to do with movies?"

"That's just a hobby with her," Cass said. "Often very gniyonna."

"I sent cute kitten photos to the members of the National Security Council," Aly said with a laugh. "Which doesn't seem like much, except I hacked into their system to do it. Through a military-grade firewall and the highest level of encryption. I was bored after finishing my homework. It seemed like a fun project."

"Did you go to jail?" I asked.

"I was nine years old." She shrugged. "I didn't know I was doing anything illegal. They didn't arrest me, they hired me. To strengthen their system. And . . ." Her face darkened. "Also to do some other stuff. I was their youngest employee ever."

"What other stuff?" I asked.

She ignored the question and jerked a thumb over toward Marco. "Believe it or not, Slacker Boy over here is good at something, too."

Marco was staring at the basketball court at the other end of the quad, near the main building. He bounced his basketball twice, rocking on his feet. "The blindfold, please."

Aly took a bandanna from Marco's rear pocket and tied it across his eyes. Slowly he reared back with the basketball.

The court was half a football field away. It was like trying to hit an airplane with a snowball. Marco crouched, then let go with a loud grunt. The ball shot high into the air. Scary high.

Marco pulled off the blindfold and watched as the ball came down like a cannon shot. It ripped the net as it dropped through the hoop.

"Three points," Aly said.

"Dang," Marco said disappointedly. "It grazed the rim."

My jaw nearly hit the ground. "I did not see that."

* * *

Cass had photo recall and could speak backward at will. Aly was a hacker genius and movie expert. Marco was Michael Jordan on steroids, without the steroids.

I was chopped liver.

I sat in my room, glumly putting on a pair of khaki pants and a button-down KI-logo shirt. I didn't have a talent. I was *eh* in school and sports. I could use computers but didn't really know how they worked. I could set up a fake volcano to launch a plastic toy. Maybe that was my talent. Dumb contraptions. Maybe I'd be able to launch an SUV using palm trees.

I was the opposite of the Select. I was the Discard Pile. Not good at anything. Maybe my lambda mark was just premature aging. I was a mistake.

And now I was supposed to go to a dinner honoring me. Were they expecting me to show off, the way Cass and Marco had?

"Ready?" Aly called out from the hallway, knocking on the door.

I opened it. She was wearing a striped knit shirt and a black leather skirt. Her wrists were full of cool, jangly jewelry that matched her pink hair, and she was wearing some makeup. "You look emosewa," I said.

"You don't look so bad yourself," she said.

She was smiling brightly, like we were about to go to the prom or something, which made me feel really uncomfortable. "I was . . . making a joke," I said, "about Cass's backward speak. Not that you don't look it—emosewa. Er, awesome. You know."

"Quit while you're ahead, McKinley." Aly took my arm

67

as we walked down the hall.

"Heeeere comes the bride . . ." Marco sang, emerging from his room.

Aly sneered. "Maturity is not part of Marco's talent profile."

We picked up Cass from his room, and Professor Bhegad met us outside our dorm. "Everyone is excited to meet you, Jack. Come."

As he walked, his massive key chain banged against his hip like tiny cymbals. He pointed out the various buildings—a library with enormous windows, a state-of-the-art gym, a museum. People joined us as we walked, all wearing clothes that showed a KI insignia over the left breast pocket. Marco seemed to have a different secret handshake for each of them. Like he'd known them his whole life.

Strange voices called out to me: "Hey, Jack, how are you feeling?" . . . "Book club meets on Tuesdays!" . . . "yoga" . . . "spinning class" . . . "surfing club" . . .

Before we went into the dining hall, Marco stopped short. "Yo, P. Beg, I want to show Jack the media room."

"It's *Professor Bhegad*," the old man said. "And I don't think we have the time. The chef has prepared—"

"One minute, that's all," Marco insisted.

As Bhegad continued to protest, Marco pulled a plastic card from the protective pouch that hung from a big key ring on the professor's belt. He quickly ran to a Colonial-style brick building, threw open the door, and announced, "Welcome to utter coolness."

Although the building looked old, the inside was amazing—long and rectangular, with a lofted area and a glass ceiling high above. Everywhere I looked there were consoles and monitors, game devices and arcade machines. The beeps and sound effects made it seem like some strange forest full of squeaking electronic rodents.

"Nerd Heaven," Cass continued. "Including board games and jigsaw puzzles."

"We're getting a foosball table on Friday," Aly said with relish. "And we're having a Preston Sturges festival. *Hail the Conquering Hero* Saturday night."

We? I could never, ever think of myself and the Karai Institute as *we*.

"Dinnertime!" Bhegad said, heading back to the door. "Oh dear, where did that access card go?"

"I gave it back to you, P. Beg," Marco said.

Now Bhegad was looking around the floor in frustration. "Achh. I've had this problem ever since I turned sixty. Honestly, I just lose *everything*! Ah, well, it will turn up. We mustn't be late. We have a surprise for you, Jack. Come."

As Professor Bhegad headed for the door, Cass and Aly followed. I turned to go with them.

Behind me, I felt Marco slipping something flat and rectangular into my pocket.

CHAPTER TEN
SECRET MESSAGE

MARCO HADN'T SAID a word. Hadn't even looked at me.

What was I doing with the card key? I didn't want it. I didn't want to be caught with it. Was this Marco's plan—to get me in trouble? Why?

I tried to look at him, to get some sort of indication. He was sitting across a crowded table from me, stuffing food into his mouth and carrying on a conversation with some young female staff member whose name tag said Ginger.

The banquet table was enormous, running the length of a vast octagonal room. Chairs were packed close together, and it seemed like the entire Karai Institute was here—fat old men with ZZ Top beards, hipsters in narrow glasses, all kinds of people. Many sported intertwining-snake KI

70

tattoos on their arms. They all seemed to know each other well, their laughter and conversation hovering like a cloud of sound.

The place was called the Comestibule. Professor Bhegad said it meant "cafeteria," and he didn't answer me when I asked why they didn't call it a cafeteria. Its walls, paneled with blond wood, rose dizzyingly upward to a kind of steeple. All around us were portraits of stern-faced scientists, who seemed to be staring at me like I owed them money.

A great chandelier, made of curled glass tubes that resembled Medusa's head of snakes, flooded the room with LED light. Across the rafters hung a banner that stretched nearly the length of the room:

WELCOME TO YOUR KARAI INSTITUTE HOME, JACK!

Professor Bhegad had made a big deal about the chef preparing quail for dinner. The thought of it made me sick.

Cass leaned over to me and mumbled a long stream of words that made absolutely no sense. "Dude, stop it," I said. "I can't do that backward-speaking thing."

As Cass stared at me, looking annoyed, Marco's voice boomed out toward a passing waitress. "Excuse me, you got any more food? There isn't much meat on these things."

"If you eat one more quail, sir, you'll fly away," the girl answered.

"Take mine," I said.

Marco reached across and vacuumed my plate away.

I kept expecting people to ask me about my Big Talent, but no one did. Fortunately, they all seemed pretty normal. Friendly.

A clinking sound rang out, and Professor Bhegad was on his feet. "Ladies and gentlemen and Scholars of Karai! Our Comestibule is a place of great joy today. We have saved a young life and we continue our adventure with renewed strength and hope. Tonight and over the next few weeks you will all have a chance to meet our newest young genius, Jack McKinley!"

"Speech! Speech!" Marco yelled through the applause.

My heart was ping-ponging. I still couldn't get used to this. *Weeks?* Here?

I felt an elbow in my side. "Hey, wake up, dude," Aly muttered. "You're getting a standing O."

All around the table, people were rising to their feet and applauding. Staring directly at me. All except Cass, who was doodling on a napkin.

"Stand up!" Aly said.

My chair was heavy and hard to push back. I felt like a dorkus maximus. I waved awkwardly and sat again.

"That was inspiring," Marco said, his mouth full of quail.

As I sat, I noticed a paper napkin and a pen lying on my chair. "Is this yours?" I asked Cass.

His eyes widened. He glanced up at the Medusa chandelier. I looked into the crazy swirl of glass tendrils, but I couldn't tell what he was acting so weird about.

Not weird. Scared, maybe. His face was tense and his fingers had the tremors.

I flipped the napkin over and saw a scribbled note. A bunch of numbers.

"The banner is cool!" Cass blurted out. "'Welcome to your Karai Institute home, Jack!' Man, I never had something this fancy. I'd remember those words forever. Wow. 'Welcome to your Karai Institute home, Jack!'"

He was trying to tell me something. I glanced at the note and figured I needed to read it in private. "I—I think I'll wash my hands," I said, pushing my chair back.

The men's room was outside the dining room, across a small hallway with a view of the kitchen. I bolted inside, ran into an open stall, and latched it shut. Carefully I spread the napkin on the wall and looked at the message.

6-27-2-8-23-20-30-15-13-4-11-21

13-5-11-30-8-28-16-2-31

15-6-1-7-13-25-20-15-1-17-10

They looked like Lotto numbers. What did they mean? Could it be some kind of code? Maybe an alphabet-number substitution thing. Like *A* = 1 and *B* = 2.

Nope. Didn't work. Some of the numbers were greater than twenty-six, and there were only twenty-six letters in the alphabet.

I sat back with a sigh. What was it Cass had been telling me? *The banner is cool . . . I'd remember those words forever.* He'd read it aloud. Twice.

Weird.

I wrote the banner's message across the top of the napkin: WELCOME TO YOUR KARAI INSTITUTE HOME, JACK.

Staring at it, I wondered if he meant it was connected to the code. I started numbering each of the letters in the banner message.

The first number on Cass's coded message was 6. That mapped to the *M* in the banner message.

I went one by one with each of his digits: 6, 27, 2, 8, 23, 20, 30, 15, 13, 4, 11, 21, 13, 5, 11, 30, 8, 28, 16, 2, 31, 15, 6, 1, 7, 13, 25, 20, 15, 1, 17, 10.

MEETINMARCOS
ROOMTHREE
AMWERUNAWAY.

Meet in Marco's room. Three A.M. we run away.

I took a deep breath. Then I ripped up the napkin and flushed it into oblivion.

CHAPTER ELEVEN
THREE A.M.

AS MY BEDROOM door clicked open, I snapped awake.
I didn't know what time it was. My brain had been dipping
in and out of sleep for hours. The night had spooked me.
I didn't trust the smiling, squeaky-clean faces at dinner.
Or Professor Bhegad.

"It's Marco," came a whisper. "Time to get up."

The little glowing clock on my bed table read 2:56. My
foggy brain was awakening. *Three A.M. we run away.*

"You're early," I mumbled.

Marco stepped inside. His backpack was slung across
his shoulder. "Just wanted to be sure you got up. I'm kind of
a control freak. But you probably figured that out. Come on
before it's too late. Aly disabled the bugs."

I turned to face him. "The *what?*"

Marco gestured toward the banner with the KI symbol. "Wake up and smell the coffee, Jethro. They've got a recording device in that banner. And in a few other places, too. Just sound, out of respect for privacy, I guess. The cameras are on the outside of the building. Now come on. Don't make me carry you out of here."

I was on my feet. I hadn't changed out of my clothes since dinner, so all I had to do was slip my feet into my Chucks.

Marco flung the door open. Conan was slumped backward in his chair, mouth open, snoring. "Aly hacked into the medical-supply security and liberated some sleeping pills," Marco explained as we walked toward his room. "Horse strength for Conan. Not that he really needed it. Sleep is his natural state."

Marco's room was the second door to the right. Cass and Aly were already waiting inside, looking grim and worried. The little smiles that had always been plastered on their faces were gone.

"We owe you an explanation," Aly said, talking very quickly. "You think we're idiots. *Children of the Corn* zombies. We had to act enthusiastic. We're under surveillance, indoors and out, twenty-four seven. I've been trying to hack into the system since day one. The encryption makes the US government look like amateurs, but I finally did it."

"So . . . everything you've been telling me . . . about how

happy you are here, how much you like this place . . ." I said.

"Lies," Cass said. "At dinner I wanted to whisper the plan to you, but that chandelier is full of unidirectional mikes. Then I tried to talk to you in Backward, but you outed me. Sorry about the code. It was my only choice. If I had my way, we would all be talking in code, just for the fun of it. Naem I tahw wonk uoy fi."

"I'm adjusting to the idea that you're all normal. Don't spoil it." I smiled. "So I was right—they're evil; they're fooling us."

"We'll talk later, bro," Marco said. "We have to move, before they notice the system is down."

"I replaced their live feed with a recording," Aly explained. "It's showing an hour-long endless loop of what happened from about one A.M. to two A.M. If they're listening to Marco's room now, they're hearing him snore, all curled up with his toy sheep, Daisy."

"Leave Daisy out of this," Marco grumbled.

Cass was peering out the window. "At two o'clock, they switch to only one guard on duty outside. We've been watching him for the last week, and he always sneaks off for a snack by five after three—at the latest. M&M's and Diet Dr Pepper. He's like clockwork."

"That's it?" I said. "Just one guard? For such a high-tech place?"

"It's *because* of the high-tech security they don't need so many guards," Marco said. "You get past the guards, and the electric eye zaps you anyway."

I must have turned green, because Aly immediately added, "They disabled it when you escaped, Jack."

"They *knew?*" I said. "But—but no one stopped me!"

"Until . . . ?" Marco said.

"This monkey appeared in the middle of nowhere," I murmured, "with a set of keys . . ."

"Led you to a clearing in the woods, right?" Marco said. "A big chopper just waiting, with ol' Sweet Cheeks in the pilot seat? Same thing happened to me. They *let* you go, Jack, and then manipulated your return. To teach you a lesson. Wear you down. That's the way they operate."

I felt as if I were emerging from a fog. For the first time since I got here, I was actually hearing things that made sense. "What about all that junk about the superpowers? How'd you make that basket from three miles away, Marco—invisible ropes?"

"He really did that," Aly said, gently taking my arm. "Look, I think the G7W marker is real. With each treatment, we get smarter, stronger, more whatever we are. *That's* what I think their goal is, Jack—to make some race of superpeople, not save us from death. They want us supercharged so we can help in their crazy missions. After this

Atlantis thing, who knows what's next? Maybe finding the abominable snowman."

"Aly's supposed to be having her treatment right now," Cass said. "She went in at eleven o'clock and is supposed to stay hooked up to machines all night. But when the docs left, she rewired the hospital monitors so it seems like she's still there."

Aly smiled. "And look at me. Skipped the treatment and I feel great! Body feels good, mind is sharp. Ask me to recite the opening lines of *Star Wars Five*."

"When we bust out of here, I'm heading for the NBA draft," Marco said.

Cass had taken twelve sheets of loose-leaf paper from under the rug and carefully taped them together. On the combined sheets was a map drawn in exacting pencil strokes. A miniature replica of the campus was at the bottom, each building labeled. At the top right was a cloud of dense trees with a dotted-line path ending at a clearing. Cass had drawn a key and a monkey on the path, and a helicopter at the end of it. "How do you know all this?" I asked.

"We have outings, nature walks," he replied. "Sometimes the guide lets us go off the beaten track. I remember it all. If I have enough data, I can mentally map a larger area according to the size and variety of the vegetation and the dispersion of light. Also spoor deposits. Patterns of animal poop can be geographically significant. Also, by the way, poop is a palindrome. The same backward and forward."

"Thank you," I said numbly.

Cass traced his finger along a path through the jungle on the upper left, a different direction from the path to the helicopter. At the very top of the map was a shoreline with a dock and a boat. "We'll head here, to a beach the guards use. Which has a boat."

On the way, his finger had crossed a line with jagged markings. "Is that the electric fence?" I asked.

Aly shook her head. "Not a fence. Filaments. Thin as cobwebs. You don't know you've been through them until you're on the ground, wriggling. They don't kill you, but you'll wish they had. The filaments were de-electrified and dropped to the ground during your escape attempt."

"And now?" I asked.

"Active again," Aly said, shaking her head. "And hard to disable. The security system is decentralized. I managed to hack the recording devices and cameras around the dorm. But the other campus cameras are still live, and so are the filaments."

"Dora the Explorer here knows where all the surveillance cameras are," Marco said, gesturing toward Cass.

"We're going to take a route to the control building that avoids the guards' sight lines."

"Once we're there, I will get to work on the security system," Aly said.

"How will we get in?" I asked.

All three of them smiled at me.

"Dude, you've got to have *some* kind of talent, right?" Marco said.

CHAPTER TWELVE

THE MOE QUADRANT

"ARE YOU SURE this will work?" Aly whispered as we raced along the back wall of the dining building.

"No!" I shot back. "I mean, I don't know!"

The moon was a ghostly blur under the cloud cover, but we could see Cass just ahead of us, pacing a precise path out of camera range. "This way," he said.

I patted my pocket nervously. In it were two shoelaces I'd taken from a pair of spare shoes in my closet, and a large rock. I was shaking with fear.

They were counting on my part of the escape plan. But my idea seemed borderline idiotic. "Okay, stay near the wall and get to the fire escape of Building D," Cass said.

We ran into the darkness, careful of the lone guard and

cameras and anything else that might give us away. Cass led us to Building D, a brick structure set all by itself away from the main campus. Just above us hung a retractable fire escape. Marco reached up and grabbed the bottom rung. His backpack was stuffed with supplies, but on his shoulders it seemed weightless. "Isn't someone going to hear this?" he said.

"I used WD-40," Cass whispered. As Marco lowered the ladder in silence, he added, "So, listen up, guys, here's what to do when you get to the top—"

"Aren't you going with us?" Aly said.

Cass shrugged. "I have this thing about h-h-heights."

Marco grabbed Cass by the waist, slung him over his shoulder, and climbed the ladder. "Don't look down," he advised.

Aly and I followed. We made our way across the rooftop, stepping lightly. As we passed a small skylight, I glanced down. The place was whirring with mechanical life. A rack of servers beeped and flickered. Laptop screens shone with Karai Institute screensavers. No people.

Marco and Aly were crouched at the opposite edge of the roof, looking down. A few feet away sat Cass, with his back to the parapet. "I think I'm going to be sick," he murmured.

"Tell Jack what to do first, Cass," Marco said. "Then hurl."

"Ok-k-kay. See if you can locate the c-c-camera," Cass said, jerking his thumb vaguely downward.

I glanced over the side of the roof. The camera was there. Fastened to the side of the wall. I calculated the distance downward as I pulled the shoelaces from my pocket.

"We're counting on you, MacGyver," Marco said.

I gulped. A great big EPIC FAIL sign flashed in my head as I took a deep breath. I tied the two shoelaces together and then knotted the rock at the bottom. I could sense my three partners staring at me, baffled. "Okay, so it's not *Mission Impossible*," I said.

Leaning ever so slightly over the roof, I eyed the maroon camera. I dropped the rock, holding on to the shoelace. Trying to gauge the distance, I swung the rock outward and let its momentum carry it back toward the lens.

Thwuck.

It struck dully against the wall, about two feet to the left of the camera.

"Let me try." Marco grabbed the shoelace from my hand and pulled up the rock. Holding the lace with his right hand, he used his left to hurl the rock up into the sky. He stood there, watching motionless until the rock reached the end of its trajectory and the string snapped it back.

It hit the lens dead center, sending a spray of glass and plastic to the ground.

My jaw dropped open. It had worked!

"Good thinking, Marco," Aly said.

"Marco?" I repeated. "It was *my* idea—"

"Get down!" Aly whispered. "That was loud. What if the guard heard it?" We ducked behind the parapet next to Cass, our breaths puffing wispily in the cool humidity.

I listened for a car, an opening door, a voice.

Nada.

After a moment, I peered over the top. "Coast is clear. Let's book."

"My knees are l-locked," Cass complained.

"At least you're not speaking backward," Aly said.

Marco yanked Cass over his shoulders again and led us back down the fire escape. We ran around to the entrance, under the remains of the camera. The door to the building had a card swiper that glowed red. "You're doing great, brother Jack," Marco said. "Now use that card I stole from Bhegad. It gives access to all the buildings."

I fished the stolen card out of my pocket and swiped it. The little light went from red to green, and Marco pushed open the door.

We raced inside. Aly tapped on a touch pad and a screen glowed to life:

> **WELCOME TO THE KARAI INSTITUTE**
> # SECURITY MATRIX
> **PLEASE INSERT FINGER FOR PRINT MATCHING**

"Oh, g-g-great," Cass said.

"You guys should have known about this," I hissed.

"We did." Aly pulled out a flash drive. "To a computer, a fingerprint is a set of data—zeroes and ones like everything else. I managed to get into the stored ID database and download Torquin's finger ID. The system will automatically upload it and conclude that he put his index finger on the pad."

She inserted the drive and the screen changed to a KI wallpaper with a new flashing message: HELLO, O MIGHTY SAVIOR OF ALL THINGS FLUFFY AND FIERCE.

"That's Torquin's welcome message?" Marco said.

"He has an odd idea of his own personal mission." Aly's fingers flew over the keyboard. The screen began flashing complex sequences of circuits. "Cafeteria . . . library . . . sewage . . ."

"No sewage pipes," Cass protested. "I'm afraid of heights *and* depths."

Aly smacked the keyboard. "Here's the security fence. But they'll only let me access one quadrant at a time."

"How do we know which is the right one to pick?" I asked.

"The one that doesn't get us killed," Aly replied. "Eeney, meeny, miney . . ."

* * *

"Moe" was the quadrant that went straight past Bhegad's house. He lived behind the library, in a little gingerbread cottage that was like something out of "Hansel and Gretel."

87

All the lights were on inside.

"We can't do this!" Cass whispered.

"He's snoring," Marco remarked. "*I* can't even hear us!"

We managed to slip by, one at a time, crouching below an open window. Cass was the last. He was frozen at the edge of the house. "Ahhh . . ." he said, his eyes narrowing for a sneeze.

"Oh, no," Marco murmured. "Please no . . ."

"Hold it in!" Aly whispered.

"CHOOO!"

We all went stiff. From inside Professor Bhegad's cottage came a snuffling sound. Then a honk.

He was still snoring.

Marco dove for Cass, grabbed him by the shoulder, and pulled him past the window. We headed for the jungle, running through a small yard and then an open, grassy field.

Aly found a well-trampled path into the underbrush. After a few dozen yards she stopped. "There," she said, pointing to what looked like a small sapling. "Careful."

The disabled electric filaments were hanging like cobwebs.

As Aly bounded into the jungle, Marco escorted Cass by the arm. "Okay, brother Cass," he said, "you're the navigation guy. Lead the way."

Cass took a deep breath and closed his eyes for a moment. Then he began walking tentatively to the right. "This way.

And if you see something, say something."

Aly and I followed close behind, with Marco bringing up the rear. His backpack clunked as he walked, and for the first time he looked uncertain. "I wish I had my basketball," he murmured. "I feel more comfortable with my basketball."

The memory of this jungle sickened me. The vines lashed just as sharply as they had the day before, the roots caught just as tightly—but in the darkness it was ten times worse. We had only the occluded light of the moon, and soon the canopy blocked even that. Through the underbrush, I could practically feel Cass shaking. He sounded like a GPS voice on a short circuit. "Go l-left here, I th-think . . ."

"Are you okay?" I asked him.

"I hate the dark," he said. "Okay, head for the shadow of that ball, tent tree. Um, sorry. Tall, bent tree . . ."

As we walked, no one wanted to talk much. The bugs swarmed all over us, and we stayed busy slapping them away.

"Um . . . this pathway to the left looks right," Cass said. "I think."

"What do you mean, you *think*?" Marco called out. "I thought you were perfect."

"Not when I'm nervous," Cass said.

"Can we slow down?" Aly asked. "I'm out of breath."

"If we go any slower, we'll be going backward—*geeaaah, horsefly!*" Marco said, slapping his forehead.

Breathing hard, Aly sat on a flat tree stump. "Feeling . . . a little . . . light-headed."

Marco stood over her, waving his arms in a regular rhythm to keep away the flies. "Hey, you just rest, sister Aly," he said. "Soon we'll be out of this horror hole. The night I disappeared, my mom was going to make a big lasagna. I'm hoping she froze it, 'cause you're all invited over."

I nodded. "My dad was cutting short a business trip to see me. He's probably worried out of his mind."

Aly was bent over, her head between her legs. We had to hunch down to hear her. "Sorry, I don't know what's wrong with me. But this feels better," she said. After a moment, she continued in a soft voice. "My mom? She knows I'm alive. I can just feel it. We have this bond. I'm worried about my dad, though. He's older. The stress is probably killing him."

"Mine probably hasn't noticed," Marco said. "It's the middle of football season. He'll figure it out after the Super Bowl. I just hope he's not defrosting the lasagna."

"How about your parents, Cass?" Aly asked.

Cass was heading farther up the path. "Um, we have to go this way . . ."

"Look who took his brave pills," Marco said. "Hey, wait up, Davy Crockett, Aly's injured!"

"It's okay," Aly insisted. "I'm ready."

As she stood up, I looked at what she'd been sitting on—a stump.

"Guys?" I said. "Does that look weird to you? A flat stump in the middle of the jungle? I mean, trees don't shear themselves flat. Someone had to have done this."

Marco took a flashlight from his pack and shone it on the stump:

"Dude, somebody carved this," Marco said.

Cass wandered over and leaned in. As he ran a finger over the grooves, a strangled scream rang out from the woods.

Aly.

We turned and ran. She was about twenty feet ahead of us, standing rigid, her hands to her mouth. "I did not see that—I am feeling sick—my eyes are playing a trick—I did not see that," she was muttering.

"See what?" asked Cass.

Aly swallowed. "Nothing. Probably a possum, or a woodchuck, or an armadillo or a hyena or whatever the heck they have in a jungle. It just—in the dark, it looked like a panther or something, only with a hog's face. And teeth."

I froze. "A hog's face?"

Marco put his arm around her. "Hey, it's okay. Lot of stress here tonight. We're almost there, right, brother Cass?"

"Should be about twenty minutes," Cass said.

Aly nodded, and she and Marco fell in behind Cass once again.

I stayed close, trying to keep my peripheral vision open. But all I could think about was my recurring dream. Of the chase and the explosion and the earthquake. And the beast I had seen so often in my imagination, the hose-beaked vromaski.

The creature with a body like a beast of prey, a snout like a hog, and teeth.

* * *

We trudged on until I felt I had no unbitten skin left. It seemed as if we'd been gone a whole night. The moon was still high but dulled by clouds that had moved in suddenly. Before long the cool sea breeze stiffened up. It tickled my lungs and I began to cough. The ground beneath us was growing sandier. I could hear the crashing of waves now. Cass stopped, his head cocked to the left.

"Akerue," he said. "We made it."

I could see a dull licking of whitish-gold ahead of us through the branches. It was the dim, defiant reflection of the now nearly obscured moon against a body of water. A wave thundered onto the shore, and one lonely seagull cawed. As its silhouette rose into the faint circle of the moon's remaining light, we all began to run toward the sound.

Marco hit the sandy beach and flew into a cartwheel. Aly started dancing but dissolved into a fit of laughter and coughing. There was a faint rotten stench, which I figured to be some washed-up dead fish, but even that seemed sweet.

It was the smell of freedom.

As I stumbled forward, my foot caught a root and I fell. I didn't care. I rolled to my feet, a laugh tearing itself upward from my throat. In the distance I could see a small wooden dock, with the shadow of a boat rising and falling on the water. The soft creak of its mooring ropes against the hull was the only sound.

Until Cass's shriek pierced the night. Directly to my right.

"Get this thing off me!" he shouted.

CHAPTER THIRTEEN

ESCAPE FROM KI

MARCO RACED BY me in a blur.

By the edge of the woods, Cass flailed against an enormous assailant. In the moon's dull light, all I could see were shadows, a changing mass of flesh and limbs.

I ran as fast as I could. But as I got closer I realized what Cass was battling. It wasn't an animal or a human.

It was a monster. And it was dead.

The thing was rolling with him, its bones all akimbo in the moonlight. Marco was pulling Cass away, but Cass's arm was in the rubbery grip of a dripping band of sinew.

I was too panicked to gag. Before I could reach them, the sinew recoiled with a *thwap*. Marco hurtled backward, tumbling head over heels with Cass down the sloping beach.

At the bottom, Cass rolled to his feet. "Never again!" he shrieked. "I will never, ever let you talk me into something like this again!"

With that he bolted toward the jungle.

"Where are you going?" Aly called out from the beach.

"I'm covered with guts!" Cass shouted. "I tripped over that stupid thing."

"So you're going into the woods?" Aly said. "The jungle flies are drooling, Cass. They can't wait to see you. Now get in the water and wash up!"

I turned to look at Cass's attacker. It stretched across the sand like the prow of some organic ship, its ribs curved upward toward the moon.

"Thar she blows," Marco muttered.

It was a whale, maybe ten or twelve feet long. It had been washed up, maybe a day or two ago, and apparently attacked by predators. Cass hadn't seen it in the darkness and had just stumbled into it. As I eyed the huge carcass, the first few droplets of rain thudded softly onto the body.

A whale this size meant we were near an ocean—this was no bay or inlet. I wasn't sure what that meant for our escape. I guess I was hoping for something a little less vast.

"Ow," came Aly's voice.

Marco and I turned to see her stumbling in the sand. She was arm in arm with Cass, heading toward the water. "'Sup?" Marco said.

"Just . . . stepped on a shell," Aly replied. "Carry on."

"Come on, brother Jackie. Let's get the boat," Marco said.

I followed him toward the dock. The rain was picking up, along with a sudden wind, and I thought I could hear a distant rumble. Marco was untying a wide, flat-bottomed boat. It was about twenty feet long or so, with wooden sides, two sets of oars in oarlocks, and two seats. "There's no motor on this thing," he said. "The darn thing is a row-boat. I'll get in first."

"We can't escape across an ocean in that!" I said. "You saw the size of that whale. What if its father is out there looking for it? What if there are sharks? It's also raining. And dark. And there's thunder."

"Okay, so it'll be a little cozy." Marco jumped in and grabbed a pair of oars. "Are you with me?"

I took a deep breath. I was not going to face Bhegad and Torquin by myself. Reluctantly I stepped in after him. Sitting down, I took hold of the other pair of oars. "I hope you know what you're doing," I said, fitting them into the locks.

Marco gestured out toward Cass. "We're traveling with a human gyroscope, dude. He'll guide us by the moon. Or the molecules in the water. Or the trail of fish poop. What-ever. In about an hour and a half, the sun rises. By that time we'll be far away and we'll see where we're going. Ready? Let's go."

We pushed off toward Cass and Aly. The boat rocked on a sudden wave that broke over the side, nearly soaking me.

Rowing with Marco was a great way to feel useless. His strokes nearly lifted the boat out of the water. As his oars struck the surface, the wind spat the splashing water into my face. I could barely keep pace. We reached the other two quickly and managed to get them aboard without capsizing. Marco had brought a blanket and some extra clothes in his pack, which he gave to Aly and Cass. Cass sat next to Aly in a seat at the stern, where Marco and I could see them. Aly was shivering and Cass put his arm around her. "Where to, Christopher Columbus?" Marco asked.

Cass peered upward, into the rain. "No chance of s-s-seeing any stars tonight. We're going to have to use d-dead reckoning. Row like crazy and keep parallel to the shore. We're traveling northwest, with the c-current. By day-break we should be one or two miles away. Then we can s-s-stop."

"You okay, Aly?" Marco asked.

"As well as can be expected, having to stare at you," she replied.

Marco's SUV-sized back loomed toward me and away, toward and away. He was pulling harder than before, the boat practically lurching out of the water. I winced with each stroke, afraid he'd break the oars and shoot straight backward.

"Can you do that a little smoother?" Aly asked. "I'm getting sick."

"You can ease up a little, Marco!" I called against the wind. "I'm rowing, too!"

"Have to . . . pull hard . . . to get over . . . these swells . . ." Marco grunted. "It's calmer . . . farther out."

Aly leaned over the side of the boat and threw up. I pulled until the skin on my palms hurt. A bright stroke of lightning rent the air. For a moment the scene in front of me was bathed in a ghostly greenish white. Marco's arm muscles were a ropy tangle as he pulled.

"Something's wrong with Aly!" Cass shouted. She was convulsing in his arms now.

"Seasickness!" Marco shouted. "She'll be better in a minute!"

Now I was rising nearly vertically. Cass screamed, his voice now below my feet. I held tight as the boat slapped back down, wrenching my stomach like a roller coaster.

"It's getting worse, not better!" Cass's cry was cut off by a crack of thunder.

"That was about ten seconds between the light and the noise!" I shouted. "We're two miles from lightning!"

"Where's land?" Cass cried out, holding tight to Aly, who now appeared to be unconscious.

"Got to . . . get farther out . . ." Marco grunted.

"I can't navigate without a shore, Marco!" Cass said.

"Sea is different from land!"

Marco dug in extra hard. "You're the genius—figure it out! I have to get the boat out of this—"

A black curtain rose up to the starboard side, as if the sky itself had been swallowed up in the storm. Marco lifted one of the oars and rowed with the other, trying to change the boat's position. *"Hang on!"* he yelled. "Get low and hold on to the boat!"

I let go of my oars and grabbed tight on both sides. I could see Aly sinking to the floor. And then she and Cass were sliding . . . colliding with Marco . . .

Marco lost control of his oars. They swung away from him, flailing against the side of the boat. His hand was bleeding. He lunged forward, trying desperately to grab them again.

The wave lifted us upward like a roller-coaster car. We paused at the top, nearly sideways, suspended for a brief moment . . .

And we flipped silently into the sea.

CHAPTER FOURTEEN
SINK OR SWIM

MY LEGS LURCHED over my head. My arms flailed as if they didn't belong to me. My body bent backward and I thought my neck would snap. I was traveling in directions I didn't know existed. I felt the grit of seaweed against my skin and had no idea which way was up.

I willed myself to be still. Soon I was floating. Upward. My lungs were about to explode from my chest. I began swimming desperately. Kicking hard.

"Geeeeeahh!" I broke through the surface with a desperate sucking of air. My body spasmed. Seawater rushed into my mouth and I thought I would choke.

"Help! Help me!"

Cass.

His voice was to my left. Not far. I took three crazy deep breaths. Swimming blindly, I called out, *"Where are you?"*

But my voice was lost in the spindrift. I fought against the swells and whitecaps, taking my direction from Cass's screams. But now his voice was getting weaker. *"Hang on!"* I shouted. *"I'm—"*

My arm hit something solid.

It was Aly, facedown in the water. I yanked her head up but she was motionless, eyes rolled back into her head. I pulled her against me, my front to her back, and squeezed her abdomen hard. Nothing.

I turned her around and put my lips over hers, inhaling as hard as I could. Then exhaling. Pumping her system with oxygen.

Her body seized up. She jerked back and coughed a gob of seawater and long-digested quail.

Marco's voice boomed from my right. *"Is she okay?"*

"I don't know." He was swimming toward us, his arms chopping through the rough water.

"Let me take her," Marco said. "You get Cass."

As he pulled Aly away, I tried to scan the area. The rain seemed to be coming horizontally, right into my eyes. *"Cass! Where are you? Say something!"*

A tiny moan was my only answer. I swam furiously until I saw a black lump emerging from the water's surface.

I reached below and grabbed an arm.

Cass's head bobbed upward. He spluttered weakly. But he was alive. "Hold on to me and I'll tow you in!" I said, flipping onto my back as I grabbed Cass's hand.

"Aly . . ." he moaned. "She . . ."

"Marco has her!" I said.

Cass was trying to shout something, but I couldn't understand him.

"I'm here!" Marco cried out in the darkness. "Follow my voice! Let's swim to shore!"

"Where is it?" I yelled.

"I don't know!"

In that moment, I knew we were dead. Left, right, forward, back—it all looked exactly the same. Marco was guessing where to go, towing Aly. And he was almost out of my sight. I was an okay swimmer but not great, and I'd swallowed a ton of seawater.

Lightning split the sky, followed almost immediately by thunder. It was getting closer. I hoped the wash of light would reveal some sign of land, but all I could see were rain and whitecaps.

Cass's grip was getting firmer. He groaned. *"Treat . . . ment . . ."*

"What?" I shot back.

"Aly . . ." he said. "Missed her . . . treatment . . ."

103

I realized what he meant. Aly wasn't seasick. Something else was wrong. Her illness was all about her treatment. The one she had blown off.

My hands plunged into the weed-choked water. I tried to measure my strokes, to conserve energy. But my fingers were weakening, and Cass slipped away. I saw in an instant that he didn't know how to swim. He was slapping the water crazily, choking.

"Going . . . to die . . ." he said.

My lungs were filling up. My body felt as if it were full of solid lead. I reached desperately for Cass's wrist and held tight.

His leg swung around and kicked up from underneath.

No. It couldn't have been his leg. Something else was down there, thick and smooth, pushing up against my own feet. It was lifting me. Lifting Cass.

His hand unclasped. We were both sliding now, off to one side.

Shark.

I tried to swim away, but my strength was gone. The beast broke the surface of the water, its skin black against the storm. It was too big for a shark. Enormous. It must have been a whale, like the one that washed ashore. I felt around desperately for Cass.

He was barely afloat. All I could see were the whites of his frightened eyes.

"Swim!" I yelled. "Move your legs and arms! Come on!"

"No," he shot back. "Jack, look—lights!"

I turned toward the undersea intruder. Its shadow was now a solid hull, its skin gleaming metal. At one end a light blinked on a small rectangular housing. As it rose, I could see shapes painted on its hull.

The letters *K* and *I*. And, between them, a star.

* * *

"She had about another half hour to live, even in the best of circumstances," Professor Bhegad announced as he emerged from a hatch in the submarine's control room. "The doctor has managed to stabilize her. She is undergoing the treatment and will continue when we dock." He stepped into the small room and eyed us meaningfully. "Without any trickery, I trust."

"Thank you," I said, shivering.

Despite the tropical climate, our body temperatures had dropped while we were in the stormy sea. I was wet and shivering beneath an oversized KI beach towel. I sat opposite Cass and Marco on wooden benches, our knees touching. The submarine was small and cramped, but the dryness felt unbelievably good. My arms shaking, I sipped a cup of hot chocolate.

"This is my fault, P. Beg—I mean, Professor," Marco said. "I did all the planning, organized the breakout all by myself—"

"You are an extraordinary athlete, Marco, not an actor," Professor Bhegad said. He was sitting next to me, his face drawn and grim. "You do not need to cover for your friends. It is enough that I found you all alive."

I glared at him. Was this another of his planned rescues, like the Miracle of the Monkey? It wasn't supposed to happen that way. Aly had rigged the surveillance system. He couldn't have seen us. "Just how *did* you find us?" I asked.

"Why did I *have* to find you?" he snapped back at me. "Do you understand the absolute folly of what you just attempted? And the consequences you may have faced? By depriving Aly of the treatment, you nearly killed her."

"Sorry, it was really stupid," said Cass feebly.

Bhegad whirled on him. "*Stupid* is a small word. What you did was unforgivably reckless. Imagine if you'd succeeded. What happened to Aly would happen to you all. The operation unlocked your G7W gate, which saved your life. But the gate is unstable and can fail. The metabolic pathways are too weak. It's like a dam—open it slowly and it will irrigate a landscape; break it and it causes a flood. Your powers will overwhelm your system and kill you. We have developed the treatments to adjust the energy flow. To preserve your lives. And you decide to take a toy boat into notoriously unnavigable waters during a storm? By the Great Qalani, this is not *stupid*, it's insane. Suicidal."

I knew I should have felt moved by Bhegad's words. He had saved us. But his tone was angry and scolding, as if we'd just spilled coffee on his favorite scientific experiment.

"We're grateful, Professor," I said, "but you're part of the reason this happened. What do you expect? Whether you lock people up in an underground bunker or in a tropical village, you're still locking them up. Saving people's lives is a *great* thing, so why do it in secret? Maybe there are hundreds more G7W carriers you could help—"

"There's a good reason for the secrecy," Professor Bhegad said.

"Atlantis!" I blurted out, staring at him levelly. "You're turning us into super-charged slaves who will find Atlantis for you."

My words hung uncomfortably in the room's dankness.

Professor Bhegad's eyes grew sad and distant, his face red from the humidity in the submarine. He paused, wiping his fogged glasses, then put them on and looked at me. "Jack, when you came out of the operating room, you were in a coma for two days. We monitored you, round the clock. You talked quite a bit in your sleep. Something about an explosion and an earthquake. A red flying beast. A hoglike thing resembling a cheetah. You called it a vromaski, I believe."

Cass choked. Marco looked stunned.

"If I'm not mistaken, Jack, you've been having these

visions for as long as you can remember," Bhegad continued. "Do they sound familiar, Marco?"

Marco swallowed nervously. "He's lying to you, Jack. Those are my dreams. You are messing with our heads, Professor."

"No, he's right, I did dream them," I said. "I dream them a lot."

"I do, too," Cass piped up.

"This is ridiculous," I said. "How can three people have the exact same dreams?"

"Four," Bhegad said. "Aly has them, too. Same event. Same location. It is a place all four of you know well."

"I thought you were a scientist, P. Beg," Marco said with a baffled laugh. "I don't need a PhD to know that's impossible."

"Do you know the term déjà vu?" Bhegad asked. "When you have this odd feeling *I've been here before*, even though you know you haven't? That feeling is considered to be a fantasy, too. But our research shows that déjà vu is a connection to something real—some past event that left an unanswered question. Any of you could feel it, say, in a small coffeehouse while visiting Paris. Chances would be that your great-great-great-great grandfather fell in love there and never saw the woman again, or was attacked by a stranger who was never found."

"So déjà vus are like memories from people who are dead?" Cass asked. "Ghosts of memories?"

"They are visions of real things," Bhegad said. "We don't pretend to understand them fully. But these visions exist—stored in that vault of mysteries, the ceresacrum! You are being called to see the destruction of Atlantis. It is a vision of what happened when its source of power was stolen, upsetting the balance that had existed for ages. We believe the power was divided into containers and hidden."

"And where are we supposed to find them?" Marco said. "Antique shops?"

"Why us?" I cut in. "Why are we having these dreams? And how does the G7W marker fit in with all of this? And why are we the ones who have to find these . . . containers?"

"They are called Loculi," Bhegad said softly. He thought for a moment and took a deep breath. "There is much I need to tell you, when you are all conscious. Suffice it to say, for now, that we are not the only ones bent on finding the Loculi. There is another group—and we must get them first."

The hatch in the floor opened, and we could hear a rhythmic mechanical beeping. A silver-haired doctor poked her head into the hole and gave Bhegad a thumbs-up. "Signs are stable," she announced. "Patient is conscious."

"Any permanent damage, Doctor Bradley?" Bhegad asked.

The doctor scratched her head. "Her first words to me were, 'We're not in Kansas anymore, Toto.'"

"*The Wizard of Oz*," Cass explained. "That means she's okay."

"Well, she will need a full day to sleep this off," the doctor replied. "Perhaps they all will."

Bhegad nodded, his eyes traveling from Cass to Marco to me. "I have no more wind to answer your questions," he said. He checked his wristwatch. "It is now six A.M. Your training begins in exactly twenty-four hours."

CHAPTER FIFTEEN

TRAINING DAY

"SORRY." TORQUIN YAWNED as he entered my room, his bare feet slapping the floor like dead fish. "Overslept. Come."

I slid off my bed and followed him down the corridor. It was nearly 7:30 A.M. on Training Day. Exactly at 6:00, a technician had arrived to take Cass to the media center. Marco had run off with a bunch of jockish-looking guards. And someone had whisked Aly off in a golf cart to the system control center. We were all supposed to have a morning of "skill building," followed by a classroom lesson at 2:00 P.M. with Professor Bhegad.

Torquin had been late. "Where are you taking me?" I asked.

"Garage," said Torquin.

Great. Either my gift had something to do with cars, or I was destined to be a world-class custodian.

As we stepped outside into a crisp, sunny day, I realized I had no idea what the weather had been for about twenty-four hours. The previous day had been spent sleeping, arguing, and eating food that Conan had wheeled to the dorm on a cart.

It took a while to fill Aly in, because she'd had no memory of the night's main events. In the end, we'd all agreed to toe the line. To go along with Bhegad's plan. Even though I, for one, still didn't believe his story.

"*Heeee-yahh!*" came a distant shout. At the other end of the compound, way across the open lawn, a group of guards seemed to be in some sort of martial-arts fight. They were dressed in robes, attacking each other with sticks.

No. Not each other. From their midst, one lone figure leaped upward, doing a complete backflip over their heads. Landing behind the line, he plowed into the backs of their knees with his own stick, sending nearly the whole group sprawling.

"Marco?" I murmured.

"Dangerous," Torquin said, waddling toward the media center. He opened the door and we walked into the huge main room, with its beanbag chairs, monitors, and games.

My heart leaped. "Cool," I said. "So you were joking about the garage!"

"Shortcut," Torquin replied. He went through a door at the other side, which led to a long, tiled corridor. As we passed one of the rooms, I could see Cass working at a desk with some scientists. Someone had placed electrodes on his head, which were attached to some machine. He and two KI guys were staring at a massive, highly detailed map of an island. In the middle stood an enormous black mountain, labeled ONYX.

"Is that where we are?" I asked.

"We are walking on floor. That is map." At the end of the corridor Torquin pushed open a door. The smell of hot rubber and grease assaulted us. "Inside. Now."

We continued across a hangar-sized building with all manner of carts, trucks, and buses being painted and repaired. Mechanics bustled about, some ducking under vehicles, others with heads buried beneath the open hoods. At the other end, what seemed to be a mile away, I saw the submarine that had plucked us out of the sea. It was now more than six feet off the ground atop a car lift. A huge square panel had been cut out of the bottom, to reveal a tangle of broken wires, tubes, and blackened steel. It looked as though it had just been through a fire.

We stopped underneath it. Torquin pointed upward.

"The night we picked you up," he said. "Hit something. Almost didn't make it."

"Looks pretty bad," I said. Was that why I was here? So Torquin could show the damage we'd caused the sub? Did he expect me to apologize? "Next time we'll send for a car. Now where do I go?"

Torquin just stood there, staring at me. After a minute or two, he bent down and picked up a wrench off the floor.

"Fix," he said. "I come back at one forty-five."

* * *

"Woo-hoo!" Marco yelled, nearly bounding across the lawn. "Hiro says I'll be double black belt in a week!"

Marco the Magnificent was the last person I wanted to see at the end of my morning of torture. Despite the fact that he'd just been deep in martial arts, he was dribbling a basketball toward me. I slumped against the outside of the garage. My face was smudged with grease. Behind me, the submarine was tilted to one side and it looked as if its intestines were hanging out.

I had managed to befriend a mechanic named Fritz, who had his entire face tattooed with the KI snake symbol. He tried to teach me how to use a welding tool and a rivet remover. I burned a hole in the hydraulic lift, managed to yank the sub's emergency hatch off its hinges, cracked a motherboard and its circuitry, and somehow hammered off one of the propellers. The sub was in worse shape now than it had been this morning. Fritz was screaming his head off in German. And a team of techs was discussing whether to commission a replacement sub.

"Whoa, what happened here?" Marco asked as he saw my face, and the sub, up close.

"You almost got a black belt," I said, walking out toward the lawn. "I almost got a *Schlag auf dem Kopf mit einem Schlussel*."

"Sounds amazing," Marco said. "What's that?"

"A smack on the head with a wrench," I replied.

Across the compound, Professor Bhegad was waving to us from the other side of the oval lawn. He was wearing a faded KI baseball cap that wasn't quite straight, and he stood at the base of a museum-like structure with wide stone steps topped by seven stone pillars. It could have passed for a courthouse in Washington, DC, but for the distant black mountain rising like a witch's hat from the jungle behind it.

I began walking across the lawn. My feet were so sweaty they squished in my shoes. My pockets were loaded down with some junk I wanted for my room, which Fritz let me take—pulleys, hooks, rope.

"So, are you some kind of car genius?" Marco asked.

"They must have thought so." I sighed. "I mean, I'm not stupid. I'm not afraid to try things. But I like to construct things *my* way, which isn't necessarily the way anyone else does it. So this afternoon was one big epic fail. I messed up everything."

Marco's brow furrowed. "This is called *training*. I think we all have to do a little bit of everything. Expand ourselves. Maybe I'm the one who gets garage duty tomorrow. Come on, brother Jack, pessimism not allowed. What are you great at? When people think of Jack McKinley, what do they say? He's an incredible . . . what?"

"Nothing," I said. "I can't even wake myself up in the morning without smacking myself in the head with a plastic toy."

Marco nodded. "Okay, that's pretty pathetic, I admit. But come on—art? Chess? Foreign languages? Angry Birds? Swimming! No, wait, you suck at that."

As we neared Professor Bhegad, I saw for the first time that the majestic building had a name, carved into a stone block above the pillars: HOUSE OF WENDERS.

"Looks like a big typo," I said, "for House of Wonders."

Marco snapped his fingers. "There's your talent—spelling!"

By now Cass and Aly were jogging toward us, laughing at some joke. A breeze had kicked up, and Aly's hair looked like a pink flame.

"Well, well, looks like you all had a splendid first day so far," Professor Bhegad called out. "Follow me, please. Jack, there is a men's locker room down the first set of steps when you enter. It has showers and fresh sets of clothing."

We followed Bhegad upstairs and into the building. A grand hallway greeted us, its floors made of polished wood, its walls of bright mosaic tile. At the opposite end, a wide carpeted stair led to a marble balcony that surrounded the hallway and opened onto rooms and offices.

But I could not take my eyes away from the hall's center, where the ceiling vaulted at least three stories high to accommodate a skeleton that nearly took my breath away. It rose up like some brontosaur on steroids, with a snakelike neck that ended in a fearsome raptor head with saber teeth. It stood on bent legs with clawed feet, and its tail was short with thick bones. "Wow, what do you call that thing?" Cass asked.

"Sir," Marco said, his head craned upward.

"The skeleton was excavated by paleontologists shortly after the island was discovered," Bhegad said, removing his baseball cap, "by one of the greatest Scholars of Karai, Herman Wenders, who died in 1897."

"Oh, well, so much for the spelling angle," Marco muttered.

"It is only one of the bizarre specimens we have uncovered, as you can see . . ." Bhegad said.

As I looked around the room, I felt something odd. Like the walls themselves were expanding and contracting in rhythm. Breathing. The light, too, seemed to be seeping through the pores of the stone, like a draft that could be seen and not felt.

Marco was peering at me oddly. "'Sup, bro?"

"I think I inhaled too many garage fumes," I said. "See you in class."

I hurried down to the showers.

* * *

Trumpets and drums and quivering violins blasted out of speakers. They echoed through a musty old classroom, where I was sitting at a wooden desk in the second row, behind Aly. An image filled a screen—a glorious castle with a great lawn on which a king and queen greeted subjects while little boys played nearby.

"The kingdom of Atlantis," Professor Bhegad announced, "existed on this spot for thousands of years. It is unlike other ancient advanced civilizations—India, Italy, Greece, China—because the historical record was completely destroyed. Or so it was thought . . ."

"Can you cut the sound track?" Marco called out from the back of the room.

Aly leaned forward and pressed the mute button.

"Yes, ahem," Bhegad said. "A transcription and several images were found by KI archaeologists shortly after the discovery of this island over a hundred years ago. They are said to be based on stone tablets, which we have not been able to locate. The transcription provided much of the history we know, and this slideshow is based on that. Behold Atlantis's last rulers, King Uhla'ar and Queen Qalani, along with their sons, Karai and Massarym."

"The Great Qalani . . ." I murmured.

He clicked the remote and another image appeared—seven globes, glowing brightly. "A pioneering genius in mathematics and physics, Queen Qalani spent her life studying the source of Atlantean power. She worried about attack from barbarians who would abuse the energy for evil intent. So she sought to analyze the power, perhaps to convert it into physical form. Imagine! It could then be transported, hidden away, kept safe. Over years, using techniques not even imaginable to our scientists today, she isolated this energy into the seven components, each to be stored in a *Loculus*."

"Like harnessing electricity and putting it in lightbulbs," Marco said.

"Not exactly," Professor Bhegad said. "Massarym, who inherited his mother's curiosity if not her intellect, found something astonishing upon handling the Loculi. Each of the seven power components had a unique property of its own. With one Loculus he could fly . . . with another become invisible . . . things of that nature. But the Loculi did not work for just anyone, only those of royal blood." He looked meaningfully at each of us. "And their descendants, too.

Which would be those carrying the G7W gene marker."

Aly's eyes widened. "The Select . . ."

"I'm a prince?" Marco said, nearly leaping out of his chair.

"Exhilarated by the discovery," Bhegad continued, "Uhla'ar, Qalani, Karai, and Massarym showed off the powers of the Loculi. Their people were in awe. They began seeing the royal family as gods. Some became envious and tried to steal the powerful spheres. Karai, who had a deep connection to Atlantean fauna, trained one type of giant raptor to protect the Loculi."

I knew the answer to this one. "The Ugliosaurus!"

The image now changed to a painting of a slavering red creature with the head and wings of an eagle and the body of a lion. "It is known in mythology as a griffin. The fiercest of beasts. When they imprinted on something, they would guard it with their lives. They tore to shreds anyone who came close, the way a hawk captures a rat. Now the game was changing. People began hating the royals. Rebel bands emerged, bent on unseating the family and stealing their magic. Karai realized that the Loculi were not preserving Atlantis but poisoning it. They needed to be destroyed."

Now we were seeing a fight scene, the dark and fair brothers in a fistfight as the queen summoned a team of burly courtiers. "Massarym would have none of Karai's talk. He loved the powers of the Loculi. So one night, when the palace was under attack, he slipped away. He commandeered a fearsome reptilian beast to kill every last griffin, and then he stole away the sacred Loculi."

The fight scene faded, replaced by a scene of horrific disaster. An explosion blackened the sky as a horrified Qalani cried out in agony. Fire swept through the jungle, and a crack opened in the earth—directly in the path of the fleeing Karai.

The dream.

I recoiled. My fingers felt scorched. I had the urge to run. My body went rigid with fear. *Fight or flight.*

Marco, Cass, and Aly were staring at me. They'd had the dream, too. Were they feeling the same thing I was?

"You okay, dude?" Marco asked.

"F—" I couldn't even say *fine*. My jaw was locked tight.

I couldn't stay here. Below me, the smooth floor seemed to vibrate like a delicately plucked string. I ran out onto the balcony that surrounded the grand entrance hall. A song seemed to be flowing from above, only it wasn't sound really, and it wasn't light either.

Bhegad had stopped talking. In a moment Cass, Marco, and Aly were by my side.

"Do you feel it?" I whispered. "Do you hear the song?"

Bhegad was standing in the door, watching us closely. Below us, the skeleton seemed to be glowing. Some of the bones were dissolving, shaking loose. They floated, re-forming in midair. The neck was shortening, the tail growing longer, as if the creature had not been put together quite right and was correcting itself. Other bones flew in from other skeletons. The beast's form was changing, its mouth growing rows of sharp teeth, its claws sharpening.

A white shroud began to form around it, slowly sapping color from the room, until a transparent film of mosaic scales had wrapped the beast from head to toe.

I felt bolted to the floor. I saw nothing now but the pale ghost of a shrouded reptilian giant. And the piercing, unmoving eyes of Professor Bhegad.

"Jack?" Aly said. "Are you okay?"

Why wasn't she looking upward? Why wasn't anyone? I blinked once, twice. I shook my head. "Look!" I said. *"Open your eyes!"*

As if in answer, the creature turned toward me.

CHAPTER SIXTEEN

THE FIRST TREATMENT

IT IS THE largest of them all. It bounds over the ridge, slashing trees in its path. The red raptors—griffins—surround it like hornets, dive-bombing, screeching. But it springs from its haunches, grabbing one of the taunting raptors out of the air and crushing its neck. I turn away as it holds the bird-lion under its claw, waiting for its twitching to stop.

I do not want it to see me. So I continue to run. Until I hear a voice.

I know the voice. It is my brother's.

He is my age, but we look nothing alike. I am angry with him, but I don't know why. He is telling me to come, to escape with him.

A fireball plunges from the sky, nearly taking my head off.

I believe my brother's plan is doomed. But I see an escape: a scorched pathway through the woods, leading over the ridge. I point that way and call to him. His name comes off my tongue, but I can't hear it.

And now I can no longer see him. Where is he? I hear his voice behind me. Then to my left. My right. Above me. I turn and turn, helpless, confused.

And I see the great creature looming above, the head of the lion-bird gripped between its teeth.

It is coming for me.

"No!" It is the first word I hear out of my own mouth.

The beast laughs, dripping blood from its jaws. "Ja-a-a-ck..." it says.

* * *

"No-o-o-o-o!"

"Jack!" a voice called out of the darkness. "You're awake, Jack. You're healthy and alive and in the real world! Welcome back."

My eyes blinked open. I saw charts and beeping LCD monitors and IV tubes. For a moment I thought I was in Belleville again, and this whole adventure had been a horrible dream.

But the voice was Professor Bhegad's, and he was dressed in a white lab coat. The silver-haired doctor from the submarine—Dr. Bradley—was adjusting my IV tube.

"What happened?" I asked.

"Your first treatment happened," Dr. Bradley replied. "It wasn't scheduled yet, but you collapsed in the House of Wenders."

"You were having visions," Bhegad said. "The timing of the first symptoms is unpredictable, which is why we've been monitoring you so closely since you arrived."

"Now you tell me!" I said.

Professor Bhegad smiled. "The hump is over, Jack. After this one we can time the other treatments nearly to the minute. From here on in, they will be given to you before anything bad happens. You will receive a schedule."

"Lucky me." I sat up, feeling weak. I thought of the museum. "I . . . felt something in there. That building . . ."

"Yes," Bhegad said. "The others did, too. To a lesser extent, but that may be because they've been here longer. For the Select, physical relics of the ancient world seem to act as conduits to the past. It as if the past and present are together."

"I saw the creature move," I said.

Bhegad cocked his head. "The others did not see that. To them, you screamed and fell to the floor. They are concerned about you."

"Why didn't they see it?" I demanded.

"I—I don't know," Bhegad replied.

"There was a song, too," I said. "Not really music, but more like . . . a call. From one of the rooms."

"The Wenders Collection?" Bhegad said. "Just above where I was standing . . . one of the rooms leading into the balcony?"

"Yes," I said.

"Fascinating . . ." Bhegad murmured. "That is where we keep the most unusual relics from Dr. Wenders's archaeological digs. We believe he alone possessed knowledge of where the heart of Atlantis lies. The place where the seven Loculi must be gathered to regain the power of the lost continent. But his studies were never completed. After his young son died, at age fourteen, he fell into grief and began trying to destroy all he had discovered. He died a broken and confused man."

"Age fourteen?" I said. "Was he . . . ?"

"Yes, young Burt Wenders was most likely a Select," Bhegad said.

I lay back in my bed and closed my eyes. I could still hear—feel—what was coming from that room. "So . . . that's one of our tasks, isn't it? To find that place where the Loculi were gathered. Which no one has done in thousands of years."

"Give yourself a night's sleep and a good shower," the professor said softly. "It's been a long day."

I spent the rest of the night in the hospital.

Wide awake.

CHAPTER SEVENTEEN

HERMAN AND BURT WENDERS

"IT'S OBSIDIAN," CASS said, staring at a jagged rock he held up to the light through the dusty windows of the Wenders Collection room.

Marco shrugged. "Seems well-behaved to me."

"Obsidian, not obstinate, you ape," Aly said.

"Oo! Oo! Oo!" Marco grunted.

I felt as if I were floating somehow. The Wenders Collection was alive to me in ways that I couldn't understand. Down the center of the room ran a solid oak table with neatly organized glass boxes full of artifacts. The dark wood walls were lined with cabinets, stuffed to bursting. Wherever I looked, I saw bones and potsherds, scraps of clothing, artwork. Each seemed to be calling to me somehow, crowding my brain. Each was its own déjà vu.

I felt stronger today. Bhegad insisted it was because of the treatment. The others assumed the same thing. But a part of me couldn't believe it. Yes, Aly had passed out, and I'd had some kind of spell. Yes, we were both whisked away behind closed doors. But maybe we would have recovered anyway. Maybe the "treatments" were nothing more than keeping us out of sight until we were well.

The better to make their story seem true.

I took the rock Cass was holding. It was palm sized, an odd, geometric shape that looked like it had been carved.

"That's sad," Aly said.

"That's gross," Marco remarked.

"This was found on Herman Wenders when he died," Bhegad said. "He had gone missing for days, mentally unraveling over the death of his son, Burt. When Wenders reappeared, he seemed haunted, babbling to himself. Claimed to have seen the center of Atlantis. The Scholars tried to take him seriously. They attempted to nurse him back to health, all the while gently coaxing him for details. But he would lapse into a confused silence and stare hopelessly at this rock."

I looked up above Professor Bhegad's head to a portrait of Herman and Burt Wenders. The father was grim and scowling, with a trim, gray beard and a waxed handlebar mustache. He sat ramrod straight in a neat, dark jacket. His son looked energetic and full of mischief, like he was dying to tell the photographer a joke.

Like he was dying to tell me something.

What?

It was amazing how a good photographer could make a person come to life. I had to glance away. "Did anyone find the place Wenders was talking about?" Marco asked.

Bhegad shook his head. "No, alas. We believe it exists, or it did. Our transcription told of a deep fissure at the center of a valley. The source of the continent's extraordinary power. A connection to the spirit of the earth. Before the creation of the Loculi, for generations the Atlantean king and queen made pilgrimages there, to find peace, wisdom, discernment."

"I had a new version of the dream—our dream," I said. "I was there at the destruction of Atlantis again. But I had a brother. He was calling to me. Did any of you guys have that one?"

Cass, Aly, and Marco shook their heads.

"Was it Karai or Massarym?" Bhegad asked, his eyes intent behind his glasses. "Which one were you?"

"I don't know," I said. "I don't remember."

"You must start writing these things down." Bhegad took a deep breath, his brow deeply creased. "As for the source of the great fissure, there are none on this island that we know of. We do know that there was a severe geological cataclysm when the island sank, which might well have changed the landscape considerably. We worry that the fissure is underwater. Some scholars thought Wenders's mysterious rock might be some sort of key. But it is likely the delusional ranting of an aggrieved father."

With a sigh, I put the rock down on the oak table.

As soon as I let go, I nearly jumped. That strange feeling jacked up a notch. Like a mild electric shock.

Look closer.

I swallowed. I wasn't sure where the suggestion had come from.

"Um, Professor Bhegad?" I said, placing my hand back on the rock. "Can I take this back to the dorm to examine?"

He looked at me curiously. "Of course. You're not going anywhere out of my purview for a long, long time."

I shuddered at that comment.

As I slipped the rock into my pocket, it was warm to the touch.

* * *

"I hate the way he talks about Wenders," I said, holding the rock up to the great Medusa chandelier in the dining room.

"I hate the way he talks about everything," Marco said. "What's a purview?"

We were sitting at dinner now, in a table by a corner. According to Aly, the chandelier mikes couldn't pick up our voices here. The great banquet table for my welcome dinner had actually been lots of square tables pushed together. Now the tables were dispersed throughout the great hall, and people were huddled together over papers, laptops, tablets, and all kinds of handheld devices, chattering busily.

"'Delusional ranting of an aggrieved father,'" Cass said, imitating Professor Bhegad's voice. "What does he know about losing someone?"

Aly shrugged. "He might. He's old enough to have lost parents, or at least grandparents."

"He's a cold fish!" Marco shouted. "And I don't care if he heard that."

I was staring at the poem, noticing the shape of the lines. "Guys," I said. "Do you think this thing is some kind of code?"

Aly looked at it closely. "It's worded funny. But it could just be old-school Victorian poetry. You know, like he couldn't stand to see the light of day. The dawn brings life and light, but it also burns—very *Romeo and Juliet*. The best version being Zeffirelli's, IMHO, but that's another discussion. Anyway, the brightness reminds him of his son's life and makes him feel bad. Also, you know, there's a similarity in the words *son* and *sun*? Another thing—he says 'I burden west.' The sun sets in the west. So maybe he's, like, wishing for his own sunset. His own death."

We all stared at her. "Did you just think of that?" Marco asked.

"Gnizama," Cass said. "I'm sitting next to you in English class."

Aly's face turned red.

"But notice the shape," I said. "The three lines of the poem are arranged funny. Like they're in two columns—one column under Burt, the other under Wenders."

Cass leaned closer. "He kind of had to write it that way. The rock is bent."

They began changing the subject, talking about Marco's martial arts exploits and Aly's improvements to the Karai security system and Cass's ability to re-create a topographical map of the sea floor around the island by memory. They were all psyched about going back to their training tomorrow.

The geek movie buff, Mr. Memory, and Athlete of the Century.

No one was taking my idea seriously.

I felt like Herman Wenders. Burnt. And not looking forward to dawn at all.

CHAPTER EIGHTEEN

THE ONES THAT DON'T BELONG

AT 6:00 A.M. my alarm went off at an ungodly volume. Which was just barely loud enough to wake me.

As I rose out of bed, I untied a string from a hook I'd screwed into the wall. The string was part of the pocketful of junk I'd borrowed from the garage. The other end of the string was tied to a wooden hanger—by way of a small pulley hooked into the ceiling. And on the hanger was my shirt. Now the shirt plunged down until its tail just brushed the sheet on my bed.

Not bad.

I took off my pajama top and thrust my arms into the sleeves of the shirt, pulling it off the hanger. Then I slid my body toward the foot of the bed, where my jeans lay waiting. The legs were held open by clothespins attached to two strings I'd hung from the ceiling on hooks. I'd clipped socks to the cuffs of the jeans, and just below the socks I'd left my sneakers open. Super-easy access for all.

Pants . . . socks . . . shoes.

I pulled off the clips, tied the shoes, and checked my watch. "Sixteen seconds," I murmured. I'd have to improve that.

I was not looking forward to another day of Find Jack's Talent.

Today I was to help the head chef, Brutus, in the kitchen for breakfast. And I had to be on time.

I ran across the compound toward the Comestibule. I passed the athletic center, a sleek glass two-story building with a track, an Olympic-sized pool, indoor basketball courts, weight rooms, and martial arts rooms. Through one of the windows I could see Marco in climbing gear, making his way up a vertical rock wall. It seemed to take no effort at all. I liked him, but I hated him.

Veering toward the back of the octagonal Comestibule, I entered the kitchen. It was enormous, its walls full of white shelves groaning with the weight of flour and sugar sacks, cans of oil and vinegar. Thick doors in the back of the room opened to meat lockers and freezers, blasting cold air every time the doors opened. Kitchen workers were preparing omelets and fruit bowls with blinding speed.

Brutus arrived late, flushed and out of breath. He had

a round, doughy face and an impressive stomach. He glared at me as if his lateness was my fault. "Make the biscuits," he said, gesturing toward a long table jammed with ingredients. "Two hundred. All the ingredients are on the table."

Two hundred biscuits? I didn't even know how to make one. "Is there a recipe?" I asked.

"Just leave out the ingredients that don't belong in a biscuit!" Brutus snapped, scurrying off to yell at someone else.

I gulped. I grabbed a cookie sheet. And I said a prayer.

* * *

"I can speak again—the dentist unglued my teeth!" Marco said, bounding into the dorm after breakfast.

I plopped onto my bed in a cloud of pastry flour. I was trying desperately to flush the morning's biscuit-making experience down my memory toilet.

Except for one thing. One comment by Brutus . . .

"I think the cinnamon-mint-mushroom combo was . . . different," Aly said cheerily, following me into the room.

"They tasted like toothpaste!" Cass added. "But I happen to love the taste of toothpaste."

I ignored them all, leaning over to take the Wenders rock from my desk drawer. The other three were just noticing the various strings hanging from my ceiling. "You making a marionette show?" Cass asked.

Just leave out the ones that don't belong . . . Brutus had said.

I held out the rock. "What if some of the letters are supposed to be left out?" I asked.

"Huh?" said Cass.

"What if this is a code, but not one where you have to
substitute a letter?" I pressed on. "What if it's about taking
away letters?"

We looked at it again:

BURT WENDERS

Truth bore Dawn herself
and reek spew
To burn burden west

Burnt !

I was seeing things in the words, recurring letters. And I had an idea what to do with them.

"Bhegad said this might be a key to the center of Atlantis—whatever that means," I said. "So maybe Wenders got to the center. Imagine being him. Imagine finding the thing you've been looking for, the find of a lifetime—and you think, so what? It's a hole in the ground. His son, Burt, had died! Think about how he would have felt."

Marco nodded. "I'd have thrown the key away."

"Part of him would want to come back announcing, 'Yo, we found the center!'" I said. "But that would have sent everyone running. It would have been disrespectful to Burt's memory. So he didn't do it. Still, Wenders was a professional, one of the best in his field. He had to feel some obligation to the Scholars of Karai. So he made it a little hard. He created a delay, a barrier to prevent people from rushing off to find the fissure."

Marco was staring oddly at me. "What made you think of all this? It's like you're reading the guy's mind."

I shrugged. I didn't know. The feeling was blindsiding me. "This was before the discovery of G7W, before the treatments," I said. "It must have felt to Wenders like a part of himself had been ripped away. So maybe he meant for the name *Burt Wenders* to be taken from the words of the poem—the way the kid was taken from him."

"Let's try it," Cass said.

I began writing the words of the poem on a sheet of paper. "Cass, you said something about the shape of the lines. It's like they're in two columns. And on top of them, there are the two words of the son's name."

"So maybe take the word *Burt* from each line in the first column and *Wenders* from the second?" Cass asked.

Exactly.

Then I wrote out the remaining letters:

THORE AHLF

ON AKPE

NI BUT

"Looks Greek to me," Marco said. "Maybe Swedish."

I exhaled. I was ready to crumple up the paper and toss it, when I looked at the bottom two lines. The word *on* began the second row. And the third began with *ni*, which could easily be *in*.

"I think they're just scrambled, that's all," I said.

I smoothed out the paper and carefully began writing.

"On peak!" Aly shouted. "That could be Mount Onyx! Maybe that's where we'll find the other half of this rock."

Marco scrunched up his brow. "So all we have to do is find . . . a *tub*? On the top of a humongous mountain?"

"Maybe that part is a mistake," Cass suggested. "Or maybe it's supposed to be *but*, not tub."

"In *but*?" Marco said. "That scares me."

Cass shrugged. "An alternate spelling for *butte*?"

"That scares me less," Marco said.

"Tomorrow," I said, folding the paper and putting it in my pocket, "we will find out."

CHAPTER NINETEEN

MOUNT ONYX

"THAT'S SPLENDID, JACK!" Bhegad said, looking at my analysis of the poem. We had managed to find him walking across the lawn toward the Comestibule for a late breakfast. Even in the morning, the low clouds seemed to trap the heat. "Very impressive. Thanks for this tip. I will have Torquin mobilize a search team at once. Come. Let's discuss today's training agenda over some of your biscuits, shall we?"

Training agenda? With my luck, they'd be testing my skills on cleaning the Karai sewer system today. I was hoping Bhegad would have had a different reaction. "I was thinking *we* would go up there," I said.

Bhegad looked alarmed. "You want to go on a hike in the jungle on a hot day like this? To find a rock?"

"Actually, some speed swimming in the pool with the Karai trainers would be great," Marco said.

I kicked him. "We're the ones who figured out the puzzle, Professor Bhegad," I said. "Isn't it our right to be the ones to find the other half?"

"Exactly my thinking," Aly said.

"It is kind of high up there . . ." Cass said dubiously.

Professor Bhegad turned and looked toward the distant black giant. "Mount Onyx looks formidable, but it's actually not terribly difficult if you use the paths our trackers have marked. Torquin, of course, knows those paths well."

"The other half of the rock may provide some clue to the big secret we're looking for!" I said. "Isn't that why we're here?"

Without breaking stride, Bhegad whipped out a walkie-talkie. "Hello, Torquin. Changing today's schedule. You are to take the children to the top of Mount Onyx . . . Oh, dear, it was your day off? Well, we'll make it up later . . . Really? Well, you know what I say to that response. See you at breakfast!"

"What did he say?" I asked as he hung up.

"Over his dead body." Bhegad mopped his brow with a handkerchief. "I can see this will be an illuminating experience."

* * *

My hiking shoes alone felt like they weighed forty pounds. My feet hurt from pounding into the hard-packed soil. My shoulders ached from my backpack, which was loaded with extra water, a change of clothing, spare ropes, some trail gorp, a flashlight, bug spray, and sunblock.

And we hadn't even reached the mountain.

The clouds hung over us like a dirty ceiling. The air was stagnant, hot, and sticky. Torquin was leading us through the jungle on a winding path, his bare feet tromping the flora flat. He had a machete, which he swung lazily from side to side.

Marco was directly ahead of me. He had a machete, too, but he preferred to keep it tucked into his belt. Instead he was listening to music through earbuds and whistling tune- lessly. His backpack was the size of a small hut. It clanked and banged with each step. "What's in there?" I called out.

Marco pulled out an earbud and glanced over his shoul- der. "Rocks. Stones. Free weights. I figured I'd get some conditioning out of this."

I knew I shouldn't have asked.

"I'm starting to have blisters already," said Aly, who was walking behind me with Cass.

"I *love* blisters," Marco said. "They're fun to pop."

"That image just ruined my frisky mood," Cass said.

That was the first thing Cass had said since we'd started out. "How are you holding up?" I asked.

"Fine, as long as I don't think of heights." He gazed upward at the black column that seemed to rise out of the mountaintop and disappear into the clouds. "That thing at the top is like Jack in the Beanstalk's beanstalk. L-like it kept growing for a thousand years and then petrified."

"AIIEEE!" Torquin shouted. "Look! Poison snake!"

He jumped out of the pathway. Something blue and shiny was slithering through the grass toward us.

I leaped away and crashed into a tree, thudding to the ground. Cass, screaming, fell into a bramble bush. Marco and Aly collided while ducking away and fell together in a heap.

The snake continued past, hissing ominously, and then stopped.

From our left came the wheezing sound of Torquin's laughter. "Need new batteries," he said.

I picked myself up and walked closer to the reptile. It was made of metal and segmented. And completely out of juice. "It's a toy," I said.

What? Marco shot back.

"Marco's backpack nearly crushed me!" Aly said.

"I want to go back," Cass said.

Torquin was sitting on the ground, holding his stomach and vibrating with laughter.

I stepped into the pathway and accidentally on purpose crushed Torquin's toy.

* * *

"Robert was old friend," Torquin grumbled, as we began our ascent up the side of the mountain.

"Robert?" Marco asked.

"Snake," Torquin growled.

"Your toy snake's name was *Robert*?" Aly said.

"What do you expect from a guy named Torquin?" Cass reminded her.

"You will pay," Torquin said.

"Sorry," I lied. "I didn't see it." I felt a little guilty. But not much. The climb was too serious for dumb practical jokes.

After about an hour of dirt, the path became rocky. We scrambled over boulders, swatting away flies. Torquin soon pulled way ahead of us, but nobody minded. With a wad of gum, Marco had stuck a sheet of paper on Torquin's backpack that said BITE ME. The flies couldn't read it, but it made us smile.

"El Torko! You're too fast for us humans!" Marco shouted.

"Watch me! Learn!" Torquin called over his shoulder.

As Torquin picked up speed, Marco stopped. He held us back and shushed us silently, waiting until Torquin grunted out of sight

With a sly grin, Marco turned to Cass. "You know this path well?"

Cass nodded. "We're at an elevation of two thousand thirty-nine feet already. The path rises here and continues to circle around, until we actually circumnavigate the circumference three times before our final—"

"Tell me this, Jonny MapQuest," Marco interrupted. "Is there a shortcut to the top—like right up those rocks?"

Cass's eyes traveled upward, toward the nearly vertical black cliff. His face took on a tinge of green and he quickly looked away. "Yes, of course, but if we follow this path we go around to the other side of the cliff. It's a gentler climb."

"Gentler and longer," Marco said.

"Right," Cass said.

"Which is where Chief TurboFeet is headed," Marco said.

"Torquin? Yeah, probably," Cass replied.

"So let's take the shortcut," Marco said. "We'll get to the top before that fat frog. He'll come huffing and puffing, like he's some kind of superhero for beating us kids. Imagine his face when he sees us, la-di-da, checking our watches."

I laughed. "It would serve him right."

"I'm not sure," Aly said.

"You guys are crazy," Cass said, peering up the sharp incline.

Torquin's voice came thundering from the top of a rock scramble. "Babies need nap? Cass want Mommy, Daddy?"

With a snort of a laugh, he turned and continued hiking.

"I loathe him," Aly said.

Cass's face was turning a deep red. His eyes were glowing

with anger. "The path is actually a few yards behind us. We make a left and climb straight upward to the base of the black rock."

"Bingo," Marco said. "You lead."

We followed Cass back down the path and found an opening—a trailhead to a very steep climb. Marco went first, shinnying up vines and over huge boulders. He pulled a rope from his pack and dropped it down to help the rest of us. We continued like this, going on our own until it became too hard, and then relying on Marco to help us over the tough parts.

We were making quick progress. After about a half hour, we climbed onto a wide rock ledge and rested. "This is it," Marco said. "The base of the cliff. Great job, guys."

Cass, Aly, and I flopped down onto our backs, breathing hard. From this perch I could look out over the island and see the Karai Institute compound. The athletic building shone like a brick of ice, steel gray in the cloudy sunlight, and the people crisscrossing the lawn looked like orderly insects. A puff of smoke went up from a chimney behind the kitchen.

Above us the black cliff rose nearly straight up to the very top of Mount Onyx. It was about the height of a twenty-story building. "Man, we're close," I said. "If we were Spider-Man—bam—we'd be at the top in seconds."

Cass gulped. His face had lost color and I could tell he

was forcing himself not to look down. "From here," he said, gesturing to a section farther along, where a pathway led away from the cliff, "we take that path, which leads us off this ledge and around the mountain again, where we connect with the main trail—"

But Marco was already unloading a pile of ropes, clips, picks, and shoes from his pack. "What the heck is that stuff?" Aly asked.

"Harnesses . . . camming devices . . . anchors . . ." Marco said.

"I thought you said you had rocks and bricks in there," Cass said.

"I lied," Marco said with a shrug. "Hey, I've been wanting to do this since I got here."

"I'm not going up that!" I said. "It's nearly vertical."

"I agree," Aly said, turning away. "This isn't *The Eiger Sanction*. Fail, Marco. Epic fail."

Cass was shaking. "Aly and J-J-Jack and I—we'll stay behind as lookouts! At least I will!"

"This kind of climbing doesn't work if one person chickens out," Marco said. "It's totally safe, and this equipment is state-of-the-art, right from the KI gym." A smile crept across his face. "So strap on those harnesses and shoes. Even you, brother Cass. 'Cause if you don't, I'm carrying you. And that will be no picnic for either of us."

CHAPTER TWENTY

BELAY ON!

CASS'S FACE WAS bone white as Marco tossed him a wrapped-up clump of equipment. "Man up, guys. Have no fear, Marco's here. We're using a belay system."

"*B-b-ballet?*" Cass squeaked and turned to us. "We're dancing up the cliff?"

"*Belay.*" Marco tossed us each our own packets. "I've done this a hundred times. Just copy what I do."

I was not expecting this. I hoped this was an elaborate practical joke.

We stood there, dumbfounded, until he shot us a no-is-not-an-option glance. He was carefully putting on a helmet, a harness, and a fancy belt that wrapped around his waist and thighs. The belt contained an arsenal of clips.

He looked like a host on the Nature channel.

"We do this in pairs," he said, as we began donning our own gear, "the climber and the belayer. Both are harnessed to the rope. The first climber is called the lead. The belayer stays at the bottom, feeding out as much rope as the lead climber needs. The rope feeds through these cool locking mechanisms on our belts. So if the climber slips . . . *shhhhk!* . . . the belayer's lock grips tight. The rope goes taut, the climber doesn't fall. When the lead climber gets to the top, he belays everyone else from up there. Got that?"

"No," Aly said.

"Not in a million years," Cass added.

"Watch." Marco lifted a cable full of hooks, slings, and eye-shaped devices from his backpack. He quickly changed into a pair of lightweight, low-cut friction shoes. "The soles are supergrippy," he explained. "I brought a pair in everybody's sizes. I'm smart that way."

"Supergrippy?" Cass mumbled. "Sounds like the lamest cartoon hero ever."

Marco reached up, holding tight to a gap in the rock. Keeping his torso close, he dug his foot into a tiny rock dimple and then began hoisting himself up—hand, foot, hand, foot. After a few steps, he let go and jumped to the ground. "See? Gravity's your friend. As long as there's the slightest incline, you can do it, no problem. Each time the lead climber sees a good place—a chink, a space between

150

rock, whatever—he or she sticks in the spring-loaded anchor. Like this."

He jammed a small metal anchor into a crack, attached a small loop of rope to it, and pulled to make sure it held tight. Then he used something I recognized—one of those pear-shaped aluminum loops with a hinge, like you put on your backpack to attach things. "This is a carabiner," he said. "Inside it, you hook the loop *and* the rope. So the rope stays fast to the anchor, but it still has freedom to move up and down. Safer than going up a flight of stairs! Okay, we need a lead climber and a belayer. Volunteers?"

"I'll watch," Aly said. "For now."

Cass opened his mouth, but no sound came out.

I thought of belaying and letting Marco climb. But I took one look at Cass and Aly, and I had a sudden fear: Without Marco to keep Aly and Cass in line, with just me on the ledge, they might refuse to go up. And then I'd have to climb alone.

I hated not to trust them. But even more, I hated the idea of being last.

"I'll do it," I blurted out. "I'll climb first."

Cass and Aly stared at me like I'd lost my mind.

"Woo-hoo, let's hear it for Jack McKinleeey!" Marco shouted. He pulled his machete out of his belt and handed it to me. "Take this."

"Why?" I asked.

"Just in case," he replied. "You never know what may be up there."

Fool. Idiot. Moron.

It's hard to put on friction shoes when your brain is screaming at you. But I had no choice now. No retreat, no surrender. Marco was hooking himself up to the belay harness. Cass and Aly looked as if they were telepathically planning my funeral.

"Okay, I'm allowing you some slack in the rope as you climb, but not too much—so if you fall, it won't be far," Marco said. "When I'm ready, I say 'Belay on!' You say 'Ready to climb.' I answer, 'Climb away.' If you need more rope, yell 'slack.' If you want me to tighten, yell 'rope.' Got that?" He turned to Cass. "And when it's your turn, no tricks. Don't say 'epor.'"

"Wasn't even thinking of it," Cass replied.

I nodded numbly. Looking up, I saw only one crack. The one Marco had already used. The rest of the rock looked like it had been gone over with a power sander.

"Belay on," Marco said. "Now you say 'Ready to climb!'"

"Ready to climb," I squeaked.

Marco put his hand on my shoulder. "Climb away, brother Jack."

"Stop calling me that," I snapped. "You make me feel like a monk." Grabbing the handhold, I pulled myself up. I tentatively dug my foot into the rock.

152

I reached up for another handhold, my fingers drumming desperately on the rock. "You don't need much, dude!" Marco called up. "Just a small indentation. Anchor with fingers, push with feet. And keep your body close to the rock."

Marco was right. The shoes made a difference. Also the angle. My head was maybe six inches forward of my feet. That gave me more balance than I'd imagined. I could push into the smallest bump with my toes and my fingers.

Push, reach. Push, reach. I was climbing!

"Find an anchor!" Marco called up.

I was staring into a deep crack that hadn't been visible from below. Perfect. "Rope!" I called out.

Marco pulled the climbing rope snug. I jammed an anchor into the crack, attached the carabiner, and snapped the rope into it. "Slack!"

I was picking up speed now. And confidence. I could see an abandoned metal tower at the top. I dropped a couple of anchors in the rush to jam them into the rock. I was getting sloppy. Marco was yelling at me from below.

Soon I was swallowing sweat. Gulping breaths. Feeling light-headed.

"Slow down!" I heard Marco's voice shout.

I forced myself to stop. Catching my breath, I looked downward.

Big mistake.

Marco was a dot next to two specks. My heart began pumping so hard I could see the movement through my sweat-soaked shirt.

Go. Get there now!

I pushed and reached. My foot slipped off, but I held on. With each climbing step I felt a stab in my thighs. My arm muscles ached. The wind rushed down on me over the top of the mountain, buffeting my ears. I could hear voices below, but I had no idea what they were saying. All I knew was that the lip of the mountain was just above me. The summit.

With a final grunt, I curled my hand around the top. The skin on my fingers had practically peeled off. I pushed as hard as I could with my legs. I hoicked one elbow over the top, and then another.

Directly above me was the old tower.

"I—I made it . . ." I gasped. *"I made it!"*

Slowly I pulled my face up over the ledge. And I came face-to-face with bloodshot eyes and gleaming sharp teeth.

CHAPTER TWENTY-ONE

THE TUB

MY FINGERS LET go.

Lurching backward, I screamed. The summit gave way to a blur of rock. I flailed my arms, trying to grasp something, anything. The weight of my pack pulled me backward. The tower gave way to the blanket of blue sky.

And then I jerked to a sudden stop. In midair. As if a giant fist had reached up and socked me. My field of vision went white. My torso seized upward.

I was traveling sideways now, flying back toward the rock. I followed the rope with my eyes. It was swinging from the anchor I'd just jammed into the topmost crack. I put my arms up for a shield.

I hit the rock full speed.

"Grab it!" Marco's voice floated up from below. *"Grab the rock!"*

My hand was bleeding. I gripped on to a crack, but my fingers slipped. With a jolt, the rope sank lower. I heard a sickening squeal as it pulled on the anchor.

My entire weight was being supported by a thin aluminum clip and Marco's grip. If either one of those gave way, I was dead.

I wiped my hand on my jeans and tried again.

There. Fingers in hole, two feet planted. "Cuh—!" I squeaked, my voice raw and parched. I swallowed and tried again. "Coming down!"

"Climb on!" Marco replied.

He hadn't heard me right. "Not *'climb on'—climb down!* There's an animal up there!"

"What kind of animal?" Marco called up.

"Hungry!" I replied. "Red eyes. Ugly. Bad. *That* kind. Can we have this discussion when I reach bottom, please?"

"You can't!" Marco said. "Go back and scare it away!"

"You are out of your mind!" I said.

"Jack, calm down. It's more afraid of you than you are of it," Marco called. "Cass says the only possible thing it could be is a bear. You startled it. As long as you're not attacking its babies, you're good. In fact, it's probably gone by now!"

"And if it's not?" I yelled.

"You have the machete, dude!" Marco replied. "Use it.

Worst-case scenario, you turn and rappel."

"What's rappel?" I asked.

Marco went silent for a second. "Oops. Guess we didn't talk about that. It's how you get down."

My blood was oozing down the rock now. "Just lower me now!"

"We don't have enough rope," Marco said. "You'd fall halfway. You'd die. Just go up, dude. Be careful. If you're safe, unhook yourself and give me a tug."

"Fall to my death . . . be eaten by a jungle mountain beast . . . Let me think about it a minute!" I yelled.

Marco, Cass, and Aly were tiny, barely discernible. It was only by some trick of acoustics—and Marco's big voice—that I could hear him.

I refused to return to the Karai Institute a flattened blob of ex–human being. I took a deep breath and felt the machete, still snug against my side. I had never hunted, never battled an animal. But there was always a first time.

You will not be scared.

"Ready to climb!" I called down.

"Climb on!"

The blood on my hands was starting to clot. My stomach was sore from the fall, and each step felt like a punch to the midsection. I willed myself to stop shaking as I made my way back up.

Slowly.

Just below the summit I stopped. If the *thing* was there, it would see my fingers reaching over the top. Instead I dug my fingers into a deep fissure just below the surface. I kept them there while I stepped upward, locking myself into a crouch. From that position I raised my head slowly over the top.

I could see the base of the abandoned black tower. A long, flat stone platform. A clump of trees. Rocks. Nothing else. The mysterious beast was gone.

"Hello?" I called out.

Holding on with my left hand, I grabbed a loose rock with my right and threw it into the trees.

No sudden motion, no attacking streak of black.

Just do it.

I pulled myself up to the top and swung my legs over. As the wind rushed over my body, my breaths came in ragged, painful gulps. Squinting to avoid the sun, I stood on shaky legs and took a few steps in. If the thing were going to surprise me, I didn't want to fall back. Pulling out the machete, I muttered, "Just try it, suckah . . ."

The beast was nowhere to be seen. The top of the mountain was an enormous flat surface that seemed to stretch out for a mile. I expected it to be barren, but a small section of it had tree cover, mostly pines, rising like a clump of hair about fifty feet to my left. I figured that was the top of the easy path—the place where Torquin would eventually emerge.

The wind whistled around me, whipping up from the jungle below. At this height it looked like a dirty carpet stretching all way to the compound, which now resembled a toy village. The distant sea surrounded the island like a scarf.

I felt a tug on the rope and remembered what I was supposed to do. Stick it through the locking mechanism on *my* harness. Belay the other climbers from above.

Cautiously I set down the machete. *"Belay on!"* I yelled as loud as I could.

I felt a tug on the rope. And a barely audible response. A frightened, high-pitched, quavery scream.

Could have been either Aly or Cass. Marco was making them go first.

For a jock, he was pretty smart.

* * *

"I don't believe this guy," Aly said, her voice hushed.

She, Cass, and I stared down the mountain at Marco.

Aly's climb had been smoother than mine—once she got past the first few minutes, she was a natural. Cass had whined and complained the whole way and had had a few major slips. But we were there, all three of us. And we were pretty proud of ourselves.

Until Marco began his climb.

"Here comes Spidey!" he screamed, scampering up like an animal. Somehow he was managing to loop the rope through his own harness as he climbed. I wasn't even belaying him.

And the worst part was that he was whistling. *Whistling.*

When he reached the top, he launched over it into a double somersault and sprang to his feet. "Ta-da!"

"I. Did. Not. See. That," Cass said.

"Wild applause," I said, looking around warily. "Now let's find this thing and go. And keep an eye out for a big beast with a snout and sharp teeth."

"Sounds like the vromaski," Aly said.

"The vromaski is fictional," I said, "from our dreams. If it ever existed, it died out a gazillion years ago. So maybe we look for something real?"

Aly raised an eyebrow. "Well, excuse me for living."

She stomped off, plopping herself down at the edge of a long, rectangular rock near the tower, her back to us.

I felt like a total jerk. I hadn't meant to sound so sarcastic. Things were too tense. I was letting my nerves get the better of me.

"Uh-oh, Romeo," Marco whispered. "A little repair work needed."

"Belay on," I said with a sigh.

I sat at the other end of the long rock. It was sunken in the center, so I had to perch carefully. "Hey. I'm sorry."

"Hi, Sorry," she said, still looking the other way. "I'm Aly."

"I shouldn't have been such a jerk," I said.

"Yup, you shouldn't have," Aly replied. "But I guess suggesting the vromaski was dumb. I have my dumb side."

She turned toward me with a hint of a smile. And then her butt began sliding down into the center of the sunken rock.

I let myself slide, too, and we collided in the middle, laughing. "First time I've ever been in a bathtub with a guy!" she said.

I could feel my face turning red.

And then we both stopped laughing at once.

Other half on peak in tub.

Together, without exchanging a word, we jumped off the rock. Dropping to our knees, we began feeling around the outside of it. The rock was solid, save a large crack that ran along the base. One part of the crack was wide enough for fingers. I pulled up, but it was heavy. "Help me," I said to Aly.

She came to my side and dug in. The rock moved a fraction of an inch. It was an entire corner of the tub, a large, loose cubic section. "Cass, Marco—we found it!" Aly shouted.

They were kneeling next to us in seconds. "We need a lever," Marco said, running into the woods.

He came back with a boulder about two feet high and dropped it near the widest part of the crack. Then he took the machete from where I'd set it down and jammed the tip into the crack. Resting the center of the blade on the rock, he pressed down hard on the hilt.

The stone started to lift. Marco's face was red with the effort. Inside the crack was a black hole. "Almost there!" I said.

"Geeeeyaaahh!" Marco grunted. The stone slid off, thudding to the ground.

With a pinging snap, the machete broke, sending the top half of the blade flying over the cliff.

Cass grimaced. "We may find some shish-kebabed toucan on the way down."

The removed corner of the tub revealed a big hole inside the rock. I pulled a flashlight out of my pack and shone it inside. The hole was thickly fretted with cobwebs, which Aly quickly pulled out. A family of small spiders and one big tarantula scurried over the edge. Cass recoiled with a choked scream.

At the bottom of the hole, covered with dirt, was another small section of rock. My heart began to beat loudly. I reached down and picked it up.

IF MISERY BE THINE
ENTER BELOW
WHERE 142857
BECOMES 999999

CHAPTER TWENTY-TWO

ATTACK

"WHAT DOES THIS mean?" Aly asked.

"No idea," I replied.

"Numbers," Marco said, scratching his head. "Very dangerous."

I looked at Cass. His face was bone white. He was looking over my shoulder. "What is it?" I asked.

"Sssh," Cass hissed.

And then I heard it. A rustling in the bushes among the evergreens. I slipped the rock into my pants pocket.

"Torquin," Marco whispered. "Let's surprise him. You guys hide behind the tower. I'll climb as high as I can go and see if I can figure out exactly where he is."

He bounded onto the big cement platform that supported

the old tower. Cass, Aly, and I ducked behind it.

In about twenty seconds, Marco was up and then back down the metal struts of the tower. "It's not Torquin," he whispered. "It's shorter. And nastier looking. And four-footed."

I glanced around, in case we needed to bolt. If something came out of the jungle, we had a lot of room to run—but I had no idea which sections of the plateau would be safest to climb down.

Marco jumped off the platform. "Listen up—you're going to rappel down, all of you. Here's how: You anchor the rope, tie it around your harness, and lock it into the belay mechanism. When you step over the edge, get your body perpendicular to the rock. That's the hardest part. Remember. Perpendicular. Once you do that, you're golden. You walk down, letting out slack as you need it. That's it. You won't fall. Got that?"

The command had barely left his mouth when a speeding gray blur erupted from the bushes. It was all sinew and flash, a red-eyed ball of muscle with a wrinkled snout. It let out a gravelly roar, flashing ivory saber teeth that looked like they could slice an elephant to shreds.

A hose-beaked vromaski.

"Marco, look out!" I shouted.

The giant predator leaped. Marco spun away with lightning reflexes, and the beast missed him by inches and crashed to the ground with a grunt. *"Run!"* Marco yelled, racing for the broken hilt of the machete.

The beast scrambled to its feet and attacked again as Marco grabbed what was left of our machete—the hilt and a jagged section of blade. Marco rolled away as the beast leapt. He thrust the weapon up, impaling the vromaski's side in midair. It let out a shriek like the scratching of glass on slate.

Aly and Cass were already running for the anchored rope. "He nailed it!" I shouted, bolting after them. I nearly tripped over a rock. The wind decided then to gust, blowing dirt and branches across the plain. I heard footfalls behind me, and Marco shot by.

The vromaski was still alive. The knife in its side only made it angrier. It had managed to shake the weapon loose, and the broken machete now lay in a pool of dark-green fluid.

At a dead sprint, Marco scooped up a branch. He looked around desperately, spotting the rock near my feet.

"Throw me that rock, Jack!" he shouted, drawing the branch back like a baseball bat. "Right down the middle!"

I tossed the rock and ducked. I heard the stick make contact and the rock whistle into the air.

It shot toward the beast and hit it square in its drooping nose. With a howl, the vromaski fell to the ground. *Now go!*" Marco shouted.

Cass was frozen at the top of the cliff. "I—I can't," he said.

165

"We're going to be killed!" Aly said.

Cass looked down again. "I—I—" His mouth froze silently. Aly and I looked at each other. In a split second, I realized this was not going to work. Cass was panicked. His body had locked down.

Trying to rappel down was one thing—doing it while carrying Cass would be suicidal.

Marco and the vromaski were near the edge of the pines. He was outleaping the beast, zigging when it zagged. Its nose was a bloody mess. It roared with fury.

I glanced back over the plateau. Our only hope was to run for the far end. The plateau dropped off, but maybe we'd find a footpath. An easier way to get to the bottom. "Go that way!" I said, pointing down the expanse of barren rock. "See if we can climb down!"

Aly urged Cass along. He began to run. I watched them for a moment, hanging back to help Marco. He had dropped his stick on the ground, and I picked it up. "Marco, here!" I shouted, throwing it toward him.

Marco grabbed it in the air, just as the vromaski pounced. In one quick move, he turned and stabbed the jagged edge of the stick into the monster's eye.

It wailed horribly, writhing on the ground, then wailed again as he pulled the stick out.

"Come on!" I said. "Follow Aly and Cass!"

Marco began to run. With one hand he held the dripping

stick, with the other he pulled me along. My feet were moving faster than they ever had in my life.

Aly and Cass raced to the end of the plateau and stopped short. I prayed that they would start walking down, and we could follow them into a wooded path, where we could lose the vromaski. But instead they turned toward us, their eyes wide and frightened. They began waving their hands frantically. *"No! Stop!"* Aly said.

Marco and I reached them at the same time. We put on the brakes. Below us yawned a deep, bottomless blackness—a crater.

Mount Onyx was a volcano, and we had reached the center.

Marco turned, the stick still in his hand. His teeth were bared.

The beast was dazed and limping. Green blood poured from its mouth as it stalked us, its eyes flashing red. Even at a distance it smelled like rotting flesh. Exactly like in my dream.

Marco backpedaled. He was a few feet from the ridge's edge now. "Scatter to the sides," he shouted. "We're safer if we're farther apart. Go as far away as you can!"

The vromaski coiled itself, holding still. Then, springing with its last ounce of strength, it hurtled toward Marco like a rocket. Its mouth widened, its teeth glinting in the sun, stained green.

Marco held the stick in front of him. Then, with a sudden motion, he stepped aside.

The beast's teeth closed around the wood—and Marco's wrist. With a sharp crack, the stick snapped. Marco bellowed in pain.

The animal's momentum carried it over the edge of the volcano. The wood went with it.

And so did Marco.

CHAPTER TWENTY-THREE

INTO THE ABYSS

"NO-O-O-O!"

I watched the two figures falling, weightless, like rag dolls. I couldn't breathe.

The thing about horror—real-life horror, not the kind you see in movies—is that it is so silent. No screaming sound track, no fancy camera angles. Just two bodies vanishing into the shadows. Gravity doing its work.

And then it hits you. Rips into your soul.

Aly leaned forward, screaming, reaching with her arms as if she could wave him back up. Cass froze and then began rocking back and forth, staring at the dirt. "This didn't happen, this didn't happen, this didn't happen . . ."

I turned away and looked back, staring into the abyss.

I don't know why. Maybe I was hoping to see him. Hoping these horrible few minutes, like the vromaski itself, were part of a dream.

But Marco was gone.

He had told us to scatter. He had faced the beast alone. He had taken one for the team.

Marco, the slacker jock. The show-off. The goofball.

He had given his life. For us.

I leaned over, my head in my hands. Tears ran down my cheeks and dropped onto the sandy crags below. A cry welled up from my gut, echoing into the chasm. "Marco . . ."

But all that came back was a hot, dry wind.

* * *

"He was attacked by a *what*?" Bhegad looked at us as if we were speaking in Gaelic.

We were gathered in his cramped office, on the second floor of the lab building. The windows were grimy, the walls a dingy shade of beige. At least seven stacks of files rose against the wall, joining at the top into one solid phalanx of paper that nearly touched the ceiling. Newspapers were stacked on the other side, paper clips marking pages that were yellowed with age. An old metal fan jutted out from where it had fallen, stuck between a file cabinet and a wall. The blades were so dusty they seemed to be made of gray felt.

Aly and I were standing. I'd given Cass the only available seat, a butt-high pile of magazines topped with *New*

England Journal of Medicine, July 23, 1979.

"He's dead, Professor Bhegad!" Aly said. "That's what matters. You didn't tell us that . . . *thing* would be there! It was a vromaski—a real one. Saber teeth, horrible snout. Just the way I dreamed it. How did that happen, Professor? What aren't you telling us?"

"I didn't know." Bhegad was wiping off his glasses. His eyes were red, his skin flushed. "There are no animals at the top of the volcano. It is barren there."

"Barren?" I exploded. "Tell Marco he was killed by an imaginary animal!"

"We didn't even have a chance to say good-bye," Cass said.

Aly shook her head in despair. "Or thank him."

"But . . . how did you get here?" Bhegad asked. "How on earth were you able to get back down so quickly?"

"Because he told us how," I snapped. "He explained how to rappel down the mountain *while the animal was attacking him.*"

"Extraordinary . . ." Bhegad leaned heavily forward on his elbows. A pile of papers shifted, sending a small alarm clock to the floor. ". . . Pushing the physical envelope under attack. Teaching . . . imparting skills. Fantastic."

"One of us dies and you call it *fantastic?*" I shot back.

"That is really cold, Professor," Cass said.

"Oh my, I meant that only as a—a tribute to this

extraordinary young man," Bhegad said, rummaging through his desk. "Tragic, tragic."

I hated his response. After what had just happened, I detested everything about the Karai Institute. Bhegad had made it seem like they cared. Like their biggest concern was our lives. Like G7W and possible superpowers were these great gifts from them to us.

They didn't care about Marco. Marco's death was another way to gather information. His murder was a new data point.

Well, I didn't care about them anymore. Or my supposed salvation.

The institute wasn't the reason I was alive right now. Not the operation or the treatment. Or the fact that I happened to be born with some fatal but magical gene marker. My life could have ended with the snap of a jaw. I was alive because of a friend's sacrifice. No matter how many more years I had left, I would have to live with that.

"We have to find his body," Cass said. "Send us down there with Torquin in his helicopter."

"I daresay Torquin is still on his way back," Bhegad said. "He radioed me. After he lost you on the mountain, he turned back. He thought you'd fallen asleep or some such. By the time he reached the top of Mount Onyx, it was long after you'd . . . left. And, my boy, we can't send a chopper into the caldera. We've tried it before. The volcano has been dormant for thousands of years, but still, there are strange updrafts that will knock a helicopter into the side walls."

"Then we'll go by foot," I said. "I'm with Cass. We can't just leave him there."

"Jack, the idea is sheer folly," Professor Bhegad said. "We have no tunneling equipment."

"There is a way into the volcano." I pulled the second half of the rock from my pocket. "We found what we were looking for, Professor Bhegad. The second part of Wenders's message was on Mount Onyx. It talks about an entrance."

Bhegad peered at the stone. "Random numbers . . . I fear this is the writing of a madman."

"The first part of the code made sense," Aly pointed out. "What makes you think this doesn't? All these years studying the island, and you have no idea what Wenders was talking about?"

He sank back into his chair, wrapped in thought. "A hundred years ago, a subgroup of Scholars—the Onyxians—hypothesized the center of Atlantis was inside the caldera. There is a mythology of a labyrinth, you know. A maze. Modern theorists know that this is unlikely within the sides of a volcano. The maze must refer to the winding paths of the castle itself, which is certainly underwater. But I will ask a team to investigate—"

"If anybody goes to try to find our friend," I said, "we're going with them."

As he reached for the phone, Bhegad shook his head. "Absolutely not. I sent you on a simple hike and you turned it into an alpine rock climb. You separated from Torquin and lost one of your closest friends. One of the Select. I plan to place you under the strictest house supervision!"

He shot us all an accusing glance, picked up the phone, and pounded a number. "Torquin? You are to assemble a search team, pronto. It will include you, me, and your three best people."

A tear made its way down Aly's cheek. Cass put his arm around her. As Bhegad moved to hang up the phone, Aly let out a sniffle.

"Now get out of here!" the professor shouted. But his voice had lost its bite and his glasses were fogging up.

None of us moved.

Bhegad's eyes flickered briefly and he coughed. Yanking the phone back to his ear, he barked, "And, Torquin . . . you will include the three remaining Select . . . No, you do not have a say in this. And, no, Torquin, I do not believe they need to be taught a lesson. I will see you in a half hour, or I will force you to work for a full month straight . . . in shoes."

I grinned. He wasn't such a lizard after all.

"Thank you . . ." Aly said.

Professor Bhegad put the phone down and hung his head. He flipped through a messy leather datebook and ran his fingers along today's date. "Don't thank me yet. We can't start this until break of day tomorrow. And at midnight the day after that, Cass is due for his next treatment." He looked at Cass. "I cannot send you, my boy."

The color drained from Cass's face. "But that's two whole days!" he protested. "We'll be back in time."

"Professor Bhegad, even your best people are no match for Cass's sense of direction," I said. "We can set a limit. If we don't reach the center by a certain time, one of the team can take Cass back."

"No to that," Bhegad said, drumming his fingers on his desk. "I have responsibilities."

"Marco used to call me brother Jack," I said. "It annoyed me. I teased him about it. Told him it made me sound like a monk. But now I understand. He really did see me—and Aly and Cass—as his family."

Cass nodded. "We have a responsibility, too, Professor. To our brother."

"To your—but that makes no—" Bhegad sat wearily in his chair, wiping his forehead with a handkerchief. His brow was knotted in a way that broadcast *no*, but his eyes were soft. "May the power of Atlantis," he finally said, "be always with you."

CHAPTER TWENTY-FOUR

THE DREAM CHANGES

The dream again.

The fire.

The beasts of air and land, in their panic, are a tangle of torsos and teeth. They're all around me, slithering, swooping, skittering. They fear the inevitable.

The end of all that's known.

A voice calls, as it always does in the scene: Run! RUN!

But this time I see a new person. Silent. Still. Someone I believe I know.

WHO ARE YOU?

I move closer but the face is shrouded, the features blurred as if seen through a dirty lens.

I'm tempted to run away, but I don't. I know where running leads. To the hole. To death.

I know I can no longer fear.

So I turn to the center of the destruction, where smoke billows blackly. Its tendrils shoot toward me, twining around my neck like curled fingers. It is at one moment sweet smelling, the next sharp and acrid. But I keep walking until I see the shaft rising from the center of the circle. It glows brightly, beckoning somehow.

Around the shaft is a circle of light. Spinning. There are objects embedded in the circle, and I must take them.

The smoke is clearing and I know I must work fast. I kneel to the circle, fighting indecision. Driving out the demons inside. What I will do—must do—defies all that I have ever stood for.

The fire rages, coming closer, licking the edges of the valley. I reach through the smoke to grab what I need.

But what I see instead is a head.

Marco's head.

It's laughing.

CHAPTER TWENTY-FIVE

IF MISERY BE THINE

"JACK, I THINK I know how to get us through it," Cass said, panting as he struggled to keep up with the search team.

The sun blazed with a special fierceness that morning, and it was hard to keep up a conversation. "Through what?" I asked.

"The ezam," he said.

"Beg your pardon?" came Professor Bhegad's voice from behind us.

Cass immediately clammed up. I was dying to hear about his plan, but not in full earshot of the old professor.

Torquin was leading the group at a breakneck pace, clomping through the bushes like an elephant on steroids. He used his machete, but he didn't need to. The guy was a human path maker. Especially when he was angry about working on his day off.

Behind him were three of the meanest, biggest guards I'd ever met in the Karai Institute. Guys I recognized from the heliport when I landed after my escape attempt. One was missing teeth, the second was missing a finger, and the third was missing his hair.

Bhegad's tweed blazer had large circular sweat stains that grew like an incoming tide. "Torquin!" he called ahead, "are you sure this is the path to the Wenders tobacco site?"

Torquin grunted something that could have been either yes or no. None of the other three seemed to have an opinion.

"Tobacco site?" I asked.

"The Onyxians searched fanatically for signs of entry to their maze," Bhegad replied. "They found a pile of pipe tobacco leaves that matched Wenders's favorite brand, near a rock wall. Although the wall was solid, they marked the place for future reference. Site One. There were other sites, too—"

"Guys, we need to pick up the pace," Aly urged. "Torquin and his goons are making tracks."

The men were way ahead of us, stepping high and fast as if on military training exercises. "Confound it, Torquin, slow down!" Bhegad shouted.

"Go slower is standing still!" Torquin's voice echoed. "Hurry. Big distance. North side of mountain!"

As we trudged on, the heat seemed to be radiating up from the ground in waves. My clothes were soaked through and my head was throbbing. But we were circling the northern side of the mountain now, and that meant we would soon be in the shadow.

Which dropped the temperature to a breezy ninety-one degrees or so.

I wiped sweat away from my eye as we walked into a clearing. The sun was behind the mountain now, and a scraggly patch of dirt led to a rock wall at its base. Torquin and his men were out of sight, and Professor Bhegad stopped, holding on to a tree. "Please . . ." he said. "Someone tell those ruffians . . . to wait . . ."

"We don't need to," Cass said. "They walked past the site. We're here."

"How do you know?" I asked.

"From one of the maps I saw in the office. I remember a marking—WTS. I'm guessing Wenders Tobacco Site?" Cass pointed to a spot on the rock wall. "It's right there."

Cass, Aly, and I ran toward the wall. It was covered with vines. We began ripping down as much as we could. I looked for some sign of an entrance—a suspicious crack, a fingerhold, a carving . . .

"Stand aside!" Torquin's voice boomed.

He and his three men were marching back, faces flushed with embarrassment. Using his machete, Torquin began swiping away more vegetation, taking down huge clumps of vines as the others joined in.

"My heroes," Aly murmured drily.

Torquin turned toward us, his chest heaving. "Is rock. No entrance. Go to Site Two."

"I'll be the one who gives marching orders," Bhegad said. "Let's rest a moment."

I was having a feeling again. Something that seemed to be vibrating up from the ground. I stepped back, holding the two parts of the stone in my hands, reading the words. Torquin's team were muttering to themselves, kicking the wall, yawning.

I looked up the side of the mountain. Maybe thirty feet above us, the rock lost its smoothness, becoming sharply cragged. To the right a cliff jutted outward, a horizontal platform attached to a diagonal outcropping, like a letter Z that had emerged from the rock and lost its bottom part.

"'If misery be thine,'" I read, "'enter below, where one, four, two, eight, five, seven becomes nine, nine, nine, nine, nine, nine.' I don't get it."

"Those numbers are familiar," Aly said. "One, four, two, eight, five, seven. They're a repeating set. For sevenths."

"Meaning . . . ?" I asked.

Professor Bhegad nodded. "One-seventh, if you change it to decimal form, is point one, four, two, eight, five, seven. Two-sevenths is expressed with the same digits, only beginning with the two."

"Look." Aly pulled a pad and pen from her pocket and quickly wrote out what she meant:

$$1/7 = .142857$$
$$2/7 = .285714$$
$$3/7 = .428571$$
$$4/7 = .571428$$
$$5/7 = .714285$$
$$6/7 = .857142$$

"The same repeating digits in the same order," she explained, "but starting at a different place."

I shook my head. "But Wenders isn't writing here about decimals. It's whole numbers—what do you call them, integers. How does one number *become* the other? And how does this get us inside?"

Cass walked closer to the wall. "Maybe he left another message somewhere . . ."

I looked up at the ledge again. At the shape of the outcropping. The incomplete letter Z.

And it hit me. The formation was the shape of a perfect seven!

Where 142857 becomes 999999 . . .

Quickly I took Aly's pen:

$$142857 \times 7 = 999999$$

"Where the first number becomes the second number," I said, "is here. At a seven! We just have to find the entrance."

Torquin stomped over to me and took the sheet of paper. He and his men stared at it.

"The slanted part of the seven points downward," I said. "Could it function like an arrow?"

I followed the diagonal downward, but the wall didn't show any obvious clue. Just rock. It was lined, like sedimentary rock formed in layers. I figured that when the volcano formed, those layers were pushed up out of the ground to form this wall. I went closer, running my hand along the rock. It was covered with spindly little roots where the vines had attached, all of which fell right off.

And then a chunk of rock peeled away, too.

Professor Bhegad came closer. "That brittle rock appears to be shale," he said. "There is no shale on this island, though."

I dug my hand in and scooped out some more. The rock crumbled easily, raining outward.

Torquin stooped down, lifted a handful of the powdery stuff, and tasted it. "Not rock," he said. "Plaster."

I cleared away as much as I could. Aly and Cass dug their hands in to help. When we were done, a sharp-edged carving stared back at us.

My hands shook slightly as I joined the two halves of the rock with Wenders's weird rhymes on them.

Then I inserted them into the carving.

CHAPTER TWENTY-SIX

THE MAZE

I WAITED.

My fingers tingled. After holding the rocks in place for a long moment, I had to let go. The two halves of Wenders's "key" did not fall out, though. They stayed snug in their place.

Torquin turned away with a dissatisfied grunt. "Now, Site Two."

"Just a minute!" Bhegad barked.

I was feeling something. I could tell from Bhegad's face that he was, too.

It began as a movement underneath us, like the passing of a subway train or a slight earthquake. Cass gasped. He and Aly looked down instinctively. But I had my eye on the wall. On a seam in the rock. Slowly it darkened into a crack and began to move with an awful scraping noise, like a boulder being pulled across a parking lot. Pulverized rock billowed out in dense clouds.

I covered my ears. We ran to a safer spot, behind bushes and away from the spewing grit, until the noise stopped. As the dust settled, we saw a slim, arched opening, barely tall enough for a human to enter standing up.

"That's it?" Cass said. "We did it?"

Professor Bhegad nodded, speechless.

We all walked cautiously closer. A horrible stench rushed out, putrid and wet, like sulfur.

"Smells like something big and disgusting died in here," Aly whispered.

"Extraordinary," Bhegad said, wiping his dirt-encrusted glasses on his tie. "The Onyxians were right about Wenders . . ."

"We lead. Kids follow," Torquin interrupted. "Mark walls. Return."

"Torquin, don't lose them," Bhegad said.

"Pah," Torquin replied with a contemptuous glare.

Bhegad turned to us with a wan, forced smile. "I'll be waiting here. And please, my young friends, stay safe."

I nodded at the old man. I couldn't bring myself to smile back.

The four goons went first into the darkness, shining

their flashlights all around. The opening was barely wide enough for Torquin.

Placing my hand over my nose, I stepped in next. Cass and Aly followed close behind.

"Narrow," Torquin grumbled, his shoulders scraping the sides.

"Diet didn't work, eh, Torq?" one of his goons remarked with a laugh.

I heard a thump and the laughing stopped.

After plodding for about ten minutes, Cass called out, "Turn right at the fork!"

"How do you know there's a fork?" I asked.

"I was trying to tell you earlier," Cass said. "That tree stump we saw in the jungle—remember the one with the carved lines? It looked suspicious to me. Like someone had carved it. Which meant there was a reason for carving it. So I memorized it."

"It was just some random thing in the middle of the jungle!" Aly said. "And you only looked at it for a moment."

Cass shrugged. "I can't help it. I memorize everything. It's like you with tech stuff. And movies. Oh, by the way, look out."

I turned and walked smack into the beefy back of one of Torquin's men. They were all standing still at a fork in the path. "Left," Torquin said.

"Right," Cass corrected.

"Right," Torquin agreed. "Left."

As the men walked off to the left, Cass's shoulders slumped. "They're just going to run into two more branches that are dead ends, and another that winds all the way around the mountain."

I called out to Torquin, "We are going to the right!"

The men stopped. I could see Torquin trying to elbow his way through them.

"Guys?" Aly called out. Just inside the right-hand turn, she had found a small rectangular panel in the rock wall. It held two buttons, one above the other in a row. "What's this doing in an ancient tunnel?"

Cass leaned closer. "Has to be from Wenders's time. But what's it for?"

Aly thought for a moment. "It looks like an early design for an on-off light switch. You see them in old movies sometimes. It's possible the correct path is rigged with lights."

"I don't see any bulbs or electrical wires," Cass pointed out.

"I said *possible*," Aly reminded him. "Of course, it could be some spectacular *Indiana Jones*–style effect, and we'll all be running from some boulder rolling down a chute. Ha-ha-ha."

Her laugh echoed unanswered.

Torquin had managed to emerge from the crowded knot of goon muscle. He stood at the opening to his tunnel, glaring at me. "Lost you before. Glued to my side now."

Out of the corner of my eye, I could see Aly pressing the top button. It was rusted and old, but it finally went in with a crisp snap.

I was hoping for something spectacular to happen— holiday lights, music, whatever—but there was nothing. Torquin stepped closer. The goons were grumbling.

"Let's just go with them," Cass said. "We need them. They're nasty enough to scare away vromaskis."

Click.

I stopped short. The sound had come from above. From within the rock ceiling. "What was that?"

"What?" Cass said. "I didn't hear—"

A deep rumble interrupted him. There was no mistaking that. Torquin looked up, grunting under his breath.

With a sudden explosion, rocks showered from above. I shoved Cass and Aly away from the noise. As we fell to the ground, arms over our heads, a clang echoed against the walls.

I peered out to see a rusted iron gate slamming down from the ceiling. It completely sealed off Torquin and his men at the opening to the left-hand tunnel.

"How?" Torquin shouted.

We stared, bug-eyed. "I don't know!" I replied.

"Sorry . . ." Aly squeaked.

The men raced to the gate and tried to lift it. Torquin wedged a machete under it as a lever. Cass, Aly, and I joined from the other side. But the thing held fast. It must have weighed a ton. "You did on purpose!" Torquin shouted.

"Like we *want* to go into this maze alone?" I shot back.

I felt helpless. Cass was right—we needed these guys. Badly. They were our first line of defense.

"We have to get some help," Cass suggested.

I was about to agree—until I considered what would happen. Bhegad would radio KI for backup. We'd have to wait. He would suspect that we'd done this on purpose and not let us go back. Our mission would be over.

"That pattern from the tree trunk—you memorized it completely?" I asked Cass.

"As well as I know my name," Cass said.

"Can Torquin and the guards meet up with us if they keep going?" I asked.

Cass thought a moment and then nodded. "But it would be a very long and twisty path."

I turned back and walked to the gate. Holding myself as tall as I could, I said, "Give me the machete, Torquin."

Torquin's eyes seemed to want to bust out of his head. "Orders, me. Following, you."

"We warned you guys—and you got trapped," I said, stepping closer. "I can go back and report that to Bhegad. He won't take it kindly. Or we can go on ahead without a weapon and be eaten by wild beasts, which Bhegad won't like either. Or you can give me the machete. We'll go ahead while you try to lift this thing—or take the path you wanted to take and meet up with us later on. Follow my instructions, and we won't say a word to your boss."

Torquin's eyes narrowed. Then, crouching slightly, he slid the machete under the bars.

"Thanks, Torquin," Aly said. "We owe you."

"Will pay," Torquin replied.

I took the weapon, tucked it into my belt, and turned. "Let's roll."

As Cass, Aly, and I headed down the right-hand corridor, I could hear one of the goons wish us good luck. It was followed by the sound of a dull blow and an agonized cry.

Torquin was not happy.

I scraped the machete along the wall, making a white line. "A marker, in case we get lost," I said. "Cass, any sense of how long this maze is?"

"If we make no mistakes, if there are no traps, no doubling back, and then we actually find . . . find Marco's . . ." Cass's voice dropped and his pace slowed.

This was going to be tough on us all.

"I'm concerned about flashlight battery life," I said. "Let's use one at a time. Cass, yours first."

As he flicked on his light, I put mine away in my pack. Although he was behind me, Cass kept the light trained on the path ahead. After a few minutes we started descending sharply. We slowed. The rock surface beneath me was slick with water. Probably from some mountain stream. To keep my balance, I stuck to the right side, walking sideways, holding the wall with my free hand. I felt an opening behind me, big enough for us to fit. I just needed to shine the flashlight into it, make sure nothing nasty was waiting for us.

"Cass, can I borrow your—" I didn't have a chance to finish the question. The floor gave way beneath me. The machete's point jammed against the stone as I fell, ejecting the weapon out of my belt. I slid downward, quickly gaining speed on the wet surface. My fingers grasped for a hold but only reached smooth stone. *"Help!"*

Cass and Aly screamed my name, but their voices were fading fast. I shielded my face with my arms as my body tumbled, out of control, down a long chute. I braced myself for impact.

But the chute ended into nothingness. I was somersaulting in midair, down to utter blackness.

CHAPTER TWENTY-SEVEN

RECALCULATING

I **FELL ON** cold, pricking knives. I tried to gasp, but the air had been displaced by . . .

Water.

The stabbing sensation slammed up through my body—the shock of cold. Colder than anything I'd ever felt. By the time my feet hit bottom I could barely feel them. I pushed as hard as I could, rising, my lungs tight as fists.

As I broke the surface, stunned and numb, I heard clattering noises. It took a second to realize they were footsteps.

"Jack! Over here!" Aly was calling.

The call seemed to come from everywhere. But I saw only blackness. "Where are you?"

"Here!" Cass said from my right. "There are stairs on the right. You didn't have to slide!"

"Th-th-thanks," I said through chattering teeth.

A flash of a light blinded me, and I felt something snake-like drop onto my shoulder. I recoiled with a yell.

"It's a rope, Jack!" Cass shouted. "Grab it!"

I managed to close my fingers around it. Cass dragged me through the water, and then two pairs of hands lifted me over the surface of a sharp rock ledge.

I flopped against a slimy wall, grateful to be out of there but shivering uncontrollably. Aly and Cass had both taken thin blankets from their packs and wrapped them around me. "Easy," Cass said. "Just sit tight."

My teeth kept chattering. My entire body shook. I'd bruised my ankle against the bottom of the underground pool. I'd lost the machete.

"Well," I said, my voice raspy and raw, "at least we're off to a good start."

* * *

I'm not exactly sure how Cass found all the wood. But it was really dry. He returned with pile after pile, proudly dropping it all on the chamber floor. "Very strange. A karst topography in a jungle environment."

"No backward words, please, Cass," Aly asked.

"*Karst* is a real word that means an area of limestone, sink holes, underground pools, cenotes," Cass said. "This must have been some kind of sacred location. There are piles of beads, stacks of wood all around. Maybe this was one of those ancient places where they sacrificed maidens to the gods."

"Why was it always *maidens*?" Aly said with disgust.

I threw a couple more pieces into the fire. The heat felt amazing. I wasn't dry yet, but getting there. We were lucky that a fissure in the ceiling served as a flue to draw the smoke upward.

Cass warmed his hands over the flame. "All the comforts of emoh. Er, home."

"Don't get too comfy." I stood up, slinging my wet backpack over my shoulder. "We have a long way to go. How many matches do you have left? Mine are soaked."

Cass shrugged. "A few."

"If we run out, I can use the flint," I said. "My matches and my flashlight are useless after that swim. Aly, you grab some wood, just in case. Cass, you, too. How are you set for other supplies?"

"Three-in-one oil, rubbing alcohol, kerosene, and peanut butter and jelly sandwich—in separate containers." Cass walked to the mouth of the pathway, shining his flashlight into the blackness. "But I forgot the monster repellant."

I took the flashlight and stepped cautiously inside. The path seemed to have been blasted through solid rock. The ceiling was about eight feet tall, the walls craggy and covered with moss. I felt a drip of water and looked up to see a small stalactite.

"Looks like there's a fork ahead," Aly remarked. "Which way, human GPS?"

"Go right," Cass called out nervously, then shook his head. "No. Recalculating. Left."

Aly and I exchanged a wary glance. Our footsteps clopped loudly. The path grew wider and warmer as we approached a blind turn. The flashlight's globe of light traced a path along the curved wall.

And then it hit a dead end.

"Want to recalculate again?" Aly asked.

"I—I don't understand . . ." Cass said, nearing the sheer rock. "I remember this. There should be a fork here, where we go right!"

As I crept closer, I noticed that the wall contained a perfectly rectangular section of stone, placed into it like a large brick. It jutted out just enough for me to wrap the fingers of both hands around it. I handed the flashlight to Aly.

"Be careful," she warned. "Remember what happened to Torquin."

I pulled. With a loud *sccccraack*, the plug slid out. Under it was a collection of dirt and cobwebs, which I blew aside. Aly shone the flashlight in.

Of sisters, gables, virtues, sins,
Of gambling men with lucky wins
Of continents and stormy seas,
Divisions are thy entry keys

"What the—?" Aly said.

"Think," Cass said. "'Keys.' Keys unlock things. Maybe this is some kind of door."

"But the keys are *divisions*," I said. "That makes no sense."

"It's a list," Aly said, staring intently. "The elements must mean something."

"Sisters, gamblers, seas—they have nothing in common!" Cass insisted.

"People are a combination of their virtues and sins . . ." I mused.

"Wait!" Aly blurted out. *"Camelot!"*

Cass and I looked at her.

"The part in the movie where the evil Mordred sings 'The

Seven Deadly Virtues'?" she said. "Seven virtues . . . seven sins? And . . . gables! That's a movie, too, *House of the Seven Gables*. Well, it started as a book. Nathaniel Hawthorne."

"Seven Sisters . . ." I murmured. "My mom went to Smith College. She called it one of the Seven Sisters schools."

"Seven continents and seven seas!" Cass blurted out. "And seven is a lucky number for gamblers! Don't ask me how I know that."

Aly's fingers were reaching toward the pad. "Seven, divided any way, gives us a fraction with the same number pattern we saw outside, remember? Let's give it a try."

Carefully Aly tapped out 1, 4, 2, 8, 5, and 7.

We held our breaths, staring at the rock. For a long moment, nothing happened. Then a noise.

"Are we . . . rising?" Cass asked.

"I don't think so," I said. "Look at the ground."

It felt like we were rising. But only because the stone wall around us was sinking into the floor.

I looked up. From the shadows behind the rock, I could see the top of two archways.

"Yes!" Cass blurted out. "I told you! A fork! Okay, when this baby sinks, we march right!"

I shone the light into the right-hand pathway.

An eyeless, skinless face stared back at me with a toothy grin.

CHAPTER TWENTY-EIGHT

DON'T LOOK UP

"AAAAAAHHHHH!" CASS'S SCREAM caromed off the stone wall.

We fell over each other trying to run away. I hit my head against a low ceiling. Aly dropped the flashlight.

"Is it behind us?" Cass said.

"It's dead, Cass!" Aly replied. "It's a skeleton!"

"So why are we running?" Cass demanded.

I took a deep breath. I stepped back and picked up the flashlight. I shone it back behind us into the empty passageway. "Okay," I said. "There's an explanation."

"S-sure. The explanation is that that used to be a live person," Cass said. "Someone who found this maze. Like us. The wall trapped him. He started knocking. And he's b-been there ever s-s-since—"

"Stop!" Aly said. "I think Wenders set this up. He found a skeleton, maybe from an ancient sacrifice. He set it up. To scare people away from getting into the tunnel."

I nodded. "Nothing to get freaked about. No big deal."

"No big deal?" Cass said. "What if there are ghosts in here, or zombies?"

"Those are mythical, Cass," Aly said.

"So are vromaskis, and superpowers, and shared dreams," Cass retorted.

Aly leaned forward, putting her hand on Cass's shoulder. "Hey. I know how you feel. We're all scared. But we have a mission. Remember?"

Cass nodded. "Marco."

"Marco," she said.

"There will be an opening off the right wall," Cass said softly. "Take it."

I trained the flashlight ahead. Cass was clinging to Aly. The opening was exactly where he said, and I scratched a mark on the corner with a piece of flint. Then we all edged past the skeleton.

This tunnel was wider. Someone had painted strange-looking animals, now faded and almost transparent. A red bird with the body of a lion. A hook-nosed beast with sharp teeth. "The vromaski and the griffin," I said.

"I need to see this," Aly said, taking out her own flashlight.

"Are you nuts?" Cass snatched the flashlight from her. "We can't sightsee! Let's get through this place. About fifty feet ahead, we turn left."

"That is rude, Cass." Aly lunged toward him and grabbed back the light.

"Guys!" I shouted. "Stop this!"

As Cass lurched away, Aly lost her balance, hurtling to the ground. She cried out, her foot wedged in a hole.

"Are you all right?" I asked.

She grimaced, looking straight downward. "I think so. Lost my flashlight, though. Thank you, Cass."

Cass and I knelt beside her. I shone my light down into the hole. It was bottomless. "Next time you guys want to fight over something," I said, "make sure it's not anything our lives depend on."

"Sorry," Cass murmured.

I helped Aly up. "We only have one working flashlight. Let's hope it lasts. How's your foot?"

She leaned on my shoulder, testing her ankle. "It's only a flesh wound," she said through gritted teeth.

Aly held on to the back of my shirt and hobbled forward. After a few steps she was limping along on her own. Our next left was a vast chamber. It vaulted upward into a dome, so high that the flashlight beam barely kissed the top. In the center of the room was a raised stone platform shaped like a keyhole, round and flat with a short walkway leading to a table on the left. The platform was surrounded by five steps. Directly across the chamber was an exit portal, an archway leading deeper into the maze.

We stepped slowly onto the floor of polished stone slabs.

"Looks like an altar," Aly said.

"Probably where the Atlanteans made the s-s-sacrifices," Cass added, setting his pack on the floor.

He took the flashlight from my hand and skimmed the beam over the wall behind the altar. It looked like an enormous grayish-green canvas.

I stepped closer to it. "Focus the light on here a minute."

Cass and Aly were examining the table, but Cass shone the light for me, and I flicked the bottom left of the canvas with a finger. Dust poofed outward. Under the coating was an image of a man wearing a toga. I shook it and saw an entire scene, some kind of ancient festival. This wasn't a canvas. It was a gigantic tapestry.

The image looked just like Professor Bhegad's scene from the classroom—the king, queen, Karai, and Massarym. But then the light beam moved, and I turned to see that Cass and Aly were examining something carved into the table.

"Guys, can I have the light back?" I asked. "This is important."

"There's some writing here," Cass said. "I want to copy it down."

I couldn't wait. I needed something brighter than a dying flashlight. Something that would show me the whole scene at once. Like a fire.

I grabbed Cass's pack and angled it so whatever light was in the room would illuminate its contents. I pulled out the kerosene can and found some stray wood. At the bottom of the pack was an old, yellowed newspaper. He hadn't included it in his inventory of the packs. But it would be useful. Quickly I set the newspaper down, piled the branches on top, and lit it with one of Cass's matches.

Flames shot upward, first consuming an advertisement for Bob's Plumbing Supplies and traveling upward to a screaming banner headline: MATTIPACK CRIME-SPREE COUPLE CAUGHT!

As the wood ignited, my mouth fell open. The tapestry came to brilliant life in the amber glow. It showed *all* the images from Bhegad's tutorial—the peaceful kingdom, the sparring brothers, the destruction of Atlantis. But I noticed something strange. In the highest right corner of the weaving, there was a man hanging by his arms from what looked like a small beach ball. It looked completely out of place in this scenario. "Cass, Aly—take a look at—"

"What did you just do?"

Cass's scream shocked me.

I spun around.

"You—you burned my *Chronicle!*" Cass lunged at me with his fists.

As we struggled, Aly tried to grab Cass from behind. The three of us stumbled back, bouncing off the altar and onto the round platform. Aly caught her heel on a slightly raised lip where two stones met. We all fell onto a disk of polished marble, directly in the center of the platform.

And after a hesitant rumble, it began to sink.

A roar echoed through the chamber, stone scraping on stone.

Cass's eyes were huge. "What's happening?"

I leaped back up to the lip of the platform. "This room is bad enough," I said, reaching down for the others. "I don't want to see the basement."

The entire chamber began to vibrate. Dust clouds shot outward from the tapestry. The stone legs of the altar table groaned against the floor as they slid.

As Cass and Aly scrambled upward, a square section of the ceiling moved. I squinted upward to see a stone door on thick metal hinges, opening to release something thick and black.

The mass spilled out, morphing and growing, changing shapes like a living thing.

"*Let's go!*" I screamed. I grabbed on to Aly. She locked her fingers around Cass.

Before we could clear the platform, the blob hit us.

CHAPTER TWENTY-NINE
CASS ON FIRE

I FELT THE impact on my left shoulder. A low *whoooomp* echoed through the chamber.

A gust of warm wind shot toward me—a compression of air from the falling mass. I hurtled away from the platform, rolling myself into a ball to cushion the fall.

I hit the floor hard. And I slid.

I was covered with something dense and grainy. It seemed pelletlike but also fine and slippery. Its stink was intense. I crashed against a wall, but I barely felt it. Everything stung—my eyes, nose, and mouth. It was as if someone had squirted ammonia in my face.

I pulled my pack around and reached frantically inside for my water bottle. With shaky fingers, I uncapped it and squirted water into my face. I tried to blink, but it was like opening my eyes in acid. I squirted again and again.

To my right Aly was writhing on the ground, clawing at her face, screaming. "Ew, ew, ew—I know that smell! It's bat guano, Jack! Like, five thousand years of it!"

"Look my way!" I shouted, scrabbling over the grime-soaked floor.

As she turned toward me, I shot streams of water into her eye sockets. The goop oozed downward in thin black fingers. "Enough . . . save the water for later . . . I can see . . ." she sputtered.

"Where's Cass?" I said.

I scanned the edge of the reeking mound. The cavern walls were glowing orange. Out of the corner of my eye I could see the right side of the tapestry, bright as day now.

"Jack, I can *see*," Aly repeated, still rubbing her eyes.

"I heard you," I said. "That's great. Now let's find—"

"I shouldn't be able to see!" Aly said. "Where is the light coming from? It should have been smothered."

That was when I saw the flames. They danced up from the back of the mountainous pile, growing, spreading, licking against the back wall. With a loud whooshing sound, the tapestry caught fire.

"This stuff is flammable!" I said.

"It's dried guano, Jack, of course it's flammable!" Aly shouted.

Cass.

In the growing brightness, I spotted a slight movement. A hand. Sticking out from the edge of the mound.

I raced toward him.

The fire skittered over the top of the guano, gaining ferocity. Aly dug into the pile, scooping the foul stuff from atop Cass. I pulled hard. His shoulders emerged. His face. He was barely breathing.

The flames were descending the slope of the mound now. Coming closer to Cass. I grabbed under his shoulders and yanked as hard as I could.

Aly took his arm, but Cass was pinned by the dense mass. The flames spat sparks all around us. *"Pull!"* I yelled.

I planted my feet. I leaned hard. Aly's face was red.

With a sudden jerk, Cass slid loose. I flew backward. The mound shifted, collapsing around the area Cass had vacated. A ball of flame arched through the air.

It landed on Cass's body. His guano-covered shirt instantly went up in flames.

"He's on fire!" Aly shouted.

I whipped off my still-wet pack and began battering the fire with it. Aly had found a bottle of water in her own pack and was pouring it on him. Finally I threw myself on top of Cass, the wet backpack between us, and held tight.

I could feel the heat radiating upward. I stayed there until I was sure the fire was out, and then rolled off.

"Is he alive?" Aly asked.

His chest wasn't moving. He was limp, motionless. I knelt and slapped his face. I'd taken a CPR class and tried to recall what we'd learned—*compressions above the lungs.* I pressed hard, in bursts of three. Cass's skin was red, and some of it looked papery.

"Geaaaahhh!" As Cass's face came to life, he spat out a hunk of guano. He began to convulse, spitting and coughing. I sat him up and doused his face with water.

He was screaming like a wounded animal. I could barely recognize his voice.

"Come on, let's get him out of here!" I shouted. "Quick."

With one of Cass's arms over draped my good shoulder, the other over Aly's, we dragged him away from the flaming guano. The fire's light showed that there were two passageways branching off ahead—one to the left and one farther ahead to the right.

"My eyes!" Cass screamed.

With my free hand, I squeezed the remaining contents of my water bottle into his face. Aly was coughing now—wracking, rattling explosions that made her body heave. Her eyes were red and swollen. We staggered forward, our lungs filling with toxic fumes.

We passed through the archway on the other side, into a narrow tunnel. Smoke was billowing from behind us.

"Where do we go?" Aly said. "There's another fork ahead."

"Guh . . . go . . ." Cass moaned. "Rrrahh . . ."

"What's he saying?" Aly asked.

"Go right?" I repeated. "Is that what you said, Cass—
go right?"

"Ssss . . ." he said, his eyes flickering shut. I took that
for a yes.

We limped into the increasing darkness. The stench
was lessening, but Aly could barely walk for her coughing.
My heart was beating too fast. My breaths were quick and
ragged, my eyes near swollen shut. "I feel . . . weak . . ." I
said, gasping for breath.

"The fire . . ." Aly paused to cough. "Toxic fumes . . ."

The fork seemed twice as far as it looked. When we
finally made the turn, we collapsed onto the floor.

The air was clearer here, the fire a dull, distant glow.

"Light . . ." Cass said. "Dropped into . . . pack."

Aly eyed his backpack, which was now nearly solid
black with fire-cured guano. I could tell she was not going
to touch it.

Cass had zipped up the pack. I hoped the interior would
be intact. I unzipped it and reached in, holding back my
own revulsion.

Incredibly, the flashlight was fine. I shone the beam to
the left. "Ready?"

Cass grimaced. "I hurt," he said.

His face was matted with blood. Welts bubbled up on

his arms. His shirt was charred and tattered, the shreds saturated with sweat and blood. Under them was an angry cross-hatching of burn marks. "We . . . we're going to have to clean you up," I said.

"Like, now." Aly pulled a water bottle out of her own pack and poured it on Cass's chest.

"Yeeeeaaaagh!" His scream was like a body blow.

Aly fell back in shock. "Sorry!"

Cass convulsed. "You're going to be fine," I said.

He grabbed my hand and Aly's. His chest was rising and falling rapidly. "I'm dying. Leave me. Go."

"We can't do that!" Aly said.

Cass flinched. "When you get out . . . send help. Go!"

I looked at Aly. We couldn't let him die. I put my arm around his shoulders and tried to hoist him up. "We'll get through. Return home to our families. All three of us."

"Stop!" Cass said, his face twisted with pain. "That news-paper . . . *Chronicle* . . ."

He was hallucinating. "Cass, the newspaper is gone!" I said.

"My family . . ." Cass said. "Gone, too. Not dead . . . gone."

As I struggled to my feet I remembered the headline, going up in flames. "Cass, that article . . . the crime-spree couple . . . ?"

"What are you talking about?" Aly demanded.

"Mom . . . Dad . . ." Cass's eyes were wild, desperate. "Never met them . . . but I found out. Life sentence . . . gave

210

me up. At birth. Four foster families. Five? I don't know. Bad . . . son. So bad. Ran away . . ."

The words hit hard.

My family isn't close . . . I remembered what Cass had said when we'd talked about our families. "Cass, we don't care who your parents are," I said. "You're coming with us."

"You have families," Cass insisted. "I have nothing. Go!"

Aly's eyes were full of tears. "Cass, we're all the same now. We're all each other has—"

"Left . . ." Cass said, his voice a raspy whisper.

"Exactly," Aly agreed.

"No . . . go left . . ." he said. "About . . . fifteen degrees. Not straight. Not too sharp either . . . fifteen degrees or so . . ."

His voice drifted off.

"Cass!" I shouted, shaking him.

Aly felt his neck for a pulse. "He's alive. Maybe we should turn back . . . get him help."

"But Marco—" I said.

"We can't save Marco," Aly said. "We may not ever find him now. But if we retrace our steps and return, we can save Cass."

I set Cass down on the floor. I couldn't go another inch with him. I was on the verge of collapse myself. His weight was killing my sore left shoulder. Aly looked half dead. "We can't go back the way we came. We'll burn alive, Aly."

"Right, you're right." She squinted ahead. "Okay. He said fifteen degrees."

"You're at a street corner . . ." I gasped. "You turn clockwise. Right turn is ninety degrees, backward one-eighty. Left turn two-seventy."

As I lifted Cass again, I slid the flashlight toward Aly with my foot. "Take this."

As Aly bent to pick it up, she coughed violently. Dark brown fluid dripped from her mouth.

She flicked on the light and shone it ahead. Its beam shook with the rhythm of her coughing. A bat chittered overhead, zigzagging among the stalactites. The light was nearly gone now, but it revealed a turn ahead. At about fifteen degrees.

"Go left," Aly said. "And pray."

Moving with Cass sent a stab of intense pain down my left side, but I held tight. Collapsing would do neither of us any good. "Okay. Ready."

"Are you sure you can do this?" Aly asked.

I nodded firmly. "For a brother, I can."

* * *

The tunnel seemed to go on forever. Bats squeaked overhead, scolding us. I could barely walk. My shoulder was completely numb.

We used the flashlight only sparingly. I was banging poor Cass into the wall. Finally I stepped into a hole and we both nearly went flying. I screamed. My body was pure agony now, shoulder to foot. "Setting him . . . down," I said through gritted teeth. "My ankle feels broken . . ."

I sank against the wall and set Cass in my lap. He needed a cushion. Holding him in a kind of modified bear hug, I felt my eyes close.

A little sleep couldn't hurt. Just a minute.

"Jack?" Aly said. "You don't look good."

I could see them in my mind now. The king and queen. They were expecting me. But they looked sad.

"I did . . . the best I could," I said. A soft, slightly cool breeze caressed my right side, sending me deeper into dreamland. Closer to Uhla'ar and Qalani.

Now the queen's face was changing. Her regal features softened, reshaping into a smile so familiar that I felt I'd been seeing every day.

"Hi, Mom," I said. I wanted to let go. I wanted to join her. It had been so long, and I had lost her so quickly. I missed her so much.

"Jack, don't go to sleep!" Aly was screaming.

I could sense a dim glow under my lids, but I wanted darkness. I was ready for it. "Please turn off . . . the light . . ."

CHAPTER THIRTY

GOING, GOING, GONE

"IT'S NOT ON!"

The sharp slap to my cheek stung. My eyes flickered open, and Mom's smile was replaced by the charred, peeling face of Aly Black. "What?" I moaned.

"The flashlight, Jack," she said. "It's not on. The light is coming from somewhere else!"

My eyes blinked open. She was right. The glow was farther ahead in the tunnel. The same direction as the breeze.

Breeze? Through the wall of pain, little bits of reality peeked through the cracks. Breeze meant air. Air meant a connection to the outside world.

"Help me up," I said, lifting Cass off my lap.

"Uhhhnn . . ." He was stirring now, reviving.

Aly helped me get him upright. I stood, once again wrapping Cass's arm around my shoulder.

We staggered toward the faint glow. The tunnel seemed to be widening. My momentary sleep must have done me good. I had a bit of strength.

I could see Aly in silhouette now. Her eyes had swollen badly. "How are you doing?" I asked.

"I look bad, huh?" she said.

I tried to shine the flashlight in her face, but the light had finally died. Still, even in the soft glow I could see that her eyes were nearly shut, her lips cracked and scabbed, her skin covered with angry red blotches. "You look fine," I lied.

"Jack, look!" She gestured to an ominous narrow floor-to-ceiling archway in the wall to the right.

The breeze was stronger now, warmer. I could hear a low, distant crashing noise. The glow—and the breeze—were clearly coming from beyond the archway.

"What is that?" she asked.

"I don't know," I said.

Aly froze. "Jack . . ." she said, her voice thin and high-pitched. "This rush of air . . . warmth, light—I think we're heading back into the fire. We've gone in a circle."

Her eyes were slitted lanterns, her red-patterned face a fright mask. Panic seized me. Cass's arm nearly slid off my shoulder.

I knew I looked as bad as she did. My own skin was pulling, my own sight lines shrinking. We all needed medical help. We were running on adrenaline and whatever advantage G7W gave us, if any. Cass was nearly dead. To march back into an advancing fire was crazy. Suicidal.

"Let me . . . try to carry him for a while," Aly said, kneeling next to Cass. "Switch off . . . we'll find another path . . ."

"Aly, no," I said. "We'll get lost—"

"What other choice do we have, Jack?"

Aly's shout echoed dully against the stone walls. Then it seemed to echo again. From beyond the archway.

A gust of warm air surrounded me. A tiny droplet of moisture formed on my nose.

Moisture.

Aly collapsed, trying to lift Cass. "Help me do this . . ."

"Aly, that's not the fire in there," I exclaimed. "Look at my nose!"

She came closer. "It's burned, Jack—"

"It's wet!" I said. "So's my face. So's yours. A fire makes the air *dry*, Aly. It sucks oxygen into itself. It doesn't send out damp breezes!"

Cass was stirring now, muttering. His heat-swollen eyes blinked. "I feel like . . . a llorggedeirf."

I dropped next to him. "What, Cass? I can't understand you."

"Fried egg roll," he said. "Sorry. Note to self: stop speaking backward."

Aly and I looked at each other. This didn't seem possible.

She knelt. Tears were making gray rivulets down her cheek. "Welcome back, Cass," she said softly.

"Easy for you to say," Cass replied.

I couldn't believe it. He was struggling to his feet.

"Cass, take it easy!" Aly said, reaching out to him.

He took her hand and put it on his shoulder. "Let me . . . lean on you . . ."

As he stood slowly, wobbling, I put his other arm around my shoulder. The tunnel would be just wide enough for the three of us. We turned back toward the dim light, the source of the moisture. At first, Cass's legs were almost useless. But things changed when we made the turn into the right-hand tunnel. He began taking more of his weight. Easing the pain in my ankle.

We picked up the pace. The light glowed brighter and the gusts picked up intensity. They soothed and tickled, seeming to wash away part of the pain. My shallow breaths grew deeper. Even my eyes seemed to be seeing more.

But the crashing sound was increasing, too—continuous, like a machine.

"We're almost there," Cass said. His eyes were open now, a pained smile growing on his face. "You did it."

He dropped his arm from my shoulder. As I lowered

mine, I caught a glimpse of his chest. It had stopped bleeding. The oozy welts down his front were now dry red swooshes. The bubbled skin on his face had receded. "Cass—your chest," I said. "It's *healing*!"

Aly smiled wanly. "You don't look like Quasimodo anymore," she said.

I smiled at Aly—and I realized her eyes were returning slowly to normal, too. "And you don't look like ET."

Her smile vanished. "I looked like ET?"

"Almost . . . there . . ." Cass interrupted.

Aly and I picked up speed. Cass's legs were stronger, and he was supporting more of his own weight. Ahead of us, the light pulsed with the rhythm of the crashing sounds. Our feet caught on rocks and bumps, but we managed to stay upright.

The tunnel veered ninety degrees to the left. We made the turn and stopped short.

Here, the wall's stones were long and lined vertically like sinew. They seemed to beckon my eyes upward, to an impossibly high ceiling, like in a cathedral.

The source of the crashing noise was a distant waterfall, surging out of the darkness above. The tunnel was suffused by a soft light that seemed to come from some unseen place.

We started forward, but Cass pushed our arms away. On wobbly legs, he stumbled toward the water. "Cass, careful!"

Aly said, reaching toward him.

I took her arm and held firm. "No," I said. "Let him."

Cass seemed to be gaining strength. He managed to rip away the remaining shreds of his tattered jeans as he walked, continuing on in a pair of grime-blackened *Simpsons* shorts, black socks, and Converse sneakers.

"I don't believe this," Aly said.

"What, that he was a Simpsons fan?" I remarked.

She jabbed me in the side. It felt good.

"Come on," she said, moving forward toward Cass.

I followed, taking care not to further injure my ankle. Cass was in the pool now, up to his neck. His head was angled upward, the ghost of a smile animating his face. As Aly waded toward him, the water rising to her waist, I stepped in.

The water was cool, not cold, with a softness that seemed to caress. Oh, did it feel nice. The waves of pain—my ankle, my arm, my shoulder—all briefly flared and then began to ease up. Aly and Cass were standing silently to my right. Aly's eyes were wide in utter bafflement.

Staying close to the edge of the pool, in water up to my chest, I moved closer to the falling stream. Standing underneath, I looked upward and felt the force on my face and chest, my back and legs. I let the water wash off the guano, the soot, the shreds of Cass's ripped clothing and mine. And other things, too—the pain and worry, the rot and weakness. The feeling that Death was digging into me, licking its greedy lips.

All going, going . . . gone.

I closed my eyes and lifted my arms. I felt Aly and Cass on either side of me. They clasped my hands and we stood there, drinking it in, gaining strength. We had no clue why any of this was happening but also the good sense not to ask any questions.

Even with my eyes closed, the light was more intense than before. I opened them. The light source seemed to be coming from *behind* the waterfall.

I let go of my friends and stepped slowly forward. The full force of the water hit me hard. The throbbing had returned to the back of my head. I waded as fast as I could until I passed completely under it.

The pool extended into a deep grotto. Almost immediately the sound of the rushing water subsided to a muffled roar. I shielded my eyes against a shocking brightness.

The lagoon's rocky bottom began to slope upward, like the steps of an outdoor pool. Soon I was emerging from the water onto a high rock platform. My eyes were adjusting to the light now, and I saw a stadium-like area flooded with light.

Sunlight.

"Jack, what are you doing?"

I spun around. It was Aly, emerging from the water. Her skin was lined only lightly, her posture strong.

Cass was behind her in a nanosecond. His boxers seemed even more ridiculous clean than dirty, but I barely noticed that.

His chest bore only the traces of scars. His face looked as if it were marked by a long-ago sunburn that had recently peeled.

"Guys . . ." I said. "You're . . . normal."

"That's the first time anyone's called me that in my life," Aly said.

Cass was gazing with squinted eyes at the area behind me. "Where on earth are we?" he said under his breath.

I turned and moved closer. The spray of the waterfall pattered lightly at my back.

As I entered the circle of light, I nearly stumbled on a thick branch I hadn't seen jutting into the entrance.

No. Not a branch. A foot.

I jumped aside and looked down.

There was no mistaking the ragged, water-soaked figure against the wall.

"Marco?" I said.

CHAPTER THIRTY-ONE
MARCO

WE RAN TOWARD the slumped body. I think we all were scared of what we'd see up close. All around us loomed vertical rock walls, impossibly high, shadowed with sharp crags and ledges. The body of the vromaski lay in a flattened heap against the wall, about fifty feet away. The walls formed a circle at the top, framing a deep blue late-afternoon sky. We had made it into the crater of the volcano. We had beaten the Atlantean maze. But as we knelt by our fallen friend, it didn't seem like such a wonderful accomplishment.

Marco was facedown on the ground, his body twisted. White fragments were scattered nearby. It took a moment to realize they were his teeth.

"Oh, no, no, no, no, no . . ." Aly moaned.

Jubilant only a moment ago, Cass was now drawn and pale.

As I knelt next to Marco, my knees shook. Taking his shoulder, I pulled gently, afraid of what I'd see. His arm slid toward me, whacking my knee. I jumped away, nearly knocking over Aly and Cass, who were clutching each other.

Marco flopped onto his back, ashen and motionless. His face was crisscrossed with cuts. His mouth looked sunken, his jaw wrenched to one side. Mist blew over his body like the fingers of a fuzzy ghost. He hadn't asked for this. He had been taken from his home, his family, just like us. To become a supposed superhero.

They didn't know what we did. That they'd failed. That he'd been a real hero.

"Jack, there's like a hundred tooth fragments over there," Cass said. "And . . . and . . . other stuff."

He turned away, looking like he was about to hurl.

I looked at Aly and then Cass. "Well, we have a mission, don't we?"

Cass nodded grimly and stood. "Let's lift him. We have to get him back."

He lifted Marco's feet off the ground, and I went around to the other side. As I dug my hands under his shoulders, I recoiled. "He's . . . warm," I said.

"He's been in the sun," Aly reminded me, in a measured voice. "Keep it together, Jack."

I knelt and grabbed his shoulders again. "One . . ." Aly said. "Two . . ."

Marco blinked.

We all screamed.

I dropped him and leaped to my feet.

His face fell to the side again. We waited. No one breathed. For a long time, nothing happened. My heart ping-ponged.

I looked upward to the top of the caldera, where we'd fought the vromaski. It was at least fifteen stories up. In sheer physical terms, Marco was like a one-hundred-eighty-pound weight dropped from a skyscraper. No one could survive that kind of fall.

I glanced at Cass and Aly and could tell they were thinking the same thing.

Okay, it was an automatic movement. Bodies do stuff like that. Man up. That's what Marco would say.

"Let's try again . . ." I said, my voice parched.

As I bent down, Marco moaned.

I fell to my knees in shock. His head twitched. His mouth was moving. I bit my lip, just to be sure I wasn't dreaming.

"M-M-Marco?" Cass said.

"His fall . . . maybe it was stopped by t-t-trees . . . growing out of the caldera walls," Aly said weakly, as if trying to ground this in some sort of logic. "Roots . . . bushes . . ."

"Yeah, and it's raining salamanders," I said, shaking my head. "It wasn't a root, Aly. Look at the vromaski. He's completely totalled. It was the water. Marco's wet. He fell close enough to get some of the spray. It kept him alive." I couldn't believe the words coming out of my mouth. *"Marco is alive!"*

Marco's eyes seemed to roll in their sockets, wild and unfocused. When he tried to speak, his voice was a grotesque squeak.

"Lift him." Cass stood, his face taut with urgency. "Don't just stand there, lift him! I'll take the feet. Jack, you take the arms, Aly take the middle."

"Cass . . . ?" I said, numb and confused.

"Now! Or I'll take him myself!" Cass cried out. "We have to get him to the waterfall."

Numbly I lifted Marco by the shoulders. His head flopped back, a trail of blood oozing from the corner of his mouth. Aly quickly folded his hands across his chest and then crouched underneath him. We lifted his body to shoulder level and walked him back through the passageway, stepping carefully down into the pool.

The crashing water pelted us as we approached. When we were almost underneath, Cass shouted, "Lower him in—now!"

I grabbed tight and slipped out from under Marco. He

was unbelievably heavy. Cass and Aly were already sub-merging his legs as I angled my body to turn around. "Slow down!" I yelled.

They didn't hear me. I tried to spin around fast, but Marco's weight put an impossible torque on my body. My foot came down on a smooth rock, and then shot out from underneath me.

I fell. Cass and Aly lost control of the body. Marco dropped into the water, his expressionless face disappear-ing under the rush of bubbles. As he floated away, his hair swirled like seaweed. Blood floated upward from his lips on a pink line of bubbles.

"We're drowning him!" Aly cried out.

Cass lunged and grabbed Marco's foot. We were almost directly under the falls now. I went around to his head and lifted it out of the water. No gasp. No choking. Nothing.

The waterfall wasn't working for him. He was too broken.

We managed to drag Marco away from the roiling pool, to a shallower part. His eyes had rolled up into his head and his mouth was slack.

"Get him on dry ground!" Aly said. "Do compressions, CPR!"

Cass was crying as we dragged Marco out of the water and onto the rocky floor. I turned him onto his back and moved his head so it was facing upward. His right arm flopped aside, bent in the wrong direction.

"Kaaashmaa . . ." he groaned.

I jumped back. Cass yelled in shock.

Marco was blinking. Moving. His arm slid slowly against the rock, then jerked upward.

With a soft, nauseating crack, it snapped itself back into place.

"I don't believe this, I don't believe this, I don't believe this . . ." Cass mumbled, as Marco's hand moved to his distorted-looking jaw—and pushed it straight.

"Owwww . . . owww," Marco moaned. Aly flinched with sympathy, tears streaming down her cheeks.

Slowly Marco raised himself up on his elbows. His brow furrowed with confusion as he saw the falls. Then he looked at us.

"Thay, doc," he said hoarsely, "will I ever play the thak-thophone again?"

CHAPTER THIRTY-TWO

THE CIRCLE IN THE DARK

ALY'S SCREAM MADE bats skitter out from the crags. She fell over Marco, wrapping her arms around him. "You cannot be alive. I am hugging a not-alive person!"

"Huh?" Marco said.

Cass leaned over Marco, his brow furrowed. "You. Fell. Marco!" he said in a barking voice, as if Marco were still in a coma. "Do you understand me, Marco? You fell! From the top of the volcano! And yet! You survived!"

Marco glanced my way. "Why ith he talking like that? And what'th with thith lithp?"

I opened my mouth to answer but my jaw just flapped open and shut. This couldn't be happening. But it was. Marco had fallen to his death. His jaw, his teeth—they lay scattered about the center of the volcano.

But he was with us again. Intact.

We were all intact. Guano free. Burn healed.

Returned from death.

"Marco, let me see your mouth," I finally said.

He obediently lowered his jaw. As I knelt closer, Aly looked, too.

I angled his face so I could catch the light. His front teeth were stubs, just breaking through the gum line. Not smashed, not ragged and pointed, but smooth edged, like Chiclets. The top of Marco's mouth—the hard palate—was pink and small as if it had been transplanted from a baby.

Aly gasped. "His teeth . . ."

"His whole jaw," Cass said softly. "It was shattered in the fall. Destroyed."

"Marco," I said, "you may not remember this, but you fell. A huge distance. You should be dead. But you landed by this waterfall, and you're okay."

Marco smiled a stubby smile. "I'm immortal?"

"It's something about the water," I said. "You're . . . regenerating."

"*I whaaaa—?*"

He nearly bit off my fingers at the *W*.

"Your teeth are growing in," I said. "Your palate—that must have been knocked out of your mouth, too. But it's coming back. That's why you're lisping!"

His face lit up. "Tho it'th not going to latht forever?"

He was sitting up now. His arms were moving. The lacerations on his face were looking less angry. "Marco," I said, "can you stand?"

Marco shrugged. He swung his legs around so they hung down over the ledge.

"Look at them, Jack!" Aly said with a gasp.

His legs dangled bizarrely, pointing every which way as if he had three knees in each one. He glanced at them curiously, swinging them right to left. "Dang," he said.

Then he kicked out twice, hard. The legs locked themselves back into a normal angle, and he let out sharp yelp of pain.

Cass groaned. "He has got to stop doing that."

"Help me up," Marco said, grimacing. "Gently, doodth."

Cass and I put our arms around him and lowered him as carefully as we could into the water. He cried out as his feet hit bottom. The backwash from the falls swirled around us, hip deep. "We have to go back under the falls," I said. "Back into the center of the volcano. That's where we found you. Can you make it?"

Marco shifted his weight. He rested in the water for a moment, taking deep breaths. Then, unhooking his arms from our shoulders, he firmly pushed us aside.

Grinning at Aly, he said, "Follow the Yellow Brick Road."

* * *

Back in the crater, Marco insisted on gathering up all his tooth fragments and lost body parts. Cass and Aly were locked in a worried conversation by an archway at the far end of the caldera, on the opposite side from which we'd come in. There were three tunnel openings there.

But my eyes were fixed on the great shadow to our left. Because of the sun's angle, a section of the crater floor was totally black. A mist, barely visible, seeped out. I figured it was water evaporating against warm rock.

"I'm pretty sure one of these connects with the path we took," Cass was saying, "but I can't remember which."

"You have to!" Aly said. "What if we walk back into the fire?"

"I'm not a machine, Aly," Cass replied. "I only got a quick look at that tree trunk. I was nervous. We were in the middle of an escape, remember? Maybe we should do a little reconnaissance—try each of them, weed out any dead ends, see if we can find some markings, leads, whatever. Maybe it'll bring it all back to me. Marco? Jack?"

"I'll wait till you figure it out," Marco called out. "I'm finding cool thtuff. Thcream if you thee a vromathki. But don't worry. We're immortal. We have the waterfall—woo-hoo!"

He was over near the waterfall entrance, practically giddy with excitement. He held a fleshy lump to the light, gazed at it in awe, then dumped it into his backpack.

"I want to explore," I called, gesturing toward the shadow. "Don't take long."

As Cass and Aly disappeared into the archway, I couldn't stop thinking about Bhegad's classroom lesson—about the heart of Atlantis, the mysterious place Wenders claimed to have seen. Now we had seen it, too. But it sure didn't match my dream, which had nothing like rock walls or this healing waterfall.

The blackness scared me a little. How could any place be that dark in the middle of the day?

Judging from the curve of the walls, I estimated the depth—the distance to the back wall—couldn't be more than twenty or thirty yards.

I stuck close to the wall as I walked in. I could see nothing now. I felt my hair lifting upward in lazy swirls.

The back of my head, which had been throbbing ever since I saw the waterfall, now pounded like a drum. I tried to shake it off. The wall was leading me straight back. I wasn't expecting that. I should have been closing a circle. Calderas were round.

I stopped when I heard faint, muffled music. It was an unearthly tangle of sounds, not like any instrument I knew but not singing either. It throbbed in rhythm with my head's pounding.

It was irresistible. Pulling me. Scaring me.

I turned, intending to call to my friends. But the voice

that emerged from my throat was compressed and garbled. Not even a word, more like the fluting of a bird.

It made me giggle in spite of myself. I kept moving inward, helpless to resist, ignoring the pain in my head.

This sound was now commandeering all my senses, exhilarating and horrifying me at the same time. It was the smell of Christmas Eve and Barry Reese's breath, the sight of Mom's smile and Marco's shattered teeth, the feel of beach sand and burning bat guano. I could no sooner escape it than turn the waterfall back up to its source. And I didn't want to.

You're not in danger. Marco is a shout away.

In the shadow's center was a bluish-white glow. A circle. It seemed to come from deep below the earth, shining through translucent rock. Pulsing with the music's rhythm. The mist hissed up through pencil-thin cracks, obscuring what was inside the shape.

I moved closer. Carved into the circle's center was a deep, wide hemisphere. Around the perimeter were seven shallower ones. Each was marked with a symbol. I leaned in, trying to make sense of them.

It looked like some weird game. The carvings looked like landmarks from some ancient country.

No. Not landmarks.

I knew what these represented.

Of sisters, gables, virtues, sins,/Of gambling men with lucky wins/Of continents and stormy seas . . .

Seven. All of Wenders's clues—even the opening to the outside—involved the number seven. And I began thinking about school, about something I'd been obsessed with in sixth grade. "The Pyramids of Egypt . . . Hanging Gardens of Babylon . . . Pharos Lighthouse . . ." I muttered.

These were the Seven Wonders of the Ancient World. But what the heck did they have to do with the Karai Institute, and this volcano—and Atlantis?

"Yo, Jack . . . where'd you go . . . ?"

Cass's voice was disembodied, as if from a TV in the

next room. I knew I should call out, but the circle was beckoning, silencing me. The mist—I could see now—it was coming from a crack in the center. Maybe that was making the sound, like breath blowing through a clarinet reed.

I edged closer. The mist caressed my face softly. It lifted my spirits. Was this the volcano's real healing source—the thing that transformed the water, gave energy to the falls?

In the eddy's midst I spotted a jagged thing, rising from the center of the circle. It was dirty and forlorn, like a spoon broken off in a bowl of petrified soup. Or the withered, split trunk of an ancient dead sapling. It seemed out of place within such an awesome force.

My head throbbed now. I felt as if someone had placed three fingers on the three points of the lambda at the back of my skull. But I was too curious to turn back. As I wrapped my hand around the little tree, a layer of dirt and rust fell off. It had more heft than I expected. It was flatter, too. Definitely not a tree. Not wood at all. Metal, probably.

I pulled and it came out easily, with a clean-sounding *shhhick*. I held it over the glow. Either the light had intensified or my eyes were getting used to it. I could see the thing pretty clearly. It was the pointy half of a rusted sword blade, marked with a finely etched design that was hard to discern. Someone had obviously gone all King Arthur on the sword and tried to pull it out of the stone, instead breaking it off midway. I looked around for the other piece but there was no sign of it.

From the center of the circle, where I'd pulled the broken weapon, came kind of a deep-earth belch. The music, so loud a moment ago, was fading.

"Jack?" Cass's voice echoed from far behind me. "'Sup? You fall into a hole or something?"

He couldn't see me in the dark. Was too scared to venture closer. I tried to answer but couldn't.

"We need your help, Jack," Cass continued, his voice growing more nervous. "We investigated three paths. Two of them are dead ends, and the other goes on forever and kind of smells of the outdoors. Marco's with us now. But the flashlight's dead. Jack . . . ? *Jack?*"

I heard Cass's footsteps retreating at a run. As my eyes fell on the circle again, I saw that the place where the sword blade had been was now glowing a garish blue-white. Something seemed to be pressing up from underneath. Trying to break out.

The ground began to shake. I could hear an avalanche of rocks all around. Through the small rip in the earth came an explosion—not of rock and soil but blinding white light. A savage wind whipped upward, lifting me off my feet, bringing me down hard.

What had I done? I needed to put the sword shard back. It had blown out of my hand and was lying on the ground. I lunged toward it. My hand closed around it just as a blast of wind spun me around.

The light was blinding me. Where was the circle?

I skidded against the wall, hitting my head. For a moment all went black. Then I heard a piercing screech and saw a wash of bright red. I felt the flapping of wings like a sudden gale wind.

My eyes were fluttering, my brain dancing in and out of consciousness.

Stay awake!

I forced myself to lean into the wind. The circle was now an angry bright white. I couldn't look into it for more than a fraction of a second. I would have to be accurate.

With a grunt, I shoved the shard back down. Hard.

It entered the rock cleanly and held.

The wind echoed up toward the sun and dispersed. The light was back underground. The circle had a swollen, angry brightness, but the sense of imminent disaster was over.

As I backed away, the mist began to rise again. My legs shook uncontrollably as I edged out of the darkness.

And I ran.

CHAPTER THIRTY-THREE

NO-DEAD-BODY ZONE

I BARRELED STRAIGHT into Marco. He was standing near the wall, just outside the umbrella of darkness, heading in my direction. Aly and Cass were close behind him.

He cocked his head curiously. "What were thossssse funky noisssessss? Dang, my s's are back."

"You heard them?" My voice was back. "Did you hear the music?"

"I heard sssomething weird, like a big old bird," he said. "Cass and Aly have been tracking tunnels. Cass said he called you and you didn't answer."

"There's a circle!" I stammered, pointing back into the darkness. "With . . . other circles in it, and carvings of the Seven Wonders—at least that's what I think they are—and they all play music! And when you get close, stuff happens to you. You lose your voice. And there's this thing in the middle, a sword actually, or part of one, which I pulled out, and this huge white light came, and wind, and earthquakes . . . Just come with me!"

I sounded like a raving maniac. Grabbing Marco's arm, I pulled him into the shadow. Dragged him directly toward the center. The glow of the circle loomed.

"Whoa . . ." Marco said.

"Calling M. Night Shyamalan," Aly muttered.

The mist seeped forward, wrapping all of us. Cass said something to me, but it was as if the wispy tendrils were siphoning away the sound.

He crept nearer, staring intently at the carvings. I could feel Aly's grip now. She was pulling me away. Marco was reaching for Cass.

I didn't resist. Didn't want to. They had seen it. Felt it. That was all I needed.

As we stumbled back into the light, Aly said, "That's it, isn't it? That's what Wenders saw. The center of Atlantis."

"Seven circles," Marco said. "For seven Loculi."

"And Seven Wonders," I added.

"What do they have to do with each other?" Aly asked.

I shrugged. "I don't know."

"Dude," Marco said, "if this is the place where the Loculi come from, we're going to have to return them here."

"If we buy into Bhegad's plan," Aly said.

"His crazy stories are starting to make sense," Marco pointed out.

"Over my dead body are we coming back here," Cass said.

Marco smiled. "This," he said, "is a no-dead-body zone."

* * *

I didn't know what to think.

We had found something real. Seven depressions in the earth. A crazy source of energy. A waterfall that gave life to the dead. A vromaski and a tapestry guarded by bat guano. Marco was right—we would have to come back.

But first we had to get out of here. And to make progress, we needed light.

A Swiss Army knife in Marco's backpack had survived the fall. It was sharp enough to help me slice three branches from the tree in the caldera wall. I put two of them in my pack. Then I took some of Cass's kindling wood and wove it into a tight ball, binding it with roots and small branches from the dead tree.

I inserted the branch through the center of the bundle and wrapped it all together with a jacket Aly had stuffed into her pack. Then I poured kerosene over the whole thing and set it aflame.

With a *whoosh*, the bundle became a makeshift torch. "I figure I can make three of these," I said. "I'm not sure how long they'll each last."

Marco gazed at the flame in awe. "Dude. I quit Cub Scouts just before Webelos."

"I'm thinking we want the second archway," Cass said uncertainly. "But I'm still not one hundred percent."

"Your instinct is good enough for me," Aly said.

"Let's move," I said, stepping quickly into the tunnel.

The ceiling was low, trapping the smoke. We hiked as fast as we could, coughing like crazy. The tunnel wove and branched. We passed at least five openings, but they all looked way too small.

Cass led us. With our new energy, we were practically sprinting. The first torch lasted longer than I expected. When it burned down I made a second.

Then later, a third.

My shirt was soaked through with sweat. I had little sense of time. It seemed we'd been gone longer than it took to get in. I was sure we'd covered more ground.

Now the third torch had burned down completely. The handle itself—the last of the three branches I'd chopped off the tree—was on fire. In a couple of minutes I would have to drop it.

"Guys, wait," Cass said nervously. "I'm tracing this path in my head, and I'm worried we may be heading toward the big fire. Maybe we should go back. Try one of those small openings."

I stopped and turned. I knew Cass was doing his best.

We'd be spun around so many times there was no way he could be perfect. We were seconds away from darkness, with no more kerosene. "Sure, no problem," I said. "In a couple of minutes we can travel by the light of my burning wrist. I wish you'd thought of this earlier."

Marco had slipped by me. From a bend just a few yards ahead, he turned around. "Dude, chill."

"Don't tell me to chill!" I said. "That was the last of the kerosene!"

"No, I mean, chill, dude—check this," Marco said.

The three of us turned. Marco was standing in the middle of the path, holding a machete high over his head. It looked like the one I'd lost in the chute. "Where'd you get that?" I asked.

Marco pointed to the ground. "It was here. Someone must have dropped it."

I ran to the bend. When the others were safely beside me, I dropped the torch to the stone floor. There the flame could die without sacrificing my hand.

The light was enough to illuminate the tunnel just ahead.

At the end of it was a mangled iron gate that had been forced halfway open.

"Torquin's gate!" I cried out.

I ran toward it, the others close behind me. The bottom of the gate hung about four feet off the floor, warped and bent. "Wow, those guys are strong," Cass said.

"We're there!" Aly cried out, wrapping Cass in a big hug. "You did it! You led us back to the entrance!"

Marco was examining the bent iron. "Who invited Torquin to this party?"

I grabbed his arm and pulled him under the gate. "We'll explain later."

We raced around to the right, retracing our original steps. In moments the light from outside was illuminating the tunnel.

I felt the tickle of a faint warmish breeze. Marco fell in beside me, whooping at the top of his lungs. Cass and Aly were laughing and shouting behind us.

At the end of the path I burst into the open air, looking up to the sky and sucking in the moist, tepid jungle air. I had never tasted anything better. "Woo-hooo!" I screamed.

"Yrotciv!" Cass whooped, leaping in the air like crazy.

As Aly and Marco joined him in a screaming victory dance, I caught sight of a lump in the grass, just a few feet ahead near the pathway. The bent elbow of a rumpled white shirtsleeve.

"Professor Bhegad?" I cried out, running toward him.

The others followed close behind. The professor was on his side, fast asleep, his hands curled up under his head. His tweed jacket had been placed neatly underneath him, and his glasses lay folded in the grass just a few inches away, along with a handheld device showing something that looked like a radar screen.

Marco knelt and shook his shoulders. "Yo, Professor, 'sup? You okay?"

Professor Bhegad turned. He muttered something incoherent. Then his eyes focused, and his jaw nearly dropped to the ground. "Marco? Is that really you, my boy? But . . . how . . . ?"

He sat up and wrapped Marco in a tight embrace. "Didn't know I was immortal, huh, P. Beg?" Marco said. "Oh. Sorry. Not supposed to call you that."

"You can call me anything you want," Bhegad said through a broad grin.

Aly was patting Marco proudly on the back. Cass was dancing to his own inner happy tune. Bhegad looked like he was about to cry.

I had to admit, I wasn't expecting that reaction.

Everyone began talking at once. Aly told the story of the rescue, the ceiling of guano, the healing waterfall. Cass described the pathway in detail. Bhegad listened in utter shock. He'd been expecting to see a corpse.

"Hey, what happened to Torquin and the Three Stooges?" Aly asked.

"They emerged without you," Bhegad said softly. "It was the second time Torquin had lost you. I gave them a severe tongue-lashing and sent all of them back to KI . . ."

As they talked, my eyes were drawn to the professor's handheld device.

I scooped it up and moved a few paces away, studying it. At the top of the screen was the word *Onyx*. Below that, pairs of letters that each were in different colors: a yellow JM, red AB, green CW, blue MR.

Jack McKinley, Aly Black, Cass Williams, Marco Ramsay.

Most of the screen was occupied by a vaguely round shape with faint concentric bar lines, like the outline of a mountain on a topographical map. Inside the shape, traces of yellow, red, and green all spiraled into the center from the outside, added a blue line, and then went back out from the center on another path that eventually merged with the first.

When I looked up, Bhegad was hurrying toward me. His eyes were dancing. "The Circle," he said. "Tell me about the Circle, Jack!"

I ignored him, looking over his shoulder toward my friends.

"Guys," I said softly. "He's been tracking us all along."

CHAPTER THIRTY-FOUR

THE HEPTAKIKLOS

MARCO AND ALY stared at Professor Bhegad in disbelief.

"But—but that's impossible," Marco stammered. "How can I be tracked if I'm not wearing a tracker? You need an ankle bracelet or a special watch."

"Please," Bhegad said. "We can discuss this later. Tell me about the Circle!"

Aly took Bhegad's device from me and examined it. "All four of us are here—time-lapse path—three going in, four coming out."

"You knew the correct pathway into the maze beforehand?" Cass asked.

"No!" Bhegad said. "Not until we tracked your paths. But—"

"Where is the tracker, Professor Bhegad?" Aly demanded angrily. "Hidden in our shoes? Have you been following us all along?"

Professor Bhegad swallowed hard. "Part of the initial operation was to install tracking devices in each of you," he said quickly. "Surgically. Not for any nefarious reason. For your own good."

My mind reeled. "So when I tried to escape that first day . . ." I said. "And when we all attempted it, the next night . . . you knew where we were. The whole time, you were following us!"

Bhegad nodded. "Well . . . yes. But I thought you'd figured that out by now. How else would I have found you with the submarine?"

"You knew I wasn't really at my treatment that night . . ." Aly said.

"You let us get onto that boat," Cass added. "We almost drowned!"

"No, no, that's not true," Bhegad protested. "You did fool us for quite some time. I confess, your tricks with the looping camera footage and so forth actually worked rather well. It's lucky that dear Torquin has a suspicious soul. After seeing a large fly crawl up Cass's window in an exactly identical path seven times, he woke me up and we tracked you, but by then you were already at the beach."

"What else aren't you telling us, Professor?" I demanded.

"What exactly have you done to us?"

"Peace, brothers and sister," Marco said, his voice unnaturally calm. "Let us not yell, but rather *show* him how we feel."

He reared his arm back and hurled the device deep into the jungle.

"*No!*" Bhegad shouted. "Do you know how much those cost?"

Cass stood over Professor Bhegad, glowering. He looked like a different person. "Marco died for your mission. If he hadn't fallen in the right place, his blood would be on your hands. You owe us, Professor. You owe us big."

"Owe you?" Bhegad said, his voice rising with impatience. "My dear boy, we planted the tracker for *your* sakes. We did not want to risk losing you. There are other forces after the secret of the Loculi. You are not as safe as you think. Now, please, tell me everything you saw in there!"

"Wait—what forces?" Marco asked.

Bhegad took a deep breath. "The Scholars of Karai discovered this island. For a century we have been dedicated to restoring Karai's lineage. He recognized the foolishness of creating the Loculi—of trying to control the great Atlantean power. But his quest to destroy them backfired. It angered Massarym. So Massarym stole them and took them off Atlantis—and that removal brought on the destruction and sinking of the great civilization. Karai somehow survived, and he devoted his life to finding what his brother had taken. He searched the world for clues, going undercover, bribing people, until at last he finally found Massarym's plans."

"Do you have those plans here?" I asked.

Bhegad shook his head. "It was long ago. They've since been lost. We believe Karai wanted to return the Loculi to Atlantis. To restore the balance, possibly to raise the continent and start anew. But he was constantly thwarted by the Massa—a group of Massarym's followers. They were in awe of the powers Massarym drew from the Loculi. They thought him a god, and he thrived on that. But after Atlantis sank, he changed. He regretted his decision to steal the Loculi. He realized Karai had been right—they were too dangerous and should not have been created in the first place. But Karai's desire to return them to the island—this horrified Massarym. He feared another cataclysm, a global one. He thought Karai had lost his mind. He considered destroying the Loculi but worried about the release of energy. So he devoted the rest of his life to hiding them away for eternity."

"These people—the Massa—are they still active?" I asked.

Bhegad nodded. "They are obsessed with finding the Loculi—and us. We believe they are close to locating this island. Our surveillance has picked up increased chatter."

"Can't we all just be friends?" Cass asked. "Work

together? We want the same things."

"Most certainly not." Bhegad shook his head. "The Massa have stayed loyal to the early aims of Massarym. They are about control. Domination. Ultimate power. We must find the Loculi before they steal them and figure out how to activate the powers."

"If we let you sic us on the Evil Empire," Marco drawled, "what do we get in return?"

"Your lives." Bhegad glared at him. "If the Massa get the Loculi, you can't return them."

"Which means . . . we die," Aly said.

Bhegad turned to me. "Now tell me about that Circle, Jack."

I gulped. "It was carved into stone and there was a . . . *bowl* dug out of the middle, with writing in it. And this mist billowing out of a crack. Jammed inside the crack was a piece of sword," I said. "And around that part were seven other bowls—"

"The Heptakiklos . . ." Bhegad said, his voice choked. "The Circle of Seven. Wenders was right. It's here—the center of Atlantis! The place where the Loculi were stolen."

"Each of the bowls had a carving," I continued. "Statues and buildings that were totally recognizable—"

"Whoa. Pause button," Marco said. "Behold the Immortal One. Marco who fell a billion feet without a scratch." He stared around at us all, his eyes blazing. "Why are we worried about G7W anymore? And treatments? We have the Magic Waterpark of Life!"

I sucked in my breath. In all the excitement, I hadn't thought of that. The water had brought Marco to life. Maybe it had cured us, too. Maybe we were free to go home.

I looked at Aly and Cass and knew they were thinking the same thing. Bhegad pulled a small, finger-shaped object out of his jacket pocket. He took Marco's hand and shoved the instrument onto his right index finger.

Marco flinched. "Yeow. Easy, P. Beg, the Immortal One is still sensitive to pain."

"Blood sample." Bhegad removed the instrument and fished a Band-Aid out of his pocket for Marco. We gathered around, watching in bafflement as the numbers changed on the instrument. When they stopped, Bhegad sighed. "Same enzyme levels, same signs of mitochondrial chaos."

"In English, please," Marco said.

"The waterfall regenerated your tissue," Bhegad said. "But it had no effect on G7W."

"You mean, if we skipped a treatment and started going haywire and then got dropped into the water . . ." Aly said.

"It would not do a thing." Bhegad shook his head sadly.

That seemed impossible. I searched Bhegad's face. He had lied to us before, and there was nothing stopping him now.

"Atlantis was about balance," the professor continued. "Clearly some of the energy has seeped through the rift.

Powerful energy indeed, which is now trapped down there in the waterfall. But you are connected to Atlantis in a deeper way. Your ceresacrum needs that connection, that balance created between the Loculi and the forces underground. We must find them, Jack."

"If Karai couldn't do it, how can we?" I asked. "Especially with the Massa breathing down our necks?"

"You said there were carvings," Bhegad said. "In each of the seven circles. Can you re-create them?"

"I can," Cass volunteered.

"You don't need to," I said. "There was a statue over a harbor, a great lighthouse, pyramids, hanging gardens. . . . They were the Seven Wonders of the Ancient World."

"By the Great Qalani . . ." Bhegad said, aghast. But before he could say a word, his phone let out a sharp beep. He glanced down and blanched.

The screen read CODE RED.

He flipped the phone up to his ear. "Bhegad here . . . A *what*?" His face darkened. "Are you sure? We're on our way."

"What happened?" I asked.

Bhegad was already heading back toward the compound. "Tell me. That blade you saw, in the middle of the Heptakiklos. Did you pull it out, Jack?"

"I put it back in afterward!" I shot back.

Bhegad went pale.

Before I could ask him to explain, an ATV crashed through the undergrowth with Torquin in the driver's seat. "In!" he commanded.

"What happened?" I asked.

"The Karai Institute," Bhegad shouted as he piled into the front seat, "is under attack!"

CHAPTER THIRTY-FIVE

CREATURE FROM THE BREACH

"WHEN THE RIFT was opened, what exactly did you see, Jack?" Bhegad was shouting over his shoulder from the front seat, as the ATV bounced over the ruts on the path.

"Nothing!" I shouted back. "I couldn't. There was this blinding light. But I felt something. Like a flapping of wings."

"Me, too!" Marco called out. "And this weird sound, like screeching."

"Impossible . . ." Bhegad said, shaking his head. "I thought they'd all been killed . . ."

"Sorry!" I said. "I really messed up, huh?"

"Yes!" Torquin turned the vehicle hard, dodging a thick tree and nearly throwing us out. "Made gate fall."

Bhegad ignored him and turned to us. His face was

etched with panic. "In Atlantean times, this area was not a volcano yet but a hidden valley. For ages, the Atlantean royal family came here to partake of the mist. The strange power. But when Queen Qalani sought to create the Loculi, she needed more of the energy. A way to control the flow. So she enlarged the fissure where the mist came out. To prevent leakage, she used a magic sword as a plug. She could remove and replace it whenever she wished."

"Leakage of what?" Aly said. "What is this energy? It heals people. It makes the island invisible. There's got to be some scientific explanation."

"We believe the fissure is an aberration in the earth's magnetic field," Bhegad said. "A flux point in the space-time continuum. A sort of time tunnel."

"That's impossible," Aly said, "according to all laws of physics—"

"*Classical* physics," Bhegad corrected. "Relativity, string theory—these tell us that space and time are fluid. That they bend and create dimensions that are difficult to see. But difficult, as we've found, is not impossible. We've suspected that a small breach existed. There have been dozens of unconfirmed sightings of ancient creatures over the years. The vromaski must have slipped through the fissure."

I did not like the sound of this. "So what happened when I pulled the sword out for that moment? What came through?"

We zoomed out of the jungle and onto the outskirts of the institute. One of the buildings looked as if it had been bombed. Its roof was a violent mass of broken shingles. From all over the campus, Scholars and guards were rushing toward it.

Torquin skidded to a stop at the building. As the guards jumped out, Torquin held one of them back. "You stay. I protect. Wait. All of you."

The moment he turned to go, a grotesque screech ripped through the air. I heard the crashing of glass and thumping of falling furniture. A KI guard dropped from a second-story window, screaming.

Inside I could see a blur of red. Another window smashed. Through the opening I glimpsed a long, whiplike object thrashing back and forth.

A tail.

"What the—?" Aly said.

Torquin was kneeling by the cart, taking aim with a gun. The other guard knelt with him.

A massive head emerged from the broken roof—a beast at least fifteen feet high. It resembled a giant eagle, but its eyes were yellow and segmented like an insect's, its skin bright red.

"Ready . . . aim . . ." Torquin said.

"*No!* Do not shoot!" Bhegad commanded.

The creature turned at the sound of the voice. Its

eyes shot pinpricks of light, the facets reflecting the sun. It glared in Bhegad's direction and tented its wings. With a sudden thrust, it propelled itself up and out of the building. The wings stretched impossibly wide. They flapped once, twice, and even at our distance we could feel the shift in air pressure.

The monster's body, covered in bright red fur, was barrel-chested and heavy like a lion's. Its legs were muscular and long, and as it took to the air I saw a row of saber-sized talons retract into its paws. It seemed impossible something this large could fly. It was too big. Its body was all wrong for flight.

It soared upward as if it had never heard of gravity. And then it dived toward us, with an ear-piercing screech.

I recognized the sound. The flash of red. The flap of wings. I had experienced them all in the volcano—during the moment when I had pulled out the broken blade.

I had let this thing through.

Bhegad was yelling at the top of his lungs, pleading with the others to hold their fire. Marco leaped out of the cart, directly in front of Professor Bhegad. "Hey, Big Bird, over here!" he shouted. In his hand was a chunk of jagged rock.

The raptor cocked its head toward Marco. He threw the rock, making a direct hit between its eyes. It let out a shriek, wings stuttering in midair.

With a sickening thump, it landed directly on Professor Bhegad.

The old man's cry was silenced by the impact. Torquin and the guards raced toward him. The thing fluffed out its wings, clipping Torquin in the jaw. He fell backward like a rag doll, taking the other guards down with him.

But the raptor's eyes were on Marco, who was taunting it, racing toward the nearest building. *"Run!"* he shouted over his shoulder. "Get to shelter!"

The creature leaped into the air, uncovering the crushed, motionless body of Bhegad. Spreading its wings, it dropped toward Marco, talons extended.

"No-o-o!" Cass yelled. He leaped out of the cart, brandishing a sharp-tipped stick. "We just rescued him, you overgrown chicken!"

Marco jumped aside with the skill of a ninja fighter. The creature crashed to the ground, its talons gripping a clod of grass.

Cass plunged forward, his momentum carrying him directly into the attacker. The stick drove into its side, releasing a gusher of greenish-black fluid.

The creature made no sound. Its head swiveled downward to see the wound. Then, with calm efficiency, it stood, took two steps, and leaped into flight.

On its way up, it grabbed Cass by his backpack.

As we watched in stony shock, the raptor soared into the darkening sky, with Cass in his underwear, swinging helplessly below.

CHAPTER THIRTY-SIX

MEANING OF THE SEVEN

"GET HIM!" MARCO raced across the quad, his feet barely touching the ground. He leaped, extending his arm upward.

His fingers just grazed the bottom of Cass's shoe.

As Marco fell empty-handed, Cass's pleas for help echoed dully.

I raced to Marco's side with Aly.

The beast gained altitude with each mighty flap of its wings. Cass's legs hung like a puppet's. We stared in horror as they receded into the distance, slowly becoming a silhouette.

A sharp *crrack* rang out. Torquin was on one knee, sighting with his rifle.

"Don't shoot!" Bhegad pleaded hoarsely. "You could hit the child!"

Bhegad.

In the horror of Cass's capture, I'd neglected him. He'd been crushed by the creature. I knelt by him, cupping his head with my right hand. "Are you all right?"

Bhegad struggled to sit up. Mustering all his strength, he called out: "My tracking device is gone, Torquin. Have someone run a trace on the boy!"

Torquin barked an order to one of his goons. Behind him I could see Aly and Marco, still frozen, eyes to the sky. Aly was sobbing.

Bhegad's eyes flickered shut. I helped him lie down, scanning his body for wounds. I saw no bleeding, but his leg was twisted like a rag doll's and his face was gray.

"I get doctor," Torquin said.

"Yes . . . thank you . . ." Bhegad said through his teeth. "And summon all three of the Select—now!"

As Torquin ran off, Bhegad looked up at me with blood-shot eyes. "We—we thought . . . they had all been killed," he said.

"All *what*, Professor?" I asked.

"The griffins," he replied. "The guardians of the Loculi. Massarym . . . slaughtered them. But in a rift . . . in time . . . there's no telling how far back . . ."

260

His head was sagging.

I didn't know what to say or do. I was stiff with shock, weighted down with guilt. This monster was here because of me. Because of my curiosity, Cass was gone.

"I'm so sorry . . ." I said.

"Get him . . ." Bhegad moaned.

"How?" I begged.

I looked up to see Torquin running our way with a tracking device. Aly and Marco were close behind him. "Professor," he said.

He knelt, holding the device in front of Bhegad's face. Behind him, a medical team began laying a stretcher near Bhegad. Aly and Marco knelt silently beside me.

"Of course . . ." Bhegad said, squinting at the screen. "It is on a quest to find a Loculus. The object it was born and bred to protect."

"Then why does it have Cass?" I asked.

"For food," Bhegad replied.

Aly gasped. Marco held her close.

"But . . . the griffin cannot . . . digest human flesh raw . . ." Bhegad continued. "Hid its prey in caves . . . cocooned it . . . macerated it with saliva. . . . You must go after it . . ."

"Prepare jet?" Torquin said.

"Yes," Bhegad said. "And Torquin . . . you will take the Select with you."

261

"No room!" Torquin snapped. "Trapped us. In cave!"

"Of course there's room," Bhegad replied. "Do not . . . let your anger get the better of you . . ."

As the medical team began to lift Bhegad, he begged them to stop. Turning to us with half-lidded eyes, he said, "The Heptakiklos carvings . . . done by Karai . . . each tells where a Loculus was hidden. I know . . . where the griffin is going . . ."

"The griffin is headed to the Seven Wonders of the Ancient World?" I said in utter disbelief.

"Yes—*yes*, my boy!" Bhegad was breathing sporadically, trying to focus. "Built by finest minds of the time . . . funded with lots of money. Secret passages . . . storage . . . hiding places . . . state of the art. Perfect for the Loculi. We should have suspected . . ."

"But they don't exist anymore, Professor Bhegad!" Aly insisted. "Haven't the Wonders all been destroyed—except for the pyramids?"

"Follow the griffin . . ." Bhegad said. "Cass's tracker . . . headed toward the Mediterranean . . ."

His voice was fading. The medics were lifting the stretcher, starting for the Karai Institute hospital. I ran along with them. He seemed desperate to tell me something. "Promise . . . bring back . . ."

"We will!" I shouted. "We'll find Cass and return him!"

"Bring . . . back . . ." Bhegad repeated.

His eyes finally fluttered shut. But not before uttering two last words.

". . . the Loculus."

CHAPTER THIRTY-SEVEN

RHODES

"BANKING LEFT," TORQUIN said. His fleshy face distorted into some strange, frightening expression that must have been his smile. He was piloting the tiny, four-seater jet as if it were a dive-bomber. The plane dipped downward so hard I was convinced I left my brain behind.

"Glurrrp . . ." I held my hand to my mouth and breathed deeply.

Torquin's antics had their advantages. They distracted me from thinking about Cass. He had been with the griffin for two hours. I worried he was going to lose his life before we found him. All I stood to lose right now was my lunch.

"Gate. Cave. Nasty trick . . ." Torquin murmured for about the tenth time.

I shared a baffled glance with Marco and Aly. "Yo, Sasquatch," Marco said, "read my lips: They didn't close the gate on purpose! It was a mistake. Understand? Or should Aly translate that into Cro-Magnon?"

Torquin banked again, rolling the plane a full three-sixty. "Banzai."

"Will you stop that?" I shouted.

The plane leveled. I tried not to look down. Below us was the Mediterranean Sea. The choppy gunmetal water seemed to stretch to the horizon. I focused on the tracking device, which Torquin had mounted to the cockpit. Cass's signal had passed east over Italy. A running line of LED text at the bottom, which had read SARDINIA and then SIC-ILY for a long time, now changed to CORFU. "Where is the griffin is taking him?" I asked.

"Could be anywhere," Aly said. "All the Seven Wonders were in Mediterranean countries."

Torquin didn't answer for a long time. His eyes were glued to the signal. The names began to change more rap-idly as it now passed over solid land—SPARTA, CORINTH, ATHENS.

It emerged off the eastern coast of Greece, into the Aegean Sea. My eyes moved ahead. I traced out the trajectory—not where it had been, but where it seemed to be going. I focused on a tear-shaped island off the coast of Turkey. I leaned closer to read the label.

"Rhodes . . ." I said.

"That's the site of one of the Seven Wonders," Aly said, peering at the device. "The great Colossus of Rhodes! Supposedly the biggest statue ever built. It straddled the entire harbor, holding up a light for all the ships."

I nodded, thinking back to a homework assignment that seemed centuries ago. "I made a replica of that. A G.I. Joe figure, wrapped in a toga. I put a toy flashlight in one hand and a pad labeled GREEK DICTIONARY in the other. I brought him to class on a Stratego board and stood him up in the Aegean Sea."

"I must have been absent that day," Marco said. "But weren't the Seven Wonders all nuked, like, eons ago? Cincinnati Red isn't going to like that."

The plane lurched. The wings dipped to the left. We were hurtling down toward Rhodes.

"*Sto-o-o-op!*" Aly yelled.

"Dude, I am about to get immortal puke all over your plane!" Marco said.

Torquin grinned evilly. "Gate. Cave. Nasty trick."

The plane went into a roll. My seat restraints dug into my body. We were all screaming now. The tracker, which was attached by one clip, went flying.

It cracked against the ceiling and went dark.

Torquin quickly righted the plane. He glanced at the useless device and flinched. "Oops."

* * *

"Face it, Samson—you *have* to tell Professor Bhegad," Marco said, leaning in toward Torquin, who was in the front passenger seat of a Greek taxicab. "He can FedEx you another device!"

"I don't think the Karai Institute has a FedEx office," Aly drawled.

"Worst-case, you let the KI do the tracking remotely," I said. "They can report Cass's location to you!"

Torquin was punching the buttons of the broken tracking device with his stubby fingers. "Fix."

I couldn't believe this.

Exhausted, I glanced out the window at the highway. We had spent the night on the airport tarmac, sleeping in the plane. We'd tried to convince Torquin to contact the KI about the tracker, but he had refused. He didn't want to admit to Professor Bhegad what he'd done.

We had to humor him like a kindergartner—while Cass was in the talons of a flesh-eating beast.

Aly and Marco were looking at me helplessly.

Think. It's the one thing you're good at.

Hotels and restaurants raced by us on one side of the road, a beach on the other. It was hard to believe we were finally in the real world again, with streetlights, highway traffic, restaurants, houses, cell towers, people in normal clothes doing normal things. The taxi's car radio was blaring ads in Greek and a news report mentioned "Nea Yorki." We were home.

Yet somehow, all this reality made everything feel more unreal.

There had to be a way to find Cass. The griffin was programmed to find and protect its Loculus. Which meant that somehow, the magical sphere still existed. Even though its hiding place, the Colossus, was gone.

If we could find the Loculus, we would find Cass.

As we approached the port, I looked closely out the window. The sides of the harbor curved around in kind of a pincer shape, like two fingers about to snap. Fishing boats were returning with their morning catches, and people were already eating early breakfasts in a sprawling line of outdoor cafés.

It was supposedly the biggest statue ever built. It straddled the entire harbor, holding up a light for all the ships . . .

"Is this the main port?" I asked the driver. "Where the Colossus of Rhodes once stood?"

"*Neh*—yes!" said the driver with pride. "You know about Colossus? Greatest Wonder of all world. The big ships? They pass under legs. My brother Niko's restaurant has view of harbor. Best food in Rhodos—"

"Wait. Passed under its *legs?*" Marco asked skeptically. "With those big old sails? That thing would have to be ginormous—like, carry the Statue of Liberty in its toga pocket."

"Is why we call it *Colossus!*" the driver declared.

"So if the Loculus fell out when the statue was destroyed," I said, "it would be underwater."

Marco squinted, shielding his eyes against the morning sun. "I don't see His Redness swimming out there, looking for it."

Torquin looked up from the broken tracker and pointed toward the road that lined the harbor. "Stop there."

"You like diving?" the driver said. "I bring you to my uncle Foti's shop!"

"Drive." Torquin went back to fiddling with the tracker. He crossed his legs, revealing a massive bare right foot.

The driver raised an eyebrow. "My cousin Irini? She has shoe store—"

Torquin brought his fist down on the dashboard, hard. The driver swerved toward the harbor.

In a moment he stopped on a cobbled road overlooking the water. A waiter, setting a table, waved to us from a nearby white stucco café. Soft bouzouki music came from inside, along with the crackle of frying foods. The smell made my mouth water. Torquin had given us some euros for pocket money. A bite of food would be great if we could do it without wasting time.

The driver held a business card out toward Torquin. "Call twenty-four seven. Taki at your service. You pay now, please."

Ignoring the card, Torquin handed the man some money and walked away. Taki counted it quickly. "No tip?"

"Talk too much," Torquin growled.

Aly glanced at him in disbelief. "He can't get away with that." Taking Taki's card, she jumped into the front passenger seat. "Torquin, that was rude. I'm not moving until you give this man a tip!"

Marco shot her a thumbs-up. "Nice one, Norma Rae."

Torquin turned. He muttered something under his breath that I'm glad I didn't hear. Then he tossed a few coins at Aly, who handed them to Taki.

"You good girl," the driver said, beaming. "I tell Niko give you free breakfast."

As she got out, I saw her putting something into her pocket. I gave her a curious glance.

She put her fingers to her lips and walked toward the harbor.

CHAPTER THIRTY-EIGHT

THE TROUBLE WITH TORQUIN

"THE COLOSSUS SITE should be somewhere just past these restaurants..." Aly said, walking briskly along the wharf.

Marco and I trudged behind her. We had gathered a bunch of brochures at a tourist stand and read them over eggs and toast at Niko's—well, Marco, Aly, and I read them. Torquin had been busy pounding on the tracking device. By now he had mangled it so badly it couldn't possibly be repaired.

It was a hot morning. Sweat was already pouring down my forehead. I had to talk to Aly. Alone. To find out what was in her pocket. And why she was keeping it secret.

As we passed a boat rental place, Torquin stopped. "Boat. Here. Into harbor."

Aly turned, a glossy brochure in hand. "Wait. According to this, the Colossus was never over the water at all. Modern scholars believe the Greeks couldn't have built a stone statue that size, straddling a huge harbor. It would have collapsed of its own weight. Even if it were made of bronze, it would have been logistically difficult to anchor its feet on the two harbor points."

Torquin stared at her blankly.

"Pay attention, dude," Marco said. "There will be a quiz later."

I looked out over the water. If a griffin had been here at the harbor, we'd know it. People would be freaking out. Cops would be all over. So it couldn't have been here.

But searching the entire island of Rhodes could take days. It was almost fifty miles long. We didn't have that time. Even if Cass was alive, he was due for a treatment at midnight tonight. If we didn't get him back in time for that, he was doomed.

"They think the Colossus actually stood on the western shore," Aly said. "Right about . . . here."

We cleared the last café. To our right, a stone wall lined the harbor. To our left, the road wound up a slight hill, to where Aly was pointing.

Her face fell.

My eyes followed the path of her finger to a building that housed a supermarket and a bank. Outside the supermarket, a clown was handing out balloons of all different colors to a group of bored-looking kids.

Marco watched one of the balloons float off into the cloudless sky. "There goes our Loculus."

Torquin let out a sarcastic snuffling sound. "We look in dairy section?"

Aly stormed away, walking up the street. The city of Rhodes was hilly when you got away from the wharf. We passed a bike shop on a triangular corner, where a clerk eyed us curiously as we passed. "Aly, wait!" I called out.

I jogged ahead to keep up with her. Now we were about a half block ahead of Torquin and Marco, who were locked in some kind of argument.

"Don't be angry," I said.

Aly looked back, then leaned in to me. "I'm not angry. I just needed to get away so I can use this."

She pulled a cell phone out of her pocket, keeping it shielded from the sight of Torquin and Marco. "When I jumped into the taxi after Torquin stiffed the driver, I took this off the front seat."

"You stole the phone!" I pointed out. "That's worse than stiffing him!"

"I *borrowed* it." Aly turned a corner onto a narrow side street of boxy apartment buildings. Moms and dads were emerging through front doors, blowing kisses to their kids who waved from the windows, in the arms of black-clad grandmothers. "I have Taki's business card. I'll call the taxi company. We need him to drive us around anyway, right? I'll return the phone and tell him it was a mistake. Look, Torquin isn't going to let us near a pay phone. This is our only chance. I just want to make contact with my mom, tell her I'm okay. It'll take me a few seconds to block the caller ID. Then, after I'm done, you can take a turn if you want."

My heart jumped. Dad probably thought I was dead. I would be able to hear his voice for the first time since I left.

I looked over my shoulder. Marco and Torquin hadn't made the turn yet. Aly took my arm and ran toward a dark alley between buildings.

My mind was racing. I imagined the call. I pictured what Dad would say. How we would both feel.

And what would happen afterward.

As we slipped into the narrow alleyway, she flipped the phone open. "Wait. You can't, Aly," I said.

She looked at me in shock. "Why not?"

"It will just make things worse," I said. "Look. You've been missing for a long time. Four of us have disappeared under the same circumstances. The police must be searching for us. Maybe the FBI. Which means they're in touch with our moms and dads—chances are they've wiretapped our families' phones. If we call them, Aly, they'll run a trace. They will find out where we are. And when they do, they will come get us. We'll never return to the Karai Institute. To our treatments."

Aly looked at me with pleading eyes. "You're the one who doesn't believe in that!"

"Here's what I believe," I said. "We have this gene that makes us sick. And Cass needs us to rescue him. Look, I don't mean to give Bhegad a free pass. I don't believe he told us the whole story. But after what we've seen in the past few days? We can't just blow it off, Aly. No one wants to call home more than I do. I wish Dad could pick me up and I could forget about what has just happened to us. You don't know how much I wish that. But we're in the middle of something we have to finish."

I put a hand on her shoulder, but she shook me off. Her face was desperate. "All phone tracing software takes at least thirty seconds to pinpoint a call. I'll use twenty seconds, tops, then hang up. Just so she knows, Jack. Please. Go distract Torquin and Marco. Just give me twenty seconds."

I took a deep breath. I knew she needed to make the call, and I didn't want to argue. No time for that. We had to get to Cass.

Torquin's and Marco's voices were drawing nearer. I ran out of the alley and jogged toward the corner, just as they made the turn.

"Aly?" Torquin demanded, looking up the street. "Where?"

I rolled my eyes. "Where do you think? She had two huge glasses of apple juice at breakfast. Nature called. Now, be nice. Turn around."

Marco turned his back. Reluctantly, Torquin followed. "Hagrid and I were having a conference," Marco said, "about where we could find information about the Colossus in a hurry. We passed this building with Greek words carved in stone. And he goes, 'Library!' I'm like, 'How do you know?'"

"You know Greek?" I asked Torquin.

"Perfect," Torquin said. "Just like English."

I heard footsteps and turned. Aly was walking toward us from the alleyway. Her face was ashen.

"It's your lucky day, sister," Marco said, bounding after her. "We're going to the library!" He stopped and squinted at her. "What's wrong? Someone put some moose in your moussaka?"

Aly didn't answer.

* * *

As we walked up the stairs of the blocky stone building, Marco pointed to a small sign in the window with the international symbols for No Smoking, No Radios, No Food, and No Bare Feet. "Did you bring your penny loafers?" he asked Torquin.

Torquin rapped loudly at the door.

I stuck close to Aly. She wasn't looking at me. I was worried. Something had happened. If she'd goofed up, if there were people coming to get us, we needed to know.

After a minute or so, the door opened slowly and a young woman's face peered out. *"Eimaste kleistoi. Pioi eisaste, eh?"*

And Torquin, without missing a beat, replied, *"Ta paithia einai Amerikani."*

Immediately the door opened wider. The woman smiled faintly. "I can open a few minutes early for Greek-American visitors," she said in a thick Greek accent. "I am Ariadne Kassis. Head librarian. Please, come in."

She took us through a nearly empty reading room, past a set of small offices, and into a spacious chamber. It had dark wooden bookshelves and a worn Oriental rug that covered nearly the whole floor. We sat in five high-backed chairs with thick red padding, arranged in a circle around a tray of sweets and tea. The place smelled of stale coffee, old leather, and ancient books. In the back of the room, a wispy-haired man who seemed more antique than them all was asleep with a book and a plate of green nuts on his lap. He looked as if he hadn't moved in several decades. Maybe even died without anyone noticing.

"We are researching the Colossus of Rhodes," I said. "We need to know everything. Where it was, what exactly happened to it, whether or not there are remains."

"You realize, of course, that you are seeking one of the great archaeological puzzles of all time," Ms. Kassis said, pouring us each a cup of tea. "But you've come to the right place. We have books, scholarly articles, internet resources—"

"Internet, just for me to use," Torquin barked. "Books, them."

"And *Papou*," Ms. Kassis continued, setting down her tea.

"Who poo?" Marco asked.

Glancing across the room, Ms. Kassis called out to the old man. *"Papou! PAPOU!"*

The man let out a series of short, sudden snorts. His head lolled around into a vaguely upright position, and his moist eyes opened into baffled slits.

"Sorry to wake you!" she said loudly in English, walking toward him. "But these are American guests! They are looking for Colossus!"

The man grabbed a gnarled cane as if to rise, but Ms. Kassis gently pushed his chair from behind. It rolled toward us on thick rubber casters. "My great-grandfather is one of the preeminent folklorists in Greece," she announced. "He just turned one hundred and seventeen—isn't that right, *Papou*?"

He shrugged. As he looked at each of us with unfocused eyes, he held up one of the shriveled little green things on his plate. "Walnuts?"

"No, thanks," I said.

"The statue depicted the ancient Greek sun god, Helios,"

Ms. Kassis said. "It was built around 280 B.C. and destroyed in an earthquake. Meaning well before *Papou*'s birth, of course. Although it may not seem that way. For years *Papou* studied an ancient sect—monks of some sort. They were devoted to preserving the Colossus's memory. Fanatics, really. Not involved with any real religion, per se. Greece, you'll find, is tolerant of eccentrics, but *Papou* took them quite seriously. Alas, his memory isn't what it used to be." She raised her voice. "*Papou*—these people are looking for the Colossus."

Papou perked up, as if just noticing we were there. "Colossus?" he said, his voice a barely audible hiss. He gestured toward a pad of paper and a pen on a nearby desk. "*Thos mou . . . thos mou . . .*"

As I gave him the pen and paper, Ms. Kassis smiled. "This may take a while. Excuse me."

She went off to answer a question from a staff member—and we waited.

After a few moments of careful writing, he handed us an address.

Bingo.

CHAPTER THIRTY-NINE

CHASING THE MONKS

"MASTAKOURI STREET." TORQUIN held out the old man's scribbled note, matching it against a street sign. "Number four-seven-seven. Long way to go."

As we walked up a steep, cobblestoned street, I stayed close to Aly. She hadn't said a word.

We were above the center of town. Here, old stone houses lined sharply curved roads. Mastakouri Street was just wide enough for a car to pass. A man with a food cart at the intersection was busy frying dough. The smell made me hungry even though we'd had breakfast only an hour ago. It seemed that everyone in Greece ate all the time.

Marco and Torquin were walking together, sharing a bag of Greek cookies covered with powdered sugar.

I slowed down, taking Aly's arm, letting them pull ahead. "Hey," I said softly, "are you okay? What happened with the phone call?"

Her eyes misted over. "Mom said hello. Like she was in the next town. Like nothing had ever happened. I had planned what to say. Twenty seconds. 'Hi, Mom. I'm in a secret place. A scientific project. But I'm safe. Don't worry.'"

"How did she react?" I asked.

"I couldn't say it," Aly said. "When I heard her voice, all I did was cry. Not even a word. G7W is supposed to make me into a superbrain, Jack. But it didn't help with this. I panicked. When I looked at my watch, eighteen seconds had gone by. So I had to hang up. But just before my thumb hit the off button, I heard her voice again. She said, 'Aly? Is that you?'"

Tears began to run down her cheeks. I put my arm around her shoulder and let her head sink. "At least she knows you're alive."

Aly shook her head. "You were right, Jack. I shouldn't have done it. I feel a thousand times worse."

We just walked in silence. Aly was sniffling, and I held her tight.

Ahead of us, Torquin's bare feet slapped loudly on the cobblestones. A couple of boys passed us by, urging along a stubborn goat. At the intersection ahead, three men in hooded robes shopped for vegetables at an outdoor display.

If you squinted, you'd think you were in the Middle Ages.

"Aha!" Torquin yelled, pointing at a street number painted on the curb. "Four-six-one . . . four-six-nine . . . four-seven-three . . ."

Torquin stopped short. He looked up at a shingled restaurant with a sandwich-board menu out front. Two young businesswomen emerged, chatting, and let out a little scream when they saw his hulking figure.

He was staring upward, over their heads.

We ran to his side and looked. Atop the entrance was a large sign:

Marco spat out a cloud of confectioner's sugar. "You asked him where the Colossus was," he said.

"Colossus . . . *Diner!*" Torquin bellowed. He ripped up the sheet and threw it to the ground, stomping on it with his feet. "Not funny!"

"Maybe you ought to contact KI for Cass's tracking info, dude," Marco said. "Not sure grilling Greek geezers is working for us."

A mother and three children were about to enter the place, but the kids took one look at the raging Torquin and began to cry. As the mom quickly shooed them away, the door opened. A man in a suit stepped out and looked forlornly at the lost customers.

"Pahhh!" Torquin shouted in disgust, kicking the sandwich board. The sign teetered, then clattered in a heap to the sidewalk.

The man looked at Torquin in disbelief. He gestured angrily, spewing Greek words that didn't sound too nice. Torquin retorted in Torquin-Greek, the two men stepping closer until they were nearly face-to-face.

"Easy, guys!" Marco said, trying to separate them.

A small crowd was beginning to gather. Behind the diner man, a frightened-looking waiter was tapping out a number on a cell phone.

Aly tugged at my sleeve. "Jack, look!"

She was gazing out into the street. The three hooded

men, finished with their shopping, were walking past us, down the hill. One of their hoods had fallen off. The man was balding on top, and he'd spun around to glance at the fight in front of the diner.

When he turned to his colleagues again, I could see the back of his head.

And a white lambda against his dark brown hair.

* * *

"Act natural!" Marco whispered. "We can't let them realize we're following them."

A block ahead of us, at the bottom of the hilly street, the monks had stopped short. The hoodless guy was talking on a cell. He seemed agitated. As the others listened to him, their peaceful expressions vanished.

We quickly turned to each other and tried to look natural. "How 'bout those Cavs?" Marco said.

A siren punctuated the quiet. I looked up the street toward the diner, where the owner was setting his sign upright again. A police car pulled away, its lights flashing. Through the back window I could see a mop of dirty red hair.

"This is so messed up," I said. "Torquin should be with us."

"Duh," Marco replied. "He would be, too, if he hadn't gotten himself arrested on a TWT charge—Trashing While Torquin."

There wasn't much we could do. It all happened so quickly. The police had cuffed Torquin despite our protests.

And even though one of them spoke English, he didn't believe Marco's claim that Torquin was our father.

We'd have to try to get him later.

Ms. Kassis's words about her *papou* were flashing in my brains. *For years he studied an ancient sect—monks of some sort. They were devoted to preserving the Colossus's memory. Fanatics, really.*

"How can that monk be a Select?" Aly said. "He's way older than fourteen!"

"Either Bhegad is lying about our fates," I said, "or these guys have some sort of secret cure."

Aly was punching out a number on the cell phone. "Where'd you get that?" Marco demanded.

"Long story," Aly said. "I'm calling us a taxi. One of those monks is holding a set of car keys. We have to tail them."

The hoodless monk snapped his phone shut and shoved it into a pocket of his robe. The men began walking again, faster, arguing. I could hear Aly muttering into the phone, giving our location. In the middle of the next block the monks entered a parking lot. Two of them headed toward an old, beat-up convertible, while the other paid the lot attendant.

"The taxi dispatcher spoke English, sort of," Aly said. "Taki's only a couple of blocks away."

The monk's car was belching and wheezing. Slowly it started up, but it bucked and died on its way out.

A taxi came zooming up from behind us, blowing its horn. We turned to see Taki beaming at us through the open driver's window. "Thank you for finding phone!" he said.

Aly handed it to him as we piled into the backseat. He didn't ask for any explanation.

"Follow those monks!" Marco said.

Taki nodded. "I give you free ride."

We took off. At about ten miles an hour. The monks' jalopy putt-putted into the street, and I wondered if we'd have to rescue them.

Finally the car began to pick up speed. In a few moments we were cruising onto the highway. "Yo, Zorba, do you have any cousins who are monks?" Marco asked.

"My uncle Stavros is priest in Greek church. He say these men not real monks. Is crazy people." Taki gave us a wink and a wry smile.

Greece, you'll find, is tolerant of eccentrics, Ms. Kassis had said.

A group of Colossus cultists with lambda hair would definitely pass as eccentric in the real world.

We were heading east, away from the city limits, past the long strip of hotels and beaches. The road followed the Mediterranean shore, and the beaches gave way to steep cliffs. A stream of black exhaust rose from the tailpipe of the monks' car. Every few minutes the engine made a popping noise.

"They're in a hurry," Aly said.

"Ms. Kassis told us these guys were devoted to the Colossus," I said. "Maybe they're not so crazy. Maybe they know something about its remains."

"A Colossus fingernail could be catnip for Turkey Lurkey," Marco said.

Finally the monks began to slow down. They pulled to a stop in front of a beat-up shack, where a lock hung from a rusted hasp. "Keep going," I said to Taki.

"We could just stop and introduce ourselves," Marco said.

"Too risky," I shot back. "You remember what Bhegad taught us. There's an enemy group after the Loculi. What if these guys are Massa?"

Taki drove for another mile or so, until I asked him to turn back around. When we arrived at the shack again, the car and the monks were gone.

A pickup truck, its cab crammed with jugs of olive oil, was parked at the side of the road. To its left was a small, rickety gate to a wooden staircase leading straight down the cliff.

Taki looked a little dubious. "Why you want to go here? I take you to beach."

As Aly and Marco walked to the gate, I tried to pay Taki but he refused. With a reminder that we could call him anytime, he took off.

I joined my two friends at the top of a cliff. The sea

was hundreds of feet below us, its waves winking in the sunlight. The stairs wound steeply downward and ended at a wide plateau that jutted from the cliffside—a ledge that was three times the size of my backyard. More stairs led downward from the ledge's left side to another ledge, and then another—three massive plateaus, connected, descending sideways along the coastal wall. Each ledge was ringed with a whitewashed wooden fence.

The highest of the three ledges, the one closest to us, contained a massive, domed, rectangular building built into the cliff. In the center of the pebbly, sun-drenched yard, monk robes dried on clotheslines. Next to the fence were three enormous stone urns, each one taller than a man. Two guys on ladders were filling these up with jugs of olive oil that had the same logo as the truck on the cliff top.

"These monks must be total Greek salad freaks," Marco commented. "That's some serious oil."

The second ledge was about sixty feet below the first. It held what looked like a greenhouse, also built right into the cliff, along with another scraggly yard.

Dozens of monks were pouring out of doors set in the cliffside on both levels. They raced down the stairs to the bottommost plateau, their flip-flops clopping loudly.

"The levels are all connected," Aly said. "Their monastery must be built into the cliff."

288

I strained to see what was happening down at that third level. But the angle was wrong. I opened the gate to the first set of stairs. "Let's get closer."

I heard a volley of shouts. Then, rising above them, came a high-pitched screech. It rang out over the sea with a volume and fierceness that nearly blew us back on our heels.

"I think we found Tweety," Marco said.

CHAPTER FORTY

BROTHER DIMITRIOS

MARCO TOOK THE steps two at a time. Aly and I were close behind him as he reached the first ledge. He snatched robes from the clothesline outside the domed building. "Put these on. Quick! Don't want to arouse suspicion."

"I don't think they care about that right now!" Aly said.

As we ran, we slipped the robes on over our packs and raced to the second set of steps. Descending to the middle ledge, I heard the griffin screech again.

We ran across the yard, past the greenhouse. Close up, it didn't seem right. I'd never seen a greenhouse with thick, brownish glass. And no evidence of plants inside.

Monks were climbing up from below now, clawing past one another, their faces panicked. Hoods were falling off left and right, and I could see that *all* of them had the lambda on the backs of their heads.

We rushed to the white fence and looked over the side.

My stomach lurched. The griffin was perched at the bottom level, its lion legs coiled. Beyond it, the cliff dropped off to the sea.

With a thrust of its wings, the beast surged toward the stairs and closed its talons on the shoulders of a black-haired monk. He screamed, his arms and legs flailing, as the griffin lifted him into the air.

We watched in horror as it flew northward along the cliffs. For the first time, I noticed that the cliff face was pocked with holes as far as the eye could see. The griffin with its prey flew directly toward one of them and disappeared inside. Aly gasped and turned away.

"I guess that's its dining room," Marco said.

Aly's eyes were like saucers. I knew what she was thinking.

Cass might be in one of those caves, too.

Marco spun around, running directly into the swarm of fleeing monks. "Did you see our friend?" he asked the crowd. "A kid! Thirteen years old! Does anybody speak English here? Did you see where that thing took our friend?"

"Careful, Marco!" I shouted.

"Don't worry, I'm immortal, remember?" Most of the monks were bouncing off Marco, not paying his words any attention. "Doesn't somebody speak English here?"

Aly grabbed my arm and began pulling me through the crowd, toward the greenhouse. "Jack, look at this," she said. "Look what's in there."

As we approached the glass-walled building, I could see enormous piles of stone rubble inside. They rose into jagged peaks high overhead.

"Look closely at those stones," she said. "They're *sculpted*. Pieces of statues. Like these guys have been scouring the world for every ruined relic they could get their hands on."

She was right. Each piece had a carved side, as if it had been broken off a larger statue. There were piles of arms, legs, feet, heads . . .

A hand.

Aly and I both saw it at the same moment—the unmistakable shape of a giant broken hand, reaching upward as if it was supposed to be holding something. Like a torch.

"Jack, what if this is the—" Before Aly could finish, two fleeing monks barreled into her. She spun and fell, her head hitting the dirt, and the men landed smack on top of her.

The three of them scuffled. I grabbed on to one of the monks, who must have weighed two hundred pounds. He had stringy, shoulder-length hair, and his eyes were circles of panic. He yanked me downward, yelling in Greek. We fell to the ground, rolling to a stop near Aly. He grabbed me by the neck and started to squeeze. Hard. I gasped for air. My eyesight started to fade.

Out of the corner of my eye I saw Aly knee the other monk in the groin. As he howled and curled up, she sprang to her feet, racing around behind my attacker. "Get your hands off him!"

She yanked the monk backward by the hair. He screamed and loosened his grip. Scrambling away, I swung my legs around to clip his ankle.

He fell with a thud as his head hit the hard-packed dirt. He was out for the count.

It took a moment for me to regain my breath. I stood carefully, still wary of the monk stampede. From their midst, Marco emerged, running toward us.

"Are you okay, Aly?" he asked.

She stood, staring down at her own palm. Her mouth hung open in shock. "Guys, look," she said, turning her hand toward us.

Her palm was streaked with white, like she'd grabbed on to a freshly painted picket fence. "It's from him," she said. Her eyes traveled to the ground, to where my attacker now lay unconscious on his stomach.

The white lambda on the back of his head was smudged. It had been painted on.

"These guys are fakes," she said. "They're not really Selects."

Marco nodded. "Shoulda known. They're not cool enough."

A massive shadow swept over us. I glanced up to see the griffin soaring overhead.

A rifle crack rang out, and the tip of the griffin's wing shattered into a spray of feathers. As I spun to look, a man in a black, embroidered robe was descending the stairs. At the top, ranged along the lip of the first ledge, three other monks knelt, their rifles pointing outward.

"Stop that!" Marco cried out, running across the plateau toward the stairs.

Aly and I followed. The man barked an order to his henchman. Then he turned to Marco and asked something in Greek.

"Do you speak English?" Marco said. "That thing has one of my friends. We think it took him into a cave. If you shoot it, we'll never find him!"

"English?" The man narrowed his eyes. He had a deep voice, his Greek accent inflected with British. "I am Brother Dimitrios. Who are you?"

"Brother Marco," Marco shot back.

The man cocked his head curiously. "From the New York or the Los Angeles Massarene?"

I shot Aly a look. *Massarene?*

Marco blinked. "Uh—the Akron, Ohio?" he said.

Brother Dimitrios eyed us warily. Then one of the henchmen began yelling, pointing south along the cliff wall. The griffin's wound had been only a graze, and it was coming back for another pass.

The men aimed their rifles. But the griffin never came in range. It soared below us and disappeared into another of the cliffside caves.

"By the Great Qalani," Brother Dimitrios said under his breath. "How many prisoners has it taken?"

I shot Aly a glance. She'd heard him say it, too.

Brother Dimitrios began shouting instructions in Greek to his henchmen. Two of them ran toward the cliff, disappearing through the door leading inside. The other man came down the steps, urging all the monks to follow him.

"What are they saying, Brother Dimitrios?" I demanded.

He ignored me, his eyes focused on something over my shoulder. I turned to see the griffin rising into the air once more.

This time, it flew straight toward us.

CHAPTER FORTY-ONE

TWEETY RETURNS

WE WERE TOAST. Aly, Marco, and I dove for the ground. We hit the dirt where the greenhouselike building met the cliff wall.

But the griffin passed right over us. It flew at the side of the cliff, digging its talons into the wall above our heads. A clod of dirt and rock shook loose.

Letting out a ferocious cry, it sprang away and attacked the wall a second time.

"It's trying to get inside!" I shouted. "It wants something in there."

"Something that starts with *L* and ends in *oculus*," Marco said.

The cliff wall shook again. We had to roll away to avoid

being crushed by an avalanche of rocks and dirt.

My mind was racing. Cass was unreachable. The Loculus was ungettable. For a split second I thought about Dad. About how he always said a problem was an answer waiting to be opened.

Help me, Dad, I thought.

As the griffin attacked the wall for a third time, I heard another rifle shot from above us. One of Brother Dimitrios's men was on his knees by an olive oil urn, pointing the rifle down at the griffin.

The griffin landed just a few yards from us, roaring angrily. The man quickly descended the steps. He planted his feet at the base of the staircase and shot a third time. We all flinched. As the bullet penetrated the griffin's skin, the beast cocked its head at the shooter. It took two quick steps toward him and lashed out with its wing. The rifleman tried to scramble away, but he wasn't fast enough.

He tumbled forward and disappeared over the edge. His scream made my stomach churn.

The griffin didn't seem concerned about either the monk or its own bullet wound. It paused a moment, looking toward the caves to the north. I didn't have to be an expert on griffin facial expressions to know that it was hungry. It had its own problem. It needed the Loculus, but it also needed to eat.

In that moment, I knew exactly what to do.

"If the Loculus is in there," I said, "we have to help the griffin get it."

"What?" Aly said at the same time.

"It's programmed to get the Loculus," I said. "It's going to do that first—and I say we let it. But look. It's starving. My bet is that once it has the Loculus it will head off for a meal."

"Yeah, fillet of Cass!" Marco added.

"Exactly," I said. "We just have to get to him before it does."

"Awesome, dude!" Marco said. "We can scale the cliff!"

Aly whirled on him. "And how do you suggest we do that, Mr. Immortal? Rappel down with our shoestrings? There are dozens of caves. We'd need a week to find him!"

"I know it's risky," I said, "but it's the only chance we have."

"Uh-oh," Marco murmured. "Heads up."

The griffin was turning slowly, as if noticing us for the first time. It blinked, then bared a set of sharp teeth, glistening with saliva. It let out a guttural hiss that whipped up the stones from the ground.

Aly's hand found mine and gripped it tight.

Marco's eyes drifted upward, above the griffin's head. He swallowed hard. "Um, Angry Bird? You can't understand what I'm saying, but you're some in serious trouble. . . ."

I looked up. The two olive oil delivery guys stood at the top of the cliff, nearly a hundred feet above the griffin, balancing an enormous boulder between them.

Behind the beast, a metal door cracked open against a wall. The griffin turned its head sharply—just as the men released the boulder.

It hurtled downward, glancing against the raptor's shoulder. Its foreleg buckled. Letting out a roar of confusion and pain, it launched itself straight upward. The olive oil men took off at a run.

As the griffin leaped, Brother Dimitrios emerged from the monastery. He began struggling up the wooden stairs toward the first level. In his arms was a huge object, covered by a gold-embroidered cloth.

Hovering in midair, the griffin turned to look.

Then it dove, shrieking, at the monk's head. Brother Dimitrios stumbled. The object fell out of his hands and bounced downstairs with a strange, ringing sound. It rolled to a stop near the fence on the far side of the ledge.

The cloth had slid off to reveal a bronze sculpture of an enormous flame, about five feet high.

"No!" Brother Dimitrios bellowed. Wrenching free of the griffin, he threw himself down the wooden steps after the flame.

And I ran toward it, trying to get there first.

I didn't know what a Loculus looked like. But I knew the Colossus had held a flaming torch in its hand, like the Statue of Liberty. And the griffin had been focused on Brother Dimitrios and his sculpture.

All of which meant to me that maybe the Loculus was *in* the sculpted flame.

Marco and Aly were right behind me. "Give it to the griffin, Brother Dimitrios!" I shouted. "Let him have it!"

"Over my dead body!" Brother Dimitrios replied. He shoved me aside, scooped up the flame, and began running, dodging the griffin as he rushed up the steps. Marco, Aly, and I dashed after him. But he stumbled as he started up the next set of stairs—and the griffin swooped down again.

The monk screamed as the griffin dug its talons into his shoulder. It shook him like a chew toy, slamming him against the wooden railing that ran along the side of the stairs. With a crack, the banister broke.

Brother Dimitrios's robe tore and he tumbled down the stairs, landing at our feet with the flame still clutched firmly in his arms. The griffin perched above us and prepared to pounce.

"Hey, Rotten Breath!" Marco called out, leaping over the monk and running right for the griffin. "Ever play Whac-a-Griffin?"

He yanked off a section of the broken banister. Holding it over his head, he raced up the steps and brought the rail down hard on the griffin's beak.

The beast let out a roar of pain. It fluttered its wings. It had endured bullets and a flying boulder. A bat to its schnozz was the last straw.

300

As Marco slipped past it and raced to the top of the cliff, it flew upward. They both disappeared out of sight on the top level where we'd first arrived.

Aly and I ran. We could hear Marco taunting the beast. It screeched back at him. I heard the crash of glass, the crunch of metal. *"Marco-o-o-o!"* I called out.

We emerged at the top and stopped in our tracks.

The griffin was hunched over, facing away from us, bent forward. All we could see was its massive wings and haunches. It looked like it was feeding.

There was only one thing it could be feeding on.

Marco.

CHAPTER FORTY-TWO

THE FLAME

I COULD HEAR Marco's voice. Shouting. He was still alive.

The creature's back was rising and falling. I had to get him. I had to do something.

I dove for the beast's legs. Fishing a pen out of my pocket, I jammed it into its thick foot. Green fluid spewed out, and the griffin let out a strange sound.

I backed off, scrabbling to my feet. I nearly knocked over Aly, who was standing still, staring.

She pulled me aside, farther to the left, and gestured toward the griffin. My jaw nearly clunked to the ground.

The griffin's head was stuck in the driver-side door of the olive oil truck.

"What the—?" Aly murmured.

Marco sauntered around from the other side of the truck. "Looks like Red Rooster's doing some window shopping." He shrugged, grinning at our astonished faces. "Hey, all I did was dive through the driver's side window and out the other door. Then I razzed this doofus through the window. It fell for the trick. Came straight for me. Got its head in, and now it can't get its head out."

"We—we thought it was eating you," I said.

"At this rate, it's going to have to settle for some pretty skanky seat upholstery." As the griffin roared, lifting the truck and slamming it back to the ground, Marco slapped its haunches. "Good exercise, Tweety. You need to lose that big butt. Now, come on, campers, let's go check on Darth Vader."

He ran ahead, down the stairs. Aly and I glanced at the trapped griffin and then followed behind Marco. Brother Dimitrios lay semiconscious at the bottom of the steps. His henchmen had surrounded him. As we approached, they reached for their rifles. "No," Brother Dimitrios said to the men. "They saved my life."

I crouched next to him. "Are you okay?"

He didn't answer the question, instead leaning in close to Marco. "May I see the back of your head, young man?"

Marco looked warily at him. "Why?"

"Is it painted?" he asked. He grasped Marco's chin and turned his head to one side. "No, it is real. The lambda.

And you two—you have it also?"

Before I could reply, Aly said, "We have a question for you, Brother Dimitrios. What is that sculpture? And why are you trying to take it away?"

The monk's eyes flickered, blood trickling from the side of his mouth. A faint smile creasing his lips. "Touch . . . the flame . . ."

His henchmen glanced uneasily at one another. Finally one of them picked up the sculpture and brought it to me with two hands. It was nearly as tall as I was. As he set it down in front of me, he groaned with its weight.

"Touch . . ." Brother Dimitrios repeated.

I reached to the flame, letting my fingers graze it. It had been dented in the fall.

For a long moment nothing happened. Aly and Marco stared, baffled. From above, I could hear the pickup truck thud onto the dirt again.

From below, I heard monks shouting.

Aly turned. "Marco, Jack—look."

One level down, the greenhouse had started glowing. It was bright enough that I had to squint. And it was getting brighter.

CHAPTER FORTY-THREE

MASSARYM

I TRIED TO let go of the flame, but it wouldn't let me.

It was warming to my touch. Brother Dimitrios's monks backed away in fright. Without really thinking, I cupped both hands around the base of the flame and pulled it toward me. I wasn't sure why. It just seemed like the right thing to do.

The metal flame felt weightless, as if filled with helium. I could lift the whole massive thing without any effort at all. I stood, turned, and walked to the top of the stairs that led to the second level. A crowd of monks had gathered around the greenhouse, which was now pulsing with an eerie light. I saw a swirling from within, like an errant gale.

"Jack?" Aly said. "You're scaring me."

"I don't know what's happening," I said. "I don't know what to do."

Marco glanced down toward the greenhouse. "The disco's calling you, dude. Better go."

As I descended, the torch in front of me, I couldn't feel the stairs beneath my feet. It was as if I were floating. The monks backed away as I neared the greenhouse. It had no entrance from the outside. The only way in, I figured, was through the monastery itself. There must have been an inner door that led into the greenhouse.

Aly and Marco went inside with me. We walked to the right, a short way down a corridor. Three ancient-looking paintings hung on the wall. One was a grand image of the Colossus. Just as Aly had said, it stood at the side of the harbor like a lighthouse. It was all made of burnished bronze, like the flame I held in my hands.

The next image was of a young man dressed in a fancy tunic, sitting on a translucent white ball. He was handsome and buff, surrounded by adoring friends, mostly girls. I had to look twice to see that he was actually floating.

Next to that painting was one of an old man, his skin wrinkled and sagging. Although his eyes were deep with suffering and his hair a tangle of white wisps, he radiated a powerful dignity.

I noticed an identical bronze plaque beneath each of the two portraits: MASSARYM.

Marco's hand was on the doorknob, but he backed away. His face was taut. "I'm not sure about this, brother Jack," he said.

"I'm not either," I said shakily.

His eyes darted toward the paintings. "This is, like, Team Massarym here. We're in the belly of the enemy. Brother Dimitrios *wants* you to do this. Doesn't that seem like a reason not to?"

"How do you know they *are* the enemy?" Aly snapped. "How do you know Bhegad and the Scholars of Karai aren't the bad guys? They've lied to us and manipulated us all along!"

"I guess we'll find out soon enough," I said. "Please, open the door."

Aly stepped forward and jiggled the knob. "It's locked," she said.

Marco leaped, launched into a spinning kick, and whacked the door open in one flying move. "Now it's not."

We stepped in. The glow from the piles of rock was so bright I had to shield my eyes. It was a kind of giant workshop, with tables placed randomly about and narrow pathways winding through the rubble. From somewhere deep in one of the piles I could hear a sound, a faint song like the one from the caldera. "Do you guys hear that?" I asked.

"I'm not sure," Marco said dubiously.

I held the flame high and wound through the pathways, searching for the giant hand I'd noticed before. It was

307

sitting askew atop one of the piles. But up close I saw that it was made of stone, not bronze. And it was nowhere near big enough to grasp this torch.

Below it were dozens of other sculpted hands, made of stone, bronze, marble, or wood. Some of them were attached to arms. They were thin and thick, feminine and masculine, childlike and wizened.

Aly moved to another pile and picked up the broken stone bust of a bull. "This is crazy. It's like a statue morgue. We could search this place for months trying to find the right pieces."

She was right. There were hundreds, maybe thousands, of statues here—people, gods, animals. If the Colossus were among them, it was impossibly buried.

The spot on the back of my head was beginning to throb again. The edges of my vision were fuzzing over. The glowing, the sound—what did it mean?

I heard the griffin shrieking in the distance. It could shake itself loose from the truck any moment. If Cass was still alive, his minutes were numbered. We didn't have time to search for the Colossus right now. That would have to wait until after we rescued our friend.

"Come on," I said, "let's get out of here."

I tossed the bronze flame onto one of the piles. I couldn't carry it up and down the side of a cliff.

It didn't fall, though.

It just hung. In midair.

Aly, Marco, and I stood gaping and the bronze began to pulse. It was changing, growing translucent, as if it were paper.

Something was trapped inside. I leaned closer to see what it was. It didn't seem solid or even liquid—just a swirl of bright, jagged objects hurtling around of their own power against the bronze flame's inner structure. They boiled and vibrated, circling so fast that they became a kind of plasma.

Before our eyes, something was being born inside. Something oblong, delicate, like a giant egg.

A long seam formed down the length of the bronze flame. Then another.

And like the petals of a flower, it began to open.

CHAPTER FORTY-FOUR

THE AWAKENING

THE BRIGHTNESS WAS like a punch. Squinting, I fell back. Marco and Aly were yelling at me, but I couldn't make out the words. The hum was excruciating. It snaked into the folds of my brain like a liquid.

The sides of the bronze flame peeled downward. Inside, a giant globe of plasma rose. It circled slowly over the piles of rubble, which began to swirl. Pieces flung themselves away against the glass, as if being thrown by an invisible hand. As we ducked to the ground, the greenhouse wall began to shatter.

Some of the shards—maybe one in a thousand—had a different fate. They rose more slowly.

One by one, they were sucked right up to the plasma

ball. They stuck to its side like skin grafts. They were forming a shell, whipping upward and locking into place like a jigsaw puzzle solving itself, until an entire sphere had formed—a sphere of bronze, about half again as large as a basketball. It hovered above the remains of the flame.

"The Loculus!" I said.

"We're supposed to *take* that thing?" Aly asked.

Marco moved closer. "Earth to Jack and Aly. Don't just stand there. Grab it!"

He began climbing one of the piles. The sphere was whirling around the greenhouse now, faster and faster, whipping the mass below into a cyclone.

"Marco, get down from there!" Aly screamed.

A flying piece of stone clipped the side of his head and he toppled downward. Aly and I ran to his side.

"Have no fear!" Marco sat up, shaking his head. "The Immortal One takes a minor tumble. This Loculus has a mind of its own. It's going to fly off to Pluto before we can figure out how to get it to—"

A shadow passed across his face and he fell silent.

We all looked up toward the glass dome. And we heard the griffin's keening, bloodthirsty caw.

"How did it get loose?" I asked.

As it descended, I could see the mangled pickup door around its neck. It had torn it loose from the truck.

"Run!" Aly shouted.

As we scrambled toward the exit, the greenhouse roof exploded.

The red beast plunged downward. Its body seemed to fill the airspace. It flapped its wings frantically, cramped by the four walls. The door had dug into its skin and formed a nasty, featherless ring around its neck. The griffin's yellow, segmented eyes were lined with black. They settled on Marco, and the beast growled.

I tried to shield Marco with my body, but he lifted me off my feet and ran me to the door as if I were a football. Aly was already through, and she pulled at Marco's arm.

The griffin smacked against the door frame. It was too big to fit. Weakened by the battle with the pickup truck, it fell backward.

And the flying Loculus whacked it on the head.

The beast seemed finally shocked out of its rage. It glanced up at the object it had been trained to protect.

The glowing orb rose higher over the debris. The rocks below swirled furiously, battering against the griffin. The lion-bird rose again, roaring in pain.

With a burst of light, three gleaming bronze shards shot up from the pile and fused in midair. Then four more, then a dozen, until the walls echoed with a fusillade of sound.

High above us, the Loculus stopped moving. The cloud of bronze shards spun around it like planets orbiting the sun. I caught sight of the Colossus's flame among them, still opened like a blooming lily.

The griffin, looking broken and confused, perched on an edge of the jagged roof to watch.

The air itself seemed to have become a shade of bronze as pieces vacuumed upward with impossible speed. They slammed against one another, fusing into shapes.

A base began to form at the bottom of the flame. It grew steadily downward, sucking up pieces large and small. It sprouted a handle, and then fingers to twine around it, followed by a palm. A wrist. A forearm. Shoulders.

At the bottom of the vortex, two enormous bronze feet expanded upward—from toes to heavy sandals to ankles and calves. Thighs became a torso, and slowly the top and bottom began to fuse together.

A gargantuan warrior of bronze, easily a hundred feet tall, stood over us. It was pocked with holes that were filling quickly as shards of bronze found their places. Its head rose higher than the shattered glass dome. Slowly it gained a face—a chiseled warrior's face with closed eyes, as if asleep on its feet.

"By the great Qalani . . ." Marco murmured.

In moments the work was complete. The Loculus zoomed upward, and for a moment I thought Marco had been right—it wouldn't stop until it reached the outer limits of the solar system. But it stopped abruptly, somewhere in the afternoon sky above the statue.

Then, slowly, it lowered itself into the flame atop the torch. Which began to close.

At that—at the sight of the Loculus disappearing—the griffin howled. It lunged off its perch toward the statue. Extending its talons, it attacked.

"What's it doing?" Marco asked.

"It wants the Loculus," I said. "Its job was to protect it— way back before the destruction of Atlantis. It doesn't know about the Colossus. It thinks the Colossus is the enemy."

Claws clanked against the statue's bronze arm and the griffin bounced back. The weight of the truck door around its neck was playing tricks with its balance. It flailed its wings, trying to steady itself in midair. It landed on a broken splinter of glass that stuck up from the wreckage of the wall. The glass buried itself deep in the bird's side.

At the sound of the beast's deathly cry, the Colossus's eyes opened.

CHAPTER FORTY-FIVE

PLAN C

"GET . . . ME . . . OUT of here . . ." Aly said faintly.

"Um, wasn't expecting *that*," Marco murmured.

I couldn't move.

The eyes of the Colossus turned from the griffin, took in its surroundings, and stopped when they reached Marco, Aly, and me. It was a blank stare—alive but not human, moving but bloodless.

Its head moved, groaning like the gears of a rusty engine. It seemed to be taking in its environment, looking for something. It ignored the caws of the injured griffin, which hung like a rag doll from the glass.

The giant statue leaned toward the center of the greenhouse, letting its left foot slide. A pile of rocks was kicked aside like so much dust. Then it lifted its right leg slowly, as if testing it. A metal, sandaled foot about the size of a moving truck came down on a stack of discarded statue pieces, instantly pulverizing them.

The plateau shook like an earthquake. Outside the monks were frantically scurrying away. In a few thundering steps, the Colossus had turned completely around and was facing the harbor. It began to walk away from us, shattering what was left of the glass wall in one step. The entire outer structure collapsed along with it, sending the griffin down into a pile of glass and stone.

Its body twitched and then went still.

The Colossus strode out onto the plateau. It turned toward the city of Rhodes.

"It's going home," I whispered. "To the harbor."

"I hope it has insurance," Marco said. "It's a long way down."

From above us came a rhythmic chopping noise. "A *helicopter?*" Marco commented. "What are those boneheaded monks doing?"

I thought about the domed structure above us. We never saw what was inside. "That big building?" I said. "It must be a hangar."

"In a monastery?" Marco remarked.

"A Massa monastery," I reminded him.

In a moment, the chuck-chuck-chucking of rotors was

unmistakable. The helicopter rose, banking high above the Colossus. I could see Brother Dimitrios at the controls. "Guess he recovered," Aly murmured.

The statue stared at the chopper, its bronze neck creaking. A red glow radiated from behind its eyes.

I looked over my shoulder toward the cliff. The sun was high overhead but starting to set. If we could save Cass, he'd need his treatment in fewer than twelve hours.

We will save Cass, I told myself.

"The Loculus is out of reach, in the Colossus's torch," I said. "The griffin is dead. Cass has to be back at the KI by midnight. Does someone here have a Plan B?"

Before anyone could answer, a searing orange beam shot out from the chopper's passenger side. It connected with the Colossus's torch, tracing a fiery line across it.

The Colossus retracted its arm. As it glanced up at the chopper, another laser beam hit it in the forehead, creating a pool of molten metal.

"What are they doing?" Marco said.

"I don't know!" I replied.

"They want the Loculus," Aly said. "That's why Brother Dimitrios told you to touch the flame. He knew that if he brought one of the Select and the Loculus together, the sphere would activate. But I bet he didn't count on the Colossus reappearing and taking it away."

"*We* made the Colossus appear," Marco said. "Brother

Jack, Sister Aly, and the Kid Who Faced Down Death."

A loud midair crunch made us look up. The Colossus had taken a swipe at the helicopter, destroying one of its landing feet. The chopper was pitching in the air, losing altitude. "They're going down!" I shouted.

The Colossus turned and began heading for the edge of the cliff. Its footsteps thudded heavily. Chunks of the cliff edge began falling away. The chopper whirled wildly, lurching toward the statue.

The top of the torch had melted from the laser hit, and from this angle I could see the Loculus floating inside. With its other arm, the Colossus reached upward and tried to grab the helicopter's whirring rotor.

The blades sheared off instantly, flying in all directions. We all hit the ground just as one of them spun past, inches away. Shrieking, Brother Dimitrios and his copilot tumbled out. They landed hard on the lowest ledge of the monastery.

The Colossus batted the empty chopper over the edge of the cliff. It hurtled out into the Aegean Sea. From above came the cracking noise of rifle shot. Bullets ricocheted off the bronze surface of the statue, leaving sharp dents.

"Oh, guns, great idea," Marco said. "Very effective against a giant metal man."

The statue turned. It stepped back toward the monastery

wall, its head peering directly at its attackers.

The men bolted as fast as they could.

Marco grabbed me by the collar. "Let's bail!" he said. "Forget about the Loculus. That thing can have it. Plan B, we go back into town and find someone with climbing equipment. We search every one of those caves until we find Cass."

"That'll take days!" I said.

"Do you have a better idea?" Marco asked.

"We created this thing," Aly said. "It's about to destroy this monastery. Then what? It walks into town and flattens Rhodes? We can't let it do that."

"We can't abandon Cass," Marco said.

I eyed the Colossus, who was now trying to get up to the top of the cliff. But the ledges were too high for it to simply use them as steps, and it didn't seem coordinated enough to climb. It was scrabbling at the cliff, scraping layers of rock loose. Before long the monastery walls would collapse.

I looked up to the first level, where the dome had been rolled back to let the chopper fly out. I thought about the monastery that was about to be trashed. The portraits on the wall, which would be crushed in the debris—the devastated old man, looking back at a life of regret. His cocky younger self, sitting on a white sphere suspended in midair.

In midair . . .

"We need that Loculus," I said. "That's how we'll get Cass."

"Say what?" Marco said.

"Just follow me," I said, running toward the stairs. "This is Plan C. For Colossus."

CHAPTER FORTY-SIX

ONE BEAST AT A TIME

I WAS THE first up. Marco followed, and then Aly. The Colossus was still on the second level. It had given up trying to climb and backed away from the wall. Above us, Brother Dimitrios's men had rearmed. Someone had retrieved a machine gun.

"Stop!" a voice called out from below.

Bloodied and bruised, Brother Dimitrios was climbing the stairs from the third level. In his right hand he held a small, oblong object. A grenade.

On the cliff top above us, his men were frozen. Brother Dimitrios stepped onto the plateau, struggling with the grenade pin. "I want the pleasure of doing this myself," he rasped.

The Colossus bent its knees. Its torch arm still aloft, it reached down with its other arm and lifted Brother Dimitrios off the ground. The grenade flew off toward the sea as the monk rose in the Colossus's hand, screaming.

The statue would crush him in moments.

I ran toward the giant urns of olive oil. *"Help me out—now!"*

Placing both hands on an urn, I tried to push. The thing was unbelievably full and heavy. It was more like an olive ocean. In a moment Aly and Marco were by my side.

"Heave . . . ho!" Marco said.

The first urn tipped over, splintering the wooden fence and spilling oil over the side of the first level. We turned over the second and third urns in quick succession. A waterfall of the gooey stuff cascaded straight down to the second ledge, spreading under the Colossus in a thin pool.

The statue took a step back and slipped on the oil. As its gigantic leg kicked upward, it toppled over. Brother Dimitrios flew out of the Colossus's hand. He smashed against the cliff wall and fell limp to the ground.

The Colossus fell with a deafening *whomp*. The torch, still in its hand, bounced against the stony soil. I could see now that the chopper's laser had cut a big hole in it. Inside, the Loculus was jammed in the jagged opening. Only two sharp edges held it in place.

Two points of bendable bronze.

I ran for the stairs.

"Jack!" Aly cried out. "What are you doing?"

I could hear Marco's footfalls behind me.

Racing back down to the second level, I ran to where the Colossus was struggling to stand.

At that moment my eye caught a sudden movement to the left. The griffin was rising out of the greenhouse debris—alive.

One beast at a time.

Splayed on the ground, the statue lifted its free hand to its eye, as if to feel for damage. As I braced myself, Marco clamped his hand on my shoulder. "Jack, you idiot, get back!"

Gritting my teeth, I pushed him aside and jumped onto the torch.

Holding tight with one arm, I reached inside with the other for the Loculus. It was shockingly cool to the touch, its soft metallic skin thin enough to give it some flexibility. As I pulled, as hard as I could, the Colossus jerked back.

The force was all the help I needed. The Loculus slipped free, into my hands.

"Got it!" I shouted.

Marco and Aly were at my side now. They pulled me away from the giant. But the olive oil had coated the ground beneath us. As we fell, the Colossus sat up. I saw for the first time that one of its eyes had been hit by the laser and melted into a zombielike droop. With a swoop of its arm, it grabbed my waist and lifted me, Loculus and all, into the air.

"No-o-o!" Aly shouted.

Slowly the Colossus staggered to its feet. I rose higher. Its fingers were tight around my midsection. I couldn't breathe.

It brought its other arm toward me, as if trying to figure out how to grab the Loculus with its blunt fingers and fit it back into its place. I held tight, looking for Aly and Marco. Maybe I could toss the orb to them. But the Colossus was whipping me about too fast. If my throw went wild, the Loculus could be dashed on the rocks below. Or lost to the sea.

Another gunshot rang out. No, not a gunshot—Marco was throwing rocks at the thing! They dinged off the statue's chest and arms. "Hey, big guy! Down here!" Marco yelled, waving his arms like a lunatic.

The Colossus took a step forward and raised its other foot high, getting ready to stomp Marco into oblivion. But once again, the olive oil did its work. I felt myself swooping right and left as the statue slipped on the slickness. It seemed to pause at the edge of the cliff. I was circling now, as the Colossus windmilled its enormous arms. I struggled again to pry its fingers from around my waist.

Out of the corner of my eye, I saw the griffin below, the

door still around its neck. Its yellow eyes stared at us, preparing for an attack.

I was the one with the Loculus now. The griffin would be coming for *me*.

And then I felt a jolt. The Colossus's fingers loosened.

I could leap out now. I looked below, hoping I was close enough to the ground.

But all I saw was the sea. Rushing closer. The Colossus had slipped over the edge of the cliff.

I was plunging down toward the rocky coast.

CHAPTER FORTY-SEVEN

THE SECRET OF THE LOCULUS

I SCREAMED, HOLDING tight to the Loculus. Ridiculously tight, as if it were a life preserver. I thought about Dad. Would he ever find out what had happened? Would his life ever be the same? I thought of my friends back home, wondering where I was. About Mom. And death.

Ever since she died, I'd always wondered what that felt like.

Now I knew.

There was no impact, no transition, no white light. Just a lot of nothing.

Death felt like floating high above the world on a gust of warm air. My hair blowing in the breeze. A bloodthirsty screech below me.

Screech?

My eyes popped open. I glanced down. The sea was still far below me. I nearly puked out my breakfast. *Don't look down. Don't look down.*

But it wasn't coming closer. Just the opposite.

I was floating.

No, not floating. I was being propelled forward. Flying!

The flying prince. I thought about the image I'd seen on the maze tapestry. And the floating Massarym on the monastery painting.

Quite exciting for a boy, no? Whoosh . . . whoosh . . . Geronimo! Bhegad had told me on that first day.

I held tight. The Loculus swung me closer to the cliffs, then swept me upward. It was real. G7W was real. The Loculus was giving me the power of flight. "Woo-HOO!" I screamed.

The bronze globe was cool against my chest. It was lifting me, ever swifter, high above the sea. The monastery was a distant set of ledges now. I could see two figures on the second one. Marco and Aly. I wanted to wave to them, but I was scared to let go of the Loculus, even a little. It occurred to me that I had no idea how to control this thing.

The griffin was below me, trying to rise in a stuttering pattern of flight. Its wings were asymmetrical now, one of them clearly mangled by the glass. The pickup door hung like a sad, squarish necklace.

I was clutching the Loculus so tightly I thought my arms would fall asleep. *Breathe*, I told myself. *One . . . two . . . three . . .*

As I soared over the cliff, I could see the empty highway snaking along the Rhodean coast. In the distance, little whitewashed houses peeked out from a cove.

And I realized something extremely profound.

This.

Was.

Fun!

"WOO-HOOOO!" My cry was lost on the wind. I had no fear of falling. As if I'd been born to do this.

I banked sharply right.

How? How could I have done that?

I had no clue. But if I could steer the Loculus, I could get back to Aly and Marco. And we could find Cass. With the Loculus, it would be a snap.

I banked left. Then upward. It was as if the Loculus was a part of me, taking my instructions by some kind of weird telepathy. "Take me to my colleagues!" I said in my best Greek-monk voice.

We—the Loculus and I—dove back toward the cliff-side. I forced myself to look down. The Colossus was now a pile of rubble on the rocky coastline. The griffin was sinking downward, too, its legs extending like landing gear as it approached the beach.

I saw my friends' gaping mouths before I could see the rest of their bodies. Behind them, the whole gaggle of monks was huddled against the cliffside.

I tried to land perfectly but hit the ground hard and stumbled, nearly letting go.

"Watch the olive oil," Marco said. "It's a killer."

"Hop on!" I said.

"Are you crazy?" Aly said. "How? We just all hug this thing at the same time?"

"What's the weight limit?" Marco asked.

"None—there's room for everybody. It's big enough." I don't know how I knew that. I just did.

Aly grabbed on, then Marco. "Belay on," he said, his voice uncharacteristically shaky.

"Ready to climb," I replied.

We rose into the orange ooze of the sun, with miles of Rhodes stretched out beneath us.

"*This . . . is . . . so . . . freakyyyy!*" Aly cried.

Marco let go with one hand and waved back toward the cliff. "*Sorry, dudes, we won't be staying for dinner!*"

"Guys," I said, "let's find Cass."

I began with the cave closest to the monastery. It was way too narrow for a human to fit through. The next one was big enough but empty. In the third cave, a monk huddled against a wall, dazed. As we flew by, his mouth dropped open in shock.

"We'll come back for you later!" Aly vowed.

We passed a couple more empty caves, and another that seemed too narrow. But as we passed it, the griffin let out a wild scream from the beach.

"Did you hear that?" Aly said.

"Of course I did," I said. "Let's keep going before it gets its strength back and comes after us!"

"No—I mean, the cry was different," Aly said. "More intense. Desperate."

"You can tell the difference?" Marco asked.

"The griffin doesn't want us going into that cave," Aly insisted. "Circle back."

I turned the Loculus and we landed inside the narrow-mouthed cave.

It widened into a large chamber just inside the entrance. I stood still, letting my eyes adjust to the darkness.

"*Ohhhh . . .*"

The sound nearly caused me to drop the Loculus. It was coming from deep within the cave. On the back wall was a narrow, arched opening. I stepped closer, and then through.

The inner chamber rose about twenty feet high to a ceiling woven with tree roots. Setting the Loculus down, I pulled a flashlight out of my pack and shone it around.

Hanging from one of the sturdiest roots was a formation like nothing I'd ever seen before. It looked like a huge yellowish-white weather balloon—oblong, maybe eight feet high, made of translucent filaments that shifted colors as it swayed. From what I could see, it was open at the top. "What is that thing?" Marco asked.

"*OHHHHHH...*" A voice cried out in pain.

We all jumped. The voice was coming from inside the shape.

Cass's voice.

CHAPTER FORTY-EIGHT
No Turning Back

I CRAWLED NEARER. The membrane was translucent, and in the flashlight beam I could see Cass's form inside. He seemed to be floating, head tilted upward. His chest rising and falling.

"He's alive!" Aly shouted.

"Brother Cass, hold tight!" Marco said. He tried to dig his fingers into the membrane, but it wouldn't give.

The griffin did not digest human flesh raw . . . Hid its prey in caves . . . cocooned it . . . macerated it with saliva . . .

"It's a cocoon," I said. "Like the one Bhegad described."

Marco recoiled. "Ugh! The griffin has been cooking him in its spit."

A crash made me jump. Aly turned, having battered her

flashlight against the rock-embedded wall. Its top was jagged and sharp. "Not a knife," she said, "but it's the closest thing we've got."

She plunged it into the skin of the cocoon.

A blast of foul air blew me back. Cass fell in a heap, his torso hanging limply through the rip in the membrane.

"Cass, it's me, Jack!" I yelled. "You're going to be all right!" I pulled him out, setting him down gently on the cave floor. His head lolled to one side. His mouth opened once, twice.

"I'll take him," Marco said, slinging Cass over his shoulder. "I can hold on to the Loculus with one hand and him with the other. We'll get him back to Rhodes and book it out of here. Somehow."

"Good," I said, snapping off the flashlight. I didn't even want to think about what we would do about Torquin. "Come on."

We crawled back into the outer chamber. As we gathered around the Loculus, the cave juddered.

The griffin's unearthly squawk was weaker but unmistakable. Its face was in the entryway, its yellow eyes desperate and angry. The truck door, which had scraped the beast's neck raw, was preventing it from getting in.

As the griffin fell away, I shouted, "Move! Let's get out of—"

The cave shook again as the beast made a second attempt.

This time it didn't fall away. It planted its feet against the cave, sprang back, and flew directly in again.

Rocks fell from the ceiling. "It's going to keep trying until it breaks its neck or widens the hole!" Marco said.

WHAM!

A low creaking sound echoed through the chamber, as a crack spread across the wall.

"Looks like the griffin's winning," Marco warned.

"What do we do?" Aly shouted.

"Protect Cass!" I said.

The griffin flew toward the cave again, at full speed. The crash knocked us all to the floor. As the opening busted wider, the beast tumbled in. Quickly it righted itself onto its haunches. Seeing the Loculus in my arms, it lunged.

Marco stepped in front of me, but the griffin swatted him aside.

From behind, Aly tried to stab it with the only thing she had—a broken flashlight. But the beast flicked her aside with its tail.

It lurched toward me, the truck door still affecting its balance. I stepped back, holding tight to the Loculus. "Lateral pass!" Marco called out, but the idea was insane. There was no room. The griffin was going to kill me for the Loculus. It would kill all of us.

My back was to the wall. I had no room to move. I had run out of ideas. Aly and Marco were both shouting my name.

The griffin crouched low, eyeing me with triumph. There was no retreat now, no surrender.

It knew it finally had me.

CHAPTER FORTY-NINE

SHOWDOWN

"STOP!"

My voice rang out in the cave. I almost didn't recognize it.

I don't know what I was thinking. I guess I didn't know what else to do. But I was staring into the creature's eyes, my hand thrust out in front of me, palm out. I knew I shouldn't be looking at the thing as it killed me. It was somehow unnatural.

The griffin cocked its head. I couldn't read the expression on its face. Maybe it thought I was the stupidest human being in the world. Maybe it wanted a good laugh before killing me.

The Loculus was tucked under my left arm like a beach ball. I could feel it warm against my side. Hadn't it been cool before? It was giving me something I couldn't describe. A kind of strength. A realization I had nothing to lose.

I stood, eyes locked on the griffin's. *Sure, take me*, I thought. Marco could steal away the Loculus while this thing was snacking on my bones. I was living on borrowed time anyway.

"Just stop," I repeated. "You don't need to guard this anymore. I will give it to Marco, and you can do what you want with me."

The griffin sat back on its haunches. Then it sprawled on the ground with a submissive whimper.

"Jack . . . ?" Aly said in a hushed voice. "What did you do?"

I swallowed hard. "I . . . I don't know."

As I sidled away, the griffin's eyes followed me. "Take this," I said to Marco. "Now. Before this spell goes away."

I could see Marco loading Cass's unconscious body back over his shoulder. "Not without you, brother," he said.

"Take it!" I repeated.

Aly grabbed me by the arm, pulling me past the lion-bird. As we stood by the entrance, it followed us with docile, sad eyes.

"Hands on," Marco whispered, holding out the Loculus.

I said a silent prayer. And we jumped.

As we soared into the clear afternoon sky, the anguished roar of the griffin bellowed from the cave. The sound made the cliff wall shake.

From just above the opening, a large section of rock and soil broke loose. It crashed downward into the opening, billowing a cloud of gray-brown debris.

As we gained altitude, it looked like a bomb had gone off inside the cave. We circled, trying to get a glimpse.

But when the noise stopped and the dust settled, there was nothing.

No hole, no sign the cave had ever been there.

The griffin, finally, was silent.

CHAPTER FIFTY

INCIDENT
AT THE
RHODEAN MANOR

"DO YOU THINK anyone saw us?" Aly asked, trudging along the beach.

We had landed on a deserted stretch, a few hundred yards short of the hotel strip. The Loculus was tucked safely under my arm as we rushed along the sand.

"The monks did," Marco said, walking with Cass slung over his back. "They're probably talking with the cops already."

"No one will believe them," Aly said.

"But Greece is tolerant of eccentrics," I pointed out.

I looked at Cass's limp body. He reeked of griffin saliva.

"No words yet," Marco said, catching my glance. "Forward *or* backward. He's breathing, though. And he needs a good shower."

339

We had a good couple of miles to go before we reached the center of town. Once we got there, our problems didn't end. We had to spring Torquin from jail and get ourselves back.

I glanced up at the nearest hotel, the Rhodean Manor, a high-rise with a small pool. "We have some money," I said. "Let's pool it and get a room. Use a different name, just in case the monks heard us using our real names and convinced the cops to look for us. Aly and I can figure out how to spring Torquin, and we'll come back to get you. Make sure no one sees the Loculus."

Marco stopped, raising a dubious eyebrow. "How do you know I won't take it for a spin back to Ohio?"

"Marco, that's not funny," Aly said, continuing to walk toward town. "And one other thing. No phone calls. There's probably a police alert on your home number. You have to keep your call to less than twenty seconds to avoid a trace, and you won't be able to. Trust me."

"You tried?" Marco asked.

Aly kept walking. I gave him a look that said *off limits*.

"I'll zip it, promise," he whispered to me. "Scout's honor."

* * *

The police station was two blocks up and one block over from the Colossus Diner. As we entered, a gale of laughter greeted us from down a corridor.

I walked up to the front desk and said, "Do you have a

prisoner here by the name of Torquin?"

The officer behind the desk smiled. She gestured for us to follow. Aly and I gave each other wary looks. I still didn't know how we were going to talk our way out of this.

We took a right into a hallway lined with jail cells. It appeared that they were all empty except for one at the far end.

Two police officers sat at a desk in the hallway outside the cell, sipping coffee and eating baklava. They were speaking in Greek to the prisoner.

All at once they burst into laughter.

From inside the cell came a retort. The officers laughed some more.

"Torquin?" I said.

We picked up the pace. I nodded to the cops and then peered inside the cell. Torquin was sitting on a padded bench, sipping his own cup of coffee. An empty plate, full of crumbs, sat on the bench next to him.

When he saw us, he sat up straight. "Late!" he said.

"We've had a busy day," Aly said. She turned to the officers and said, "Um, any English speakers? If so, listen up. If you don't release this man, someone will die. I will march right to the American consulate if I have to in order to free him. I will contact the ambassador and the president, and you will have an international incident on your hands."

"I'm impressed," I murmured.

The two Greek officers stood. One of them bowed politely and pulled on Torquin's cell. It swung open. "I am Detective Haralambos. He is yours, young lady. No need to summon your Congress. If only all Americans were like this fascinating gentleman! He should be allowed a brief moment of temper." He smiled. "Between you and me, Kostas, the owner of the Colossus, is a bit of a crank."

Torquin stood. With a swagger, he padded out of the cell. "*Yia sou*," he said.

"Later," answered Detective Haralambos.

* * *

Torquin was waiting in the taxi outside the hotel when Aly and I knocked on the door of Marco's room.

"It's open," said a groggy voice.

Cass's voice.

I pushed open the door. Aly and I ran in. Cass was lying on the bed, a wet washcloth on his forehead. He was in a bathrobe, looking all cleaned up, but his skin was mottled from what had happened in the cocoon.

"I don't believe this!" Aly gushed, leaning over the bed and giving him a gentle hug.

Cass winced painfully. "Ouch."

"Sorry!" Aly said, springing back. "Are you all right?"

"I feel like gnicnad," he groaned.

Aly shot me a smile. Cass, we knew, was going to be fine.

342

"I brought you some clothes," I said, laying out a T-shirt, pair of shorts, underwear, and flip-flops I'd bought in town. "Greek sizes. I hope they fit."

"Anything's better than what I had," Cass said. "It was embarrassing flying over the KI in *Simpsons* boxers."

Aly looked around. "Where's Marco?" she asked.

"Was Marco here?" Cass asked.

"Marco brought you here," I said. "With the Loculus. And now we have to go. Torquin's waiting outside."

I stood and glanced around the room. The only sign of Marco was a plate with chocolate crumbs and three candy wrappers. I figured he was out getting a soda or something.

"Jack?" Aly said. "Where's the Loculus?"

My body stiffened.

I looked under the bed. I pulled open every drawer. I checked the bathroom.

No Loculus.

"What are you guys talking about?" Cass demanded. "We have a Loculus?"

As Aly explained what had happened, I sank onto the bed. Marco's words were spinning in my head. *How do you know I won't take it for a spin back to Ohio?*

Could he have done it?

Marco the Immortal . . . the Kid Who Faced Down Death . . .

"Jack . . . ?" Aly said. She and Cass were both staring at me now.

"Marco thinks he's okay," I replied. "Immortal. He doesn't believe what Bhegad said about the finger prick. He isn't scared about missing the treatments anymore."

"You think he . . . ?" Aly said.

"Gamed us," I said, staring out the window into the blue Greek sky. "Yes."

"I don't believe it, Jack," Aly said. "What if he just decided to fly back to the Karai Institute on his own? To race us. That's his style."

"How would he know where the island is, Aly?" I asked. "Even Cass couldn't find it."

"Maybe I could," Cass said. He sat up, the washcloth falling from his head. "Oww."

"Get dressed, brother Cass," I said softly. "We have a long ride back."

CHAPTER FIFTY-ONE

SOLDIER, SAILOR, TINKER, TAILOR

"HE'S WHAT?" PROFESSOR Bhegad was ashen in his wheelchair. I couldn't bring myself to look him in the eye. Tired and sweaty, I stared at the tarmac.

"Gone," I said. "With the Loculus."

"Why did no one tell me?" Bhegad demanded. "Why the radio silence until now?"

Torquin glanced guiltily away. "Technical difficulties."

"Our difficulties have just begun. All of us." Bhegad spun around and began wheeling himself back toward the campus, ignoring the hospital orderlies who scurried along on either side of him. "Come."

"We're . . . glad you're feeling better, Professor," Aly offered weakly.

Bhegad looked over his shoulder. "Thank you," he said. "And I'm glad Cass is alive and well. How are you feeling, my boy?"

"Peachy," Cass said with a weak smile.

"Good," Bhegad snapped back, "because I am going to need all your brainpower to track down Marco. If he is indeed headed home, it could destroy us. It could undo centuries of work."

"This is my fault," I blurted out. "I lost Marco. It was my plan to leave him in the hotel room while we went to get Torquin out of—"

"HRRRMMMM!" Torquin belched.

"I'm the wrong guy for this," I barreled on. "You picked someone who had no talents, Professor Bhegad. I don't deserve to be here, because I can't contribute like the others. I will volunteer to go find Marco. If I miss a treatment and drop dead, what's the difference? I'm no help here, anyway. I only mess things up—"

Professor Bhegad stopped short and stared at me coldly. "Do you really believe that?" he asked.

"That's ridiculous!" Aly said, stepping in front of me. "You were the one who brought the Loculus to life, Jack. And you rescued Cass. And defeated both the griffin and the Colossus. You gave me good advice—which *I* didn't follow. And whenever the rest of us couldn't figure out what to do, you were the one who made a plan."

Bhegad sighed. His eyes softened. "You know, here at the KI we have nicknames for you four. Tinker, Tailor, Soldier, Sailor. Marco was—is—the Soldier, the bravest and most fit. Cass is the Sailor, who can navigate in a blind fog. Aly is the Tinker, the one who can understand how anything works and fix it."

"And I'm . . . the Tailor?" I asked. "I sew?"

"In a manner of speaking, yes," Bhegad said. "You, Jack, are the one who puts it all together."

I laughed. But when I looked up, no one was laughing with me.

My headache was coming on strong. I needed sleep badly. The sky was pitch-black but I had no idea what time it was.

Cass. "What time is it?" I blurted out. "Cass is due for his treatment!"

"Yes, we know. It's ten forty-five," Professor Bhegad said calmly. He glanced up at the orderlies. "Please take the young man to the hospital. And make sure he gets to bed immediately afterward. We need him, rested and ready."

Aly and I gave Cass a hug. "Thank you," he said softly to me. "You are my oreh."

As the workers escorted him away, Bhegad began to wheel himself back toward his cottage. "As for you two, I trust you slept on the plane," he said as we followed along.

"Because I expect you in my office in a half hour for a planning session. So change, shower, do what you need to do. We must find your friend immediately and bring him back before he's done any damage."

"And if he has?" Aly asked fearfully.

"Eliminate," Torquin growled.

We stopped. As Torquin padded after the professor, the old man didn't say a word.

Aly crumpled to a small bench against the airport building.

I couldn't look at her. My blood was running cold.

Soldier, Sailor, Tinker, Tailor.

The night was cloudless and moonless. Stars spread across the sky like spattered blood. My thoughts raced. Somewhere up there, I knew, was Marco.

I scanned the horizon, looking.

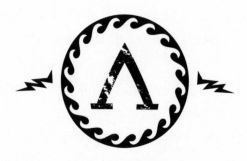

ABOUT THE AUTHOR

PETER LERANGIS

is the author of more than 160 books, which have sold five million copies and been translated into twenty-eight different languages, including books in two *New York Times* bestselling series: The 39 Clues (Book 3: *The Sword Thief*, Book 7: *The Viper's Nest*, and Book 11: *Vespers Rising*) and Cahills vs. Vespers (Book 3: *The Dead of Night*). He wrote the popular Spy X and Drama Club series; the two-book adventure *Antarctica*; and the Watchers series (winner of Children's Choice and Quick Pick awards). With Harry Mazer, he co-authored the YA novel *Somebody, Please Tell Me Who I Am*. Peter's novel *Smiler's Bones*, based on the true story of a polar Eskimo boy orphaned in New York City at the turn of the twentieth century, was selected as a New York Public Library Best Books for Teens 2006, a Bank Street Best Books of 2006, and a Junior Library Guild pick. He is also author of the hilarious, edgy YA novel *wtf*. Peter was one of three authors, along with R. L. Stine and Marc Brown, invited by the White House to represent the United States at the first Russian Book Festival in 2003. He is a Harvard graduate with a degree in biochemistry. After college he became a Broadway musical theater actor. He has run a marathon and gone rock climbing during an earthquake, but not on the same day. He lives in New York City with his wife, musician Tina deVaron, and their two sons, Nick and Joe. In his spare time, he likes to eat chocolate. Lots of it. Seriously, he loves chocolate.

SEVEN WONDERS

LOST in BABYLON

COMING

FALL 2013

SEVEN·WONDERS
of the Ancient World

BLACK·SEA

THE·TEMPLE·OF·ARTEMIS
AT·EPHESUS

ATHENS

THE·MAUSOLEUM
AT·HALICARNASSUS

THE·STATUE·OF·ZEUS
AT·OLYMPIA

THE·COLOSSUS
OF·RHODES

MEDITERRANEAN·SEA

THE·LIGHTHOUSE·OF·ALEXANDRIA

THE·GREAT·PYRAMID·OF·GIZA

NILE